continued . . .

Books by Rebecca York

KILLING MOON
EDGE OF THE MOON
WITCHING MOON
CRIMSON MOON
SHADOW OF THE MOON
NEW MOON
GHOST MOON
ETERNAL MOON
DRAGON MOON

BEYOND CONTROL
BEYOND FEARLESS

Anthologies

CRAVINGS
(with Laurell K. Hamilton, MaryJanice Davidson, Eileen Wilks)
ELEMENTAL MAGIC
(with Sharon Shinn, Carol Berg, and Jean Johnson)

DRAGON
MOON

REBECCA YORK

BERKLEY SENSATION, NEW YORK

THE BERKLEY PUBLISHING GROUP
Published by the Penguin Group
Penguin Group (USA) Inc.
375 Hudson Street, New York, New York 10014, USA
Penguin Group (Canada), 90 Eglinton Avenue East, Suite 700, Toronto, Ontario M4P 2Y3, Canada
(a division of Pearson Penguin Canada Inc.)
Penguin Books Ltd., 80 Strand, London WC2R 0RL, England
Penguin Group Ireland, 25 St. Stephen's Green, Dublin 2, Ireland (a division of Penguin Books Ltd.)
Penguin Group (Australia), 250 Camberwell Road, Camberwell, Victoria 3124, Australia
(a division of Pearson Australia Group Pty. Ltd.)
Penguin Books India Pvt. Ltd., 11 Community Centre, Panchsheel Park, New Delhi—110 017, India
Penguin Group (NZ), 67 Apollo Drive, Rosedale, North Shore 0632, New Zealand
(a division of Pearson New Zealand Ltd.)
Penguin Books (South Africa) (Pty.) Ltd., 24 Sturdee Avenue, Rosebank, Johannesburg 2196,
South Africa

Penguin Books Ltd., Registered Offices: 80 Strand, London WC2R 0RL, England

This is a work of fiction. Names, characters, places, and incidents either are the product of the author's imagination or are used fictitiously, and any resemblance to actual persons, living or dead, business establishments, events, or locales is entirely coincidental. The publisher does not have any control over and does not assume any responsibility for author or third-party websites or their content.

DRAGON MOON

A Berkley Sensation Book / published by arrangement with the author

PRINTING HISTORY
Berkley Sensation mass-market edition / October 2009

Copyright © 2009 by Ruth Glick.
Excerpt from *Skin Game* by Ava Gray copyright © by Ann Aguirre.
Cover design by Springer Design Group.

ISBN: 978-0-425-23098-5

BERKLEY® SENSATION
Berkley Sensation Books are published by The Berkley Publishing Group,
a division of Penguin Group (USA) Inc.,
375 Hudson Street, New York, New York 10014.
BERKLEY® SENSATION and the "B" design are trademarks of Penguin Group (USA) Inc.

PRINTED IN THE UNITED STATES OF AMERICA

10 9 8 7 6 5 4 3 2 1

DRAGON
MOON

CHAPTER
ONE

HIS NAME WAS Vandar, and he was a creature from an ancient nightmare. A creature who had lived for centuries relying on his psychic powers, his cunning.

Now he lifted his massive head and roared for the pleasure of feeling his slaves cringe.

In his present incarnation, he was a huge, scaled being with glittering red eyes, a reptilian body, and wings shaped like those of a bat—only enormously larger. But he was just as likely to take human form.

Leaping into the air, he circled his lair, looking down with a feeling of satisfaction as he churned up the chemicals in his belly, then spewed out a blast of fire that singed the already blackened landscape.

His huge mouth stretched into a parody of a smile as he viewed the circle of destruction. It was a warning to any enemies who dared approach this blighted place. And a warning to the slaves who lived in the huge cave he had blasted out of a mountainside. If any tried to escape, he could turn them to ash as easily as he had charred the land.

Now he was widening his circle of influence, not just here but into a world parallel to this one. A world where the people would be helpless to fight him.

But he hadn't lived for more than a thousand years by leaping unprepared into the unknown.

As he flew over his territory, he thought of the tasks that must be accomplished before the big invasion. He had already started his preparations for the assault by sending spies to the other universe. They were all men who had stayed for a few days and come back to give him a sense of the place. In the next phase, his agent would remain longer and provide a more detailed report.

And this time he would send an attractive woman because she would seem weak and vulnerable, yet her pretty face, sexy figure, and psychic powers would give her an advantage over the men she met.

Satisfied with the plan, he circled back and landed in the ceremonial site fifty yards from the mouth of his cave. Lifting his head to the skies, he roared out four notes. Two long and two short. A signal to the people who did his bidding.

Three hundred slaves instantly dropped what they were doing and hurried to answer his call.

One by one and in groups, they stepped outside the cave, blinking in the morning sunshine.

He watched their stiff postures, their wary eyes as they stood in their color-coded tunics. White for adepts. Gray for house servants. Brown for those who did the dirtiest jobs like washing the floors and mucking out the toilets. And burgundy for his troops.

They knew what was coming, and they cringed, even as they came toward him with hesitant steps.

Standing before them, he began to change form. His wings folded inward. His claws and his great tail retracted back into his body. The shape of his torso shrunk and transmuted into the incarnation he used when he walked among his minions.

He was vulnerable when he changed, but they didn't know that, and they trembled as he transformed from silver-scaled monster to a tall, dark-haired man. He stood before them naked for several moments, letting them take in his well-muscled body with its impressive male equipment.

Satisfied that they had had enough time to contemplate his magnificence, he snapped his fingers. Two blond-haired women clad in white came forward and walked to the carved wooden chest where he kept a set of clothing. From its depths, one of them removed a long black tunic of fine linen, edged with gold braid. As he held out his arms, one of them slipped the garment over his head and the other knelt and strapped a pair of supple leather sandals onto his feet.

When he was dressed and they'd stepped back into the crowd, he turned and smiled at the waiting throng, feeling the waves of tension rolling toward him.

They knew he would feed now. On one of them. He could have done that in his dragon form, of course. But this was so much more intimate, and it impressed upon them that, even when he looked like a man, he was as far above them as an eagle was above an ant.

Long moments passed as he let them sweat. Let them wonder which of them he would select. And why.

A man or a woman?

They didn't know he had already made that decision. In his mind, he kept a running assessment of his slaves' deeds—of the times they pleased him and of their transgressions. One man above all the others had earned the privilege of participating in this ceremony.

Finally, he raised his voice. "Bendel, come forward."

The man gasped. Everyone else breathed out a sigh of relief.

For a long moment, nothing happened. Then Bendel broke and ran.

Vandar was ready for the slave's futile bid for freedom. His tongue flicked out, lengthening like a whip, catching the man and pulling him back.

Bendel's face turned white. His eyes were wide and pleading.

"Were you foolish enough to think you could outrun me?" Vandar murmured, his voice silky. "And foolish enough to steal food from the larder?"

The slave's jaw worked, but no words came out of his mouth.

Vandar spread his lips, baring his teeth as he sent out his fangs, his gaze never leaving the man's terrified eyes. Grabbing his victim's hair, he arched his neck before sinking his fangs into the pale flesh.

The first draft of blood sent a burst of warmth through him. He felt the life-giving liquid flow into his mouth, down his throat, and into his stomach.

The nourishment brought him a satisfying glow of energy. In his childhood, he hadn't known what kind of creature he really was, and he had subsisted on a human diet. He could still eat small amounts of food and drink if he wanted. He had tried wine made from grapes and other fruit, and to his taste buds, the wine had a tang that was similar to blood.

He could have spared his victim's life. Draining the life-blood from any one individual wasn't necessary to quench his thirst. He didn't even need to drink human blood. An animal would do. But an animal could not fear him with the intellect of a man, and that was part of the pleasure for him. He loved feeling a victim's terror swell, then the inevitable acceptance as his life force slipped away.

When he had drained the last drop of sweet-tasting nectar, he cast the husk of the body onto the ground and wiped his mouth on the sleeve of his tunic before raising his head to stare at the other slaves.

As he searched their faces, he let the moment stretch, prolonging the little ceremony and impressing the gravity of the occasion on the group of terrified watchers. Then he snapped his fingers, calling on the two men who would take out the garbage.

FEELING an unaccustomed restlessness, Talon Marshall exited the former hunting lodge where he lived in the woods of rural Pennsylvania and walked to a stand of pines that he'd planted years ago. In maturity, they formed a tight circle, shielding him from view. But there was one place where he had trimmed some lower branches so it was easy to push through.

Once inside, he pulled off his clothes and stowed them in the wooden storage box he'd built. Standing naked among the pines, he enjoyed the feel of the humid air on his well-muscled body.

Did normal men chafe at the confinement of clothing? Did they long for the freedom that he had claimed for himself?

In a clear voice, he began to say the ancient words that had turned the men of the Marshall family into werewolves since Druid times.

"Taranis, Epona, Cerridwen," he chanted, repeating the phrase and going on to another.

"Ga. Feart. Cleas. Duais. Aithriocht. Go gcumhdai is dtreorai na deithe thu."

The human part of his mind screamed in protest as bones crunched, muscles jerked, and cells transformed from one shape to another.

No matter how many times he changed form, it was never easy to feel his jaw elongate, his teeth sharpen, his body contort as muscles and limbs transformed themselves.

The first time, he'd been terrified that the pain would kill him—the way it had killed his older brother.

But he'd willed himself to steadiness, and once he'd understood what to expect, he'd learned to rise above the terrifying physical sensations.

Thick gray hair formed along his flanks, covering his body in a silver-tipped pelt. The color—the very structure—of his eyes changed as he dropped to all fours. A magnificent beast of the forest. Unrecognizable as a member of the human race.

With the transformation completed, everything changed. In animal awareness, he lifted his head and dragged in the familiar smells of the forest: leafy vegetation, rotting leaves, and the creatures that made their homes here.

Racing past a stand of oaks, he caught the scent of a fox and automatically corrected his course to follow the trail. The animal gave a good chase, taking him to a patch of wilderness that he hadn't visited in months.

As he stopped for a moment, breathing hard, a scent

came to him. Not a familiar odor. Something that didn't belong in this wilderness environment.

A threat?

Slowly, he walked around the area, sniffing, until he came to a place where the forest floor had been disturbed. As he pawed the earth, he found it was soft, with leaves brushed over the top to hide freshly disturbed dirt.

The wolf dug down several inches, sure there was something buried here that didn't belong in the woods. A body? Or something that might leach into the soil, spreading poison?

He dragged in more of the scent and decided it wasn't anything that had been alive. But that was as far as he could go as a wolf. He needed hands to get to the bottom of this mystery.

Turning, he raced back the way he'd come, to the circle of pine trees where he pushed through the change. As soon as he had morphed back to his human form, he pulled on his clothing, then strode to the five-door garage where he kept his outdoor equipment: some of it for his business—leading wilderness expeditions—and some of it for maintaining the property around the lodge.

With a short-handled shovel slung easily over his shoulder, he strode back to the place where he'd pawed the earth.

His human senses were no longer as keen. But he dragged in a draft of the forest air and looked around carefully before beginning to dig in earnest, scooping out the dirt and piling it to the right of the hole where he could easily replace it when he was finished.

When the shovel scraped against something hard, he widened the hole around the object. Then, using the shovel as a lever, he pried up a metal box, which he hauled out and set on the ground.

Obviously, the box was private property, but it was buried on public land. With the shovel blade, he whacked at the padlock securing the top until the hasp broke. Then he knelt and lifted the lid.

What he saw inside made his breath catch.

CHAPTER
TWO

AS SHE HURRIED toward her workstation in Vandar's cave, Kenna slid her eyes left and right. When she was sure nobody was looking at her, she said a silent little prayer to the Great Mother that she would get through this day without incident.

Prayer was forbidden in this place of horror, and she knew that if anyone realized what she was doing, they would report her to their master. Then she might be the next victim of his bloodlust.

Great Mother, what had she come to? A slave quaking in her sandals.

She hated herself. Hated her existence. Yet she saw no way to escape.

A few months ago, she'd had choices for the future. Marriage—to the right man. Or not, if that suited her better.

Until she'd been carried away to this nightmare place, she'd been a free citizen of Breezewood. Her father owned a shop that sold well-made sandals and boots to nobles and common people alike. After finishing her education at the city's school for adepts, she had worked for two years, using her talent to cure leather for the merchants who had paid for her schooling. With her obligation fulfilled, she'd become a tutor in the house of a powerful man named Cardon—one of the leaders of Breezewood.

His children had shown signs of early psychic talent, and he and his wife, Donda, had wanted to give them a head start in the school for adepts.

So they had asked the teachers who would be a good

tutor, then hired Kenna. She'd only been in the household a few months, but she had already met a number of highborn men who were attracted to her—men who might want a pretty young wife with powers, a wife who would improve the chances of advancement for their own children.

She pressed her hand against her mouth, wondering if she was remembering her old life accurately. Or was she just trying to distract herself from the horrors of the present?

She'd been on a visit to her parents when Vandar's warriors had burst through the city gate and swarmed up the cobblestone street. They'd grabbed Kenna and taken her away with twenty other unfortunates.

Now she was afraid that death at Vandar's hands was the only way she would leave this outpost of Carfolian hell. That might be a relief, because life as one of his slaves was no life at all.

Around her, others hurried down the corridors of the huge cave, each of them alone in the crowd.

When they'd arrived, Vandar had tested each of them in a horrible ceremony where he probed their minds as he drank their blood. If they had no psychic powers, their lives would be hard, because they were only good for manual labor. They would likely be slaughtered quickly, or work themselves to death at an early age.

But if they had powers, then the evaluation was trickier. He wanted to use the talents of his slaves, but if he discovered an adept was strong enough to challenge his authority, that person might be killed on the spot.

Kenna had almost met that fate. During the selection ceremony, she had sensed his mental jaws clamping onto her mind, and she had instinctively tried to pull away. But he'd been stronger than she was. And he'd held her fast.

Maybe that had saved her life, but now she was a slave in the most basic sense of the word.

At first, alone in her narrow bed at night, she'd thought about trying to escape under cover of darkness and flee across the black plains that surrounded the cave. Beyond were the badlands, full of lawless men who belonged to no city.

She longed to risk that route, but she couldn't make herself leave the vicinity of the cave. No one could, and she was sure it was because Vandar had put some silent orders into their heads that kept them chained to this place.

As she passed the dormitory where she slept with twenty other women, she repressed a sigh.

She couldn't go there now. Unless she was too sick to work, and that was risky, because a sick slave might easily become a dead slave.

Her job was in the library, a large room by cave standards, with desks and wooden tables and shelves of books lining the walls.

The volumes were on many subjects, and most of them came from the old times. Today books were copied by scribes, but these volumes had been made by another process that she didn't understand.

In the library, she hurried to the wide worktable where a volume lay open. It was about something called chemistry. The words meant very little to her, but she wasn't there to read and understand a complicated subject from the past.

The book had been damaged by dry rot, and the edges of the paper were crumbling. Deftly she used her telekinetic skills to even out the rough places. Then she dipped her horsehair brush into a pot of preserving solution and swished it across the page. It was impossible to give the paper an even coat with the brush alone, but she could smooth it out with her mind, leaving the thinnest layer of transparent film on the page.

After she had smoothed out the coating, she used her telekinetic skills again to dry the paper. When it was no longer sticky, she went on to the next page, repeating the process. As she did the purely physical part of the job, she thought of Bendel, the man who had died so publicly a few days ago.

She had seen him stealing food, and she had thought he was taking a terrible chance for a little bread and fruit.

But she hadn't warned him to stop. Because that could get her into trouble, and she'd known he wasn't worth it.

With the brushwork finished, she began the psychic part of her task again, thinning out the preservative. The process was tedious, but she knew that she could be doing far more unpleasant work, like cleaning the toilets or burying bodies.

Instead, she got to sit in a room alone for most of the day, engaged in her special project, a luxury in this communal environment.

She heard a bell chime nine times and knew that she still had three hours to go before she could stop for the noon meal, which she would eat in the communal dining room with the other women. In this place, men and women were separated at meals and at work, to keep them from forming relationships.

Taking a short rest, she stretched her arms and legs, sipped some water from a pottery mug, and went back to her task.

She was about halfway through the chemistry book when a shadow filled the doorway.

Glancing up, she saw a man named Wendon giving her a speculative look as though he were considering whether to send a horse off to auction. He was short, with thinning hair, and it was rumored that he had been with Vandar for years. Whether that was true or not, he was certainly one of the adepts who worked most closely with the master.

When Kenna saw the smirking expression on his face, her hand froze.

"Vandar wants to see you."

Fear leaped inside her, and she couldn't stop herself from gasping out, "Why? I'm working as fast as I can on these books."

She knew she wasn't slacking off at her job. Had one of the other slaves reported her for some real or imagined infraction? Or did someone in the cave want to get even with her? That was always a possibility. Maybe someone thought that she was getting off too easily.

"The master will tell you what he wants when you get there. Hurry up; don't keep him waiting."

She jumped up, her hands suddenly clammy.

Her heart was pounding as she followed Wendon out of the room and down the hall toward the master's quarters.

A flash of movement in the late summer woods made Talon freeze.

Pivoting to the right, he saw a white police cruiser with a shield on the side driving slowly up the access road to his converted hunting lodge.

As the cruiser pulled up at his front door, Talon set down the Husqvarna chain saw he'd been using to cut up a fallen log for firewood. Then he removed his safety helmet and pulled off his leather gloves before walking out of the woods.

Two gray-clad cops wearing Smokey the Bear hats had gotten out of the black-and-white and were striding toward the front door of the lodge when they heard his heavy boots crushing the dry leaves.

Both of them turned toward him, each with his service revolver within easy reach.

"Talon Marshall?" one of them asked.

As he drew closer, he saw from the speaker's plastic tag that his name was Eckert. The other one was Milner. Eckert was blond. Milner was dark. Both of them were around six feet tall, square-jawed men with military-short haircuts and the spit and polish look of young cops poised to move up in the ranks.

Talon knew they were sizing him up, too, seeing a dark-haired man in his late twenties, about their own height, dressed like a lumberjack—in a plaid shirt, jeans, and chaps to guard against a leg injury with the saw. Not that Talon was ever careless with the Husqvarna.

"Yes. Can I help you?"

Eckert pulled out a notebook and flipped it open. "We'd like to ask you some questions about that box you found in the woods."

Talon shifted his weight from one foot to the other. "I already told the desk sergeant everything I know when I turned in the damn thing."

"When you find over a million bucks under a bush, there are going to be questions," Eckert said.

Talon sighed, wishing he'd never dug up the damn box. But once he'd known something was under the ground, he'd been compelled to do it. "What do you want to know?"

"We want to see where you found it."

He gestured toward the fallen poplar behind him. "I'm kind of busy."

"You can get back to work as soon as we identify the spot where the box turned up."

He could see he wasn't going to get out of this without giving them what they wanted.

Eckert looked down at his notebook. "The box was in the middle of the woods?"

"Yeah."

"What were you doing out there?"

"Hiking."

"You run wilderness trips for a living?"

"Yeah."

"And the box was buried?"

"Yes," he answered, trying not to sound impatient.

"How did you happen to find it?"

Right. Would anyone besides a werewolf have known where to dig? Not unless they knew where to look.

"The forest floor was disturbed. I was curious. When I started poking around, I figured something was down there. Maybe a body."

"Let's have a look."

Talon shrugged. Since he'd found the buried money, he'd realized that it wasn't far from an old dirt road that ran through the forest.

"Do you want to duplicate my original route on foot? Or do you want to drive?" he asked.

"Drive," Eckert said immediately.

Before they could suggest he ride in the back of the cruiser, he said, "I'll lead you."

He backed his four-wheel-drive hybrid out of the garage, reversed direction, and angled around the cop car before starting down his drive.

After leading them onto the two-lane highway in front of his property, he slowed down to find the track through the woods. It was badly rutted, and he wondered what it was doing to the cops' suspension, but that wasn't his problem.

Fifteen minutes after they'd started, he pulled to a stop near the place where he'd found the box.

The two officers followed him into the woods, where they all gathered at the place where Talon had dug up the box.

"Right there." He pointed.

Milner squatted down and ran his hand over the leaves. "I can't see anything."

"I put it back the way it's supposed to be."

"Uh-huh."

He kept from clenching his fists, because he didn't want to look like he was guilty of anything. He wasn't, unless you counted being a nonhuman monster.

"And you found this—how?" Eckert asked, watching him carefully.

He'd already answered that question when the cops first arrived, but he went through it again. "The forest floor didn't look natural."

"You must have good eyes."

He shrugged. "I'm good at reading the natural environment. That's my job."

Both cops nodded.

Eckert kept his gaze on Talon. "And what motivated you to turn in the money?"

Ah. The sixty-four-thousand-dollar question.

"Good citizenship," he snapped. "I assume you got an inventory from the bank, and the cash was all there."

"How do you know it was from a bank?"

"I don't! I was making an assumption."

"Yeah, we traced the serial numbers to a Phoenix National branch. And thirty thousand bucks were missing."

"What are you suggesting?"

This time it was the cop who shrugged. "The guy who buried the box could have held some out."

"I didn't keep any of the money," Talon said. "Did you find my fingerprints on it?"

"No."

So what were these guys really thinking? That he and someone else had pulled off a bank job in Arizona, and now he was trying to make sure he didn't get nailed for the crime? Or that he had killed his partner?

If so, why would he have turned in the loot? It didn't make sense, but maybe cops were constitutionally suspicious. He wanted to ask if they'd checked his schedule for the day of the holdup, but he figured the less he said, the better.

"Anything else I can help you with?" he asked, making an effort to keep his voice conversational.

"We just needed to have a look at the crime scene," Eckert answered.

And get my reaction to the missing money, Talon silently added.

"Okay. I'm going back to work now. Just continue up the road. It comes out on the highway a couple of miles from where we entered the woods."

Before either of them could answer, he climbed back into his four-wheeler and started the engine, wishing he'd never found the damn box, because he had the feeling that it was going to cause him more trouble.

CHAPTER
THREE

KENNA HAD BEEN to the private quarters of the master only a few times before. As she followed Wendon through a stone arch, the walls changed abruptly from mud blocks to narrow wooden boards, nailed together, painted with a variety of scenes and illuminated by candles set into iron brackets fixed to the wall. Some of the decorations were just designs of swirling colors. Others depicted people and animals. She walked past pictures of men harvesting grain, swimming in a river, and herding cattle. Some showed both sexes working at various trades. The scene of a shoemaker's shop made her eyes blur. Blinking, she struggled to focus on the murals again, to keep from thinking about the end of the journey.

How many years had it taken to decorate these hallways? And when had it been done? As far as she knew, none of the artists still lived in the compound. Had Vandar worked them to death, or drained their blood when they no longer pleased him? Behind Wendon's back, she clenched her teeth.

He led her around several turns, until they came to a wide wooden door where he knocked and waited.

When Vandar called, "Come in," Kenna felt goose bumps rise on her arms.

The adept opened the door and said in a voice dripping with ceremony, "I have brought you the woman you requested."

There was a low answer of acknowledgment. Wendon faded back, put his hands on her shoulders, and pushed her forward. When she stumbled inside, the door closed behind her, leaving her alone with the master.

She was vaguely aware of an ancient, patterned rug under her feet, rich draperies hanging on the walls, and several low-slung easy chairs, grouped in a circle.

Her gaze zeroed in on Vandar. He was sitting in a leather chair with a high back. One metal spoke of a leg came down to several horizontal pieces like the shafts of a wheel.

His feet moved, swinging the chair body back and forth as his glittering eyes focused on her. She had been twenty yards away when he'd killed Bendel. Now she was closer, much too close.

She longed to look away yet she kept her gaze focused on him. If he were a man, she would have called him handsome. He looked like a noble who was entirely comfortable in his surroundings, and he appeared to be young—no more than a man in his thirties. But it was said that he had lived much longer. Maybe hundreds of years.

She had no way to verify that, or anything else besides the cruelty and the power tactics she had seen for herself. But she knew he was so much more than he appeared to be.

Pressing her hands against her sides, she struggled to keep from trembling as her gaze darted to his mouth.

She hated Vandar. And she hated her fear of him. Probably, he knew that.

When he climbed out of the chair and walked forward, her heart stopped, then started again in double time.

As she stood in the center of the room, he circled her, giving her a close inspection. "Move your arms away from your body."

Somehow she made her muscles work, standing with her arms sticking out stiffly as he traced the indentation of her waist, then raised his hand to cup her breast.

When her breath caught, he laughed. "Is my touch repulsive to you?"

"No, sir," she managed to say, although it was a lie. Would he kill her for having the wrong thoughts?

It was no idle question. She knew he had done it before.

"Sit down," he said abruptly, pointing to a chair a few feet from the door.

Quickly, she sat down and folded her hands into her lap, casting her eyes down.

"You are very attractive, by the standards of human-kind," he said when she was seated. "Your curly brown hair is appealing. Your features are delicate. Your hips curve out below your waist, and your breasts are nicely shaped."

"Thank you," she managed, hating the catalogue of her physical attributes. She knew that he sometimes took female slaves to his bed. Great Mother, was he going to do that with her?

"You lived in a noble's household," he said.

"Yes, sir," she answered, struggling to keep her voice from shaking and wondering if he remembered the history of every slave.

He returned to his own chair, putting more blessed distance between them.

"And you are educated in the ways of the adepts and also in the ordinary subjects. You can read and do simple mathematical problems."

"Yes, sir," she answered, unsure where this conversation was going. At least it didn't sound like he was planning to bed her or kill her. Not right away.

He tipped his head to the side, studying her. "Did you learn in your school for psychics that there is more than one world, which runs along a similar but separate track?"

"Yes. I learned that theory."

"It's more than a theory. This is not the only universe, but going from this world to another is not so easy."

She waited for him to continue.

"It takes a lot of energy to open a portal between the worlds. One person cannot do it by himself, but several of my adepts have pooled their resources and accomplished it. I've sent a few men through the portal, for brief periods.

To a world that had developed much differently from this one."

Despite the circumstances, she listened, fascinated.

"In the other universe, because the people lack psychic abilities, they have developed technology we don't have here. We run equipment by mental energy. They have electricity and gasoline."

She nodded, wondering if he often called slaves into his private rooms to share his theories of the universe.

"In many ways, our psychic talents limit us. This world did not develop the creature comforts that are available on the other side of the portal. Just to give you a few examples, they have music you can carry around in a small case. They have carriages that do not need horses to pull them. They have foods that come in rectangular packages. And clothing that any woman here would envy. You'll like living there."

The last words made her head jerk up. "What?" she gasped.

"I plan to expand my influence into that universe, and you will be my advance scout. You will go there to find out what it is like, then come back and report to me."

A mixture of fear and hope leaped inside her. Fear of the unknown. And hope that if he was sending her to that other world, perhaps she would be beyond his reach. Probably, the hope showed on her face, because his eyes narrowed. As they did, she felt a stab of pain inside her head.

"No!" she cried out.

"You are foolish if you think I cannot reach you there."

She tried to fend him off, and for a moment the pain stopped.

"How dare you!"

Long seconds passed before pain jolted her again.

She screamed, slipping to the side, then off the chair so that she lay sprawled on the rug.

Run, the part of her mind that was still free ordered. But she couldn't push herself up. She could only lie on her side, rocking back and forth, clutching her head with her hands, trying to tear her way through her own flesh so that she could rip away the pain blasting at her.

"Please, no," she managed to croak.

Ignoring her plea, he spoke again. "You will be my eyes and ears on the other side of the portal. You will do as you are ordered. You will observe that new world. You will find out what those people are like. Their strengths and their weaknesses. But you will tell no one about me, and when I summon you back, you will return here."

His voice droned on, giving her more orders. She hardly heard them, but she knew they were etching themselves into the fibers of her mind.

To reinforce his words, the pain flared, dimming all of her senses, and the only escape was into a world of blackness.

She wasn't unconscious. She wasn't asleep. But she wasn't exactly awake either, and she could hear Vandar's voice still whispering in her mind, reinforcing what he had already said.

"You will obey my orders. You will have an advantage over the people who live on the other side of the portal. Because they lack psychic powers, they won't expect you to have them. You can use your telekinetic abilities. Try not to let anyone catch you." He laughed. "But even if they do, they won't believe what they've seen. They'll dismiss it because they'll think that what they're seeing is impossible. Do you understand?"

Yes, she managed to answer inside her mind.

"Say it out loud!"

"Yes," she whispered, because that was her only option.

She could feel him looking down at her with satisfaction. Finally, he began to speak again.

"When you get there, you must find a place of refuge from which you can gather information. Make friends with one of the natives. You are an attractive woman. A man will fall under your sway. Use him for your own purposes. Do you understand?"

"Yes," she answered again, hating herself. She didn't want to use anyone. She only wanted . . .

Before she could form the word "freedom," another blast of pain seared her.

This time, when blackness took her, she tumbled into a bottomless well.

VANDAR stood looking down at the unconscious woman lying on the Oriental rug. He had felt her trying to resist his orders. She had fought him as best she could, and her spirit had surprised him. She was strong, stronger than she knew. And resourceful. It might have been safer to kill her. Instead, he had chosen her for this vital assignment.

In the beginning, he had thought a man would serve him better than a woman. But the three men he had sent to the other side of the portal had ended up failing him. They had collected useful information, but each of them had come running back to this world in a panic when they'd encountered a situation they weren't prepared to handle.

One had gotten drunk in an establishment called a bar and killed a citizen of the other universe. Another had almost been caught stealing artifacts from a house. And a third had thought he could drive one of their horseless vehicles and had crashed it into a tree, barely escaping serious injury.

He hoped Kenna would do better, but he must test her ability to cram in the facts she needed to function effectively in the other world. If she wasn't up to the job, he would kill her and choose another slave for the mission.

CHAPTER
FOUR

FIGHTING THE IMPULSE to fold her arms across her chest, Kenna stood very still with her hands at her sides. She was wearing clothing that she had never seen until today. Clothing that revealed her form in a way that made her want to run back to her sleeping chamber and put on her familiar tunic.

In public, she had always dressed in modest garments with a skirt. Now she was clad in tight blue pants and a thin shirt. Under her clothing, she had on filmy panties and a kind of halter that lifted her breasts and thrust them forward.

Only her sandals were familiar.

She stopped worrying about her clothing when Vandar asked a sharp question.

"Who rules the United States of America?"

Kenna moistened her lips. "The president."

"What is a toaster?"

"A machine that puts a burnt crust on the outside of bread slices."

"Not burnt!"

She dragged in a breath and let it out. "A brown crust."

Vandar kept his gaze on her as he threw question after question at her.

"Where do Americans keep milk?"

"In a refrigerator."

"What is the underwear that confines your breasts?"

"A bra."

"What pants do you have on?"

She looked down at her legs. "Jeans. Or blue jeans, they're sometimes called."

"What does 'okay' mean?"

"Yes. Or all right."

The questions went on and on as Kenna stood in front of Vandar, doing her best to respond, because she was sure from the intensity of her master's expression that her life depended on her answers.

She had studied for two weeks, in a luxurious apartment, far back in the cave, drilled for hours by a squad of adepts and scholars. Now she must prove that she had learned the facts.

She tensed the muscles in her legs, struggling not to waver on her feet through the rapid-fire assault.

When Vandar finally said, "You have proved yourself ready. The adepts will take you to the portal now," she wondered if she had heard him correctly.

She didn't feel ready, but she wasn't going to argue. Instead, she breathed a sigh of relief as she followed Wendon out of the master's chamber and then down the hallway to the cave's entrance. She hadn't been outside since the morning of Bendel's death, and the late afternoon light made her blink.

She'd been relieved to leave Vandar. Her heart started to pound as Wendon gestured toward an outcropping of rock about a quarter mile away. "The portal is there. Hurry."

He took up a position behind her, as if to prevent her escape. Two other white-clad adepts walked in front of her.

And the long shadow of the rock formation reached out like a barbed hook, dragging her forward.

In this land that had been forsaken by the gods, no birds sang. No animal or insect scurried across the ruined earth. And no wind blew.

The still air felt cold against her clammy skin, and she shivered, wondering if Vandar was watching the troupe of slaves heading for the portal. He was nowhere in sight, but she felt the unseen touch of his strong powers. Probably, he was using his powers to view her progress toward the rock.

So why, exactly, did Vandar need *her*?

She hadn't dared ask the question. All she knew was that she was going to an unknown place where people put a toasted coating on bread. Did it crunch like the blackened land under her feet?

She had no idea what came next. Except that she must carry out Vandar's assignment—or die. But maybe the rules were not what they seemed. Maybe when she got to the other side of the portal, she could break his hold on her.

And what?

She struggled to push the word "escape" out of her mind, lest he dip into her thoughts and discover that she was contemplating something forbidden.

A shrieking sound from the heavens broke the silence, making her cringe. Involuntarily, she glanced up and saw a silver-scaled dragon in the sky above her.

He was *here*.

Not as she had last seen him inside the cave, but as a great winged creature circling in the sky, ready to swoop down at any moment on the mortals below him.

While he circled above them, they all speeded up, bunching closer together as they headed for the portal. Wendon walked in back of her. The men in front were Barthime and Swee, two of the most powerful adepts among Vandar's slaves. Men he trusted—at least as far as he trusted anyone.

When they reached the pile of rocks, the shadow was deeper, making her shiver. Clenching her teeth to keep them from chattering, she raised her head and saw that the rock sheltered the entrance to a small cave. Without a word, Wendon lit a lamp and disappeared into the darkness, the flame receding down a narrow passage.

Barthime turned to look her up and down, giving her a final inspection. Again, she fought the impulse to fold her arms protectively in front of her breasts.

Swee smirked at her. "You look lovely, my dear."

She didn't bother to answer.

Before the adept could make another comment, Wendon reappeared at the cave entrance.

"Everything is in order."

Kenna shifted her carry bag from one hand to the other. It had a change of clothing and a few other things she would need. She was glad Vandar hadn't asked her the name of the thing. It was a knapsack, but she kept forgetting the right word.

With a rush of wings Vandar landed fifty feet away, his hot breath warming the cool air, his glittering eyes fixed on them.

Kenna and the others froze in place. She almost expected the enormous creature to roar out words at them, although she had never heard him speak when he was in the form of a beast.

"Get inside the cave," Barthime whispered, as if disappearing from sight would save them from Vandar's wrath if he meant to kill them.

Without another word they all hurried inside the dark passage, and Kenna rejoiced that she wouldn't be coming back this way. At least not immediately.

Would Vandar drink from one of the men when they reappeared from the shelter of the rocks? Or was he just amusing himself by frightening them?

She didn't like his adepts, but she wouldn't wish death on them at Vandar's hands.

Pushing the thought out of her mind, she followed Swee to the back of the cave.

He gestured toward the solid rock wall. "The portal is there."

Kenna peered at the rough surface. "I can't see anything."

He made a scoffing sound. "Of course not. It's hidden, so nobody can escape through it, or come here by accident from the other world."

Kenna nodded, imagining a horde of slaves who would escape if they could, but she would be sorry for anyone who came here from the other world by mistake.

"It took the mental powers of ten men to make this gateway. Now that it exists, it can be opened with a trigger mechanism," he continued, pointing to a patch of rock at the level of her right shoulder. "You press your palm against it, and the rock appears to thin, revealing the entrance. You must go through quickly, because the panel stays open less than a minute. There is an identical trigger point on the other side. That's how you get back. Do you understand?"

"Yes."

"Repeat the instructions."

She repeated what she had heard, just as she had earlier repeated all the facts she had learned about the other universe.

"Do you have any questions?" Wendon asked.

She managed to repress a hysterical laugh. She had thousands.

"What if I get into trouble? Can you rescue me?"

"We won't know if you are in trouble," Swee answered.

"And we are not permitted to come through," Barthime added.

When she opened her mouth again, he shook his head. "We are wasting time. Open the portal," he ordered.

She swallowed, flexed her fingers, then raised her hand and pressed against the rough surface, feeling a slight tingling on her skin. At the same time, the rock in front of her seemed to dissolve, so that she was facing an open doorway.

The portal.

She marveled at the opening and what she saw. On the other side was a landscape very different from the territory around Vandar's cave.

Instead of blackened land stretching in all directions, she saw trees.

"You've been there?"

"Yes," Barthime hissed.

"How was it?"

"Go. Before we have to do this all over again."

"May the gods protect you," Swee whispered.

She was shocked at the benediction—and touched,

because she knew he was risking Vandar's wrath to call on the gods.

In the next moment, he gave her a little push, and she stumbled into a place where the thick air held her in place.

Panic seized her as she imagined the rock reforming with her still standing in the opening. With a gasp, she struggled forward through the clinging air and broke free—into the other universe.

She stumbled for a few more steps, catching her hand against a tree trunk. Whirling, she looked back through the portal into the world where she had come from.

At first she could still see the men in the cave, all of them staring solemnly at her.

Swee raised his hand in farewell. Then, as she stood with her heart pounding, the rock quickly solidified back into place, and she was left alone in the forest.

For a long moment she stood with her pulse pounding and her breath wheezing in and out of her lungs. Then she lifted her head, looking around in wonder at the unfamiliar surroundings. She had been preparing for this for weeks, but she had never really believed it would happen.

From one moment to the next, she was plunged into a world of differences, large and small. On this side of the portal, there was no cave, only the rocks and forest, which stretched away in all directions.

She had never seen so many trees in one place.

And the air smelled different here.

Of course it did. She wasn't breathing in the smell of burned vegetation. But there were more differences. This place wasn't like Breezewood, either, the city where she had lived. There was something in the atmosphere that wasn't entirely pleasant.

Vandar's words came back to her. He had said that this society was more advanced than the one she came from. Could the smell be from the gasoline or the electricity he had spoken of?

Perhaps. But all she saw was the vast expanse of virgin forest.

As she stood among the trees, a blast of wind shook the branches above her, and she shivered as thunder rumbled.

A storm was coming on this side of the portal. Was it on the other side, too?

TALON grimaced as he looked up from the computer screen. He loved taking people out on wilderness trips, but keeping track of all the details made him crazy.

Like now. He had a canoe trip coming up, and the dehydrated food his clients would eat hadn't been delivered. When he'd checked the order, he'd found that his supplier was out of beef stew, so they'd held up the whole shipment.

He'd switched to chili.

Of course, dehydrated meat was never the first choice of a werewolf. But they'd be able to catch fish for a couple of meals.

Speaking of which, it was time to fix dinner now. Which wasn't too much of a problem. All he had to do was pull a package of steak out of the refrigerator and open it up. When he was alone, he didn't bother with the fiction of pretending to broil or fry it.

A noise outside made him tense, and he turned toward the office window. Since the visit from the cops, he'd been waiting for something else to happen. What that was, he wasn't sure.

Through the glass, he saw the wind kicking up the branches of the trees. Then thunder rumbled. Storms could be fierce out here in the woods, and he'd better bring in the tents that were airing outside.

PUSHING away from the tree, Kenna peered through the gathering darkness.

With no idea which way to go, she chose the easiest direction—downhill—her mind racing as she hurried through the forest.

For months she had been living in a terrible place where

an evil creature dictated every move, dividing the people and setting them against each other. But it hadn't been that way in Breezewood, and there was no reason to think that she wouldn't encounter ordinary human kindness here.

Or would she?

As she hurried into the unknown, the rain broke, and she heard drops hitting the leaves far above her head. When they began to fall on her, she raised her arms over her head—not that it did much good. Her clothing would be soaked soon.

She stopped under a tree with thick foliage. It helped to shelter her a little, and she wanted to huddle there. But she remembered a school lesson from long ago. Lightning was attracted to trees. You could get hit if you were too close to one.

Yet how could she get away from them? They were all around her.

Somewhere to her right, a blast of light flashed. It was followed by a crack of thunder so close that it shook the ground around her. Then, through the rain, she saw a massive tree come crashing to the ground, taking other trees with it.

Gasping, she tried to sprint in the other direction, but her sandals slipped against the wet ground, and she almost fell. When she felt steadier on her feet, she looked around, shading her eyes from the downpour. Through the branches to her right, a light shone out. Not a flash from the storm, but a steady, warm glow that called her forward.

Even through the rain it looked brighter than any artificial light she had seen in her universe.

Electricity. That's what made it so bright. She didn't know how it worked, but she knew that it did other things, too, like run refrigerators and televisions.

She had learned about those things in her recent studies, although she wasn't sure she believed what the adepts had told her.

The light looked like it might come from the window of a house, although she couldn't be sure. Still, she thought that heading toward it was her best option.

She kept her gaze focused firmly in the distance, which turned out to be a mistake. In the darkness, her foot caught on a root, shooting pain through her toe and almost sending her crashing to the ground.

Somehow she kept upright, then marched onward. Bursts of rain drummed down on her, making her shiver.

But at least the light was growing closer.

When she thought she saw the outline of a house through the gloom, she thanked the Great Mother. Probably, someone was home. Either that or they were rich enough to leave their lights on while they were out.

Trying not to slip again, she quickened her pace, heading for the dwelling.

Just as she broke into a clearing, another jagged spear split the sky, and thunder shook the ground.

When a huge tree came crashing toward her, she screamed and sprinted across the slippery leaves, trying to escape the toppling giant.

Though she ran as fast as she could, she felt branches clawing at her back. There was no way she could outrun the falling monster, but she instinctively used her telekinetic powers to keep the massive limbs from crushing her.

CHAPTER
FIVE

CAUGHT BY THE sudden torrent, Talon stood inside the entrance of his storage garage, watching the rain pelt down and debating whether to wait out the storm or make a dash for the house.

In his human form he'd be soaked to the skin. As a wolf he'd get just as wet, but his thick fur would keep the water from penetrating to his skin.

Another bolt of energy speared the sky, lighting up the forest as the rain poured down with renewed force.

The power of the storm called to him, making the decision for him. Quickly, he began taking off his clothing. Naked, still standing inside the shed, he began to say the chant that turned him from man to wolf.

Once again, the familiar pain took hold as his body transmuted from one form to another.

In the middle of the change, he sensed another lightning bolt above him, followed quickly by a bone-jarring roll of thunder.

As he came down on all fours, he thought he heard two sounds over the wind and rain—a massive tree hitting the ground and a woman's scream.

Silently cursing, he thought about changing back from wolf to man so he could shout out the questions, "Who's there? Are you hurt?"

But that would only waste time. If someone was out there, he could find her more quickly as a wolf.

On all fours, he raced into the rain, stopping when he saw a great oak sprawled across the clearing at the edge of the woods, its branches still quivering from the fall.

As another sword of lightning split the sky above him, he sped toward the tangle of tree limbs.

THE tree was still rocking around Kenna, splashing water in her face and turning her hair into a dripping mass, but she had saved herself from getting flattened.

Cautiously, she moved her arms, relieved that they were not pinned down. They were sore, but the lack of serious pain told her that no bones were broken. Thank the Great Mother.

When she tried to shift her legs, the news wasn't quite so good. Her right foot was stuck.

Grasping the branches beside her, she braced herself and gave a mighty yank on her leg, but all she accomplished was scraping her skin.

Closing her eyes for a moment, she considered her options. Perhaps she could use her telekinetic abilities again.

She'd never tackled such a daunting task, but what if she could just lift the branch an inch or two?

She was gathering the energy to try it when the sound of wet leaves rustling made her head jerk around.

At first she saw nothing through the screen of greenery. When she encountered a pair of yellow eyes staring at her, she gasped.

Unable to turn away, she saw the eyes were centered in a gray, furry face. Taking in the whole picture, she made out a canine muzzle, pointed ears, light facial hair, and a ruff of creamy fur around the creature's neck. When he opened his mouth she was treated to a view of sharp, pointed teeth.

A guard dog? A wolf? She had never seen a natural wolf, although a werewolf had once come to her class for young psychics. From what Vandar and his adepts had told her about this world, she was sure they didn't have such beings here. Still, the shape was the same as what she'd seen.

As he approached, she smelled his wet fur and heard his panting breath.

He looked like he could rip out her throat in one savage lunge, and she would have run if she could, but the branch held her captive. Unable to escape, she raised her chin and stared at the animal as he took a careful step into the tangle of branches around her, then another. When he reached her, his eyes sought her face, and she had the strange feeling that he was going to speak to her. The moment stretched. Of course he didn't say anything because animals didn't talk. Instead, he brushed past her arm, and she felt the rain on his fur.

Shifting his body, he pawed at the place where her leg disappeared under a stretch of wet bark.

The tree limb didn't move for him any more than it had for her.

She lay on her sopping bed of branches and leaves, breathing hard, watching the wolf. If he'd wanted to hurt her, he could easily have done it already, she reasoned as he sniffed around the natural trap that held her fast.

When he took a step back, she made a small sound of distress. "Can you bring help?" she asked, knowing that he didn't understand her and that he couldn't answer.

To her surprise, he raised and lowered his head, like a man nodding, and his expression seemed to say, *Wait right there.*

In the next moment he disappeared, leaving her alone and shivering in the rain and wondering if she had made up her unlikely visitor. Maybe she had gotten hit on the head, and her brain was serving up strange visions.

Like the light flickering off to her left.

She turned in that direction, wondering if she'd gotten turned around and misplaced the direction of the house.

Then the smell of smoke drifted toward her, and she realized that the lightning had started a fire in the forest.

Could it keep burning in this damp environment? She didn't know, but she saw that the flames were coming closer to where she lay trapped.

When panic constricted her chest, she ordered herself to steadiness. Fear wasn't going to help anything.

She could get out of this. She had to, because there was no alternative, and there was one thing in her favor. The rain was still falling, although more gently. Maybe it would put out the fire before it reached her.

Drifting smoke made her cough. Trying to ignore the distraction, she flexed her fingers and leaned forward, putting her hands on the heavy branch holding her fast. Eyes closed, she pressed her fingers against the bark and used her mind to extend the reach of her hand, sending her thoughts through the surface and into the living tissue beneath. She needed to learn the mass and weight. Learn how the branch was connected to the central tree trunk.

As the answers fell into place, she formed a plan of action. Pulling the branch up wasn't enough. She had to rotate it as she lifted; otherwise the trunk would hold the limb down.

Opening her eyes, she saw the fire creeping closer, heard the hissing of the wet wood.

Terrible images leaped into her mind—of herself, surrounded by flames. In Breezewood, teams of adepts would have come to pull water from a nearby well and shoot it toward any fire that threatened the city. But she was the only one here, and she couldn't stop a fire by herself.

Unable to hold back a whimper, she watched for a moment, then tore her gaze away and sent out her invisible energy, trying with every shred of power she had to make the branch shift.

Fear made her desperate as she poured out her psychic power. Despite the cold, sweat broke out on her forehead, and her muscles trembled. When the limb quivered under her fingers, she took hope and increased her efforts. To her dismay, the quivering was all she could accomplish—for now.

Unwilling to give up, she lay back, sucking in great drafts of air and shivering from the wet clothing plastered against her skin.

She'd been in this world less than an hour, and she was already in more trouble than she could have imagined.

Still, iron determination made her reach out again with her mind. Before she got very far into the process, she heard something moving rapidly through the forest—coming from the direction where the wolf had disappeared.

Was the animal circling back? This time to attack?

She tensed, probing the darkness. In the flickering light from the fire, she made out a dark shape hurrying toward her. A beam of light ran along in front of it, and as the figure drew closer, she saw it was a man holding a thing called a flashlight.

She'd seen it in a training exercise with Vandar's adepts. And also long ago in one of her classrooms.

Her teacher had made each of the students try to turn it on with his or her mind. She'd been one of the few who could do it. Here she knew that something called batteries made it work.

"Are you all right?" a man called.

"I'm caught. And . . . and . . . the fire's coming."

"Yeah. I'll take care of the fire."

Despite the circumstances, a spurt of wonder leaped inside her. This was her first encounter with a person from the other side of the portal.

She listened to his voice. It was strong and confident, and his accent was different from the people she knew in her own world.

"Hang on. I've got a fire extinguisher."

He backed away. As she listened to the sound of his footsteps receding, fear rose in her throat.

Then she heard a hissing sound, and the flames that had been lapping closer died away.

Moments later, he was back, clambering to her side and hunkering down.

"You put out the fire?" she whispered.

"I can't be sure it's dead. I'll have to check it later."

He kept the beam of his light out of her eyes as he studied her face, apparently as interested in her as she was in him. Up close, in the light from the flashlight, she saw that his hair and eyes were both dark and his features were hard-etched.

And he had a . . . knapsack over his shoulder. Squatting beside her, he took something from the carry bag. It was a small rectangle that unfolded into a surprisingly large blanket, which he spread over her.

The blessed warmth made her want to weep, but she held on to her emotions by force of will while he turned and played his light over the place where her leg disappeared under the branch.

"This is a nice mess," he muttered. "You're lucky your leg isn't broken. Or is it?"

"I don't think so. I mean, I'm not in pain." Switching the subject, she asked. "How . . . how did you find me?"

"I was putting some things in my storage building. I saw the tree fall, and I thought I heard a scream. It took me a while to locate the tree."

Her own situation had made her sensitive to half-truths. "What happened to the wolf?"

He tipped his head to the side, staring at her with a steady gaze. "What wolf?"

"He was here."

He shrugged. "I didn't see him."

She nodded, wondering if she had made up the encounter with the beast. No. He had been too real. His animal smell. His wet fur. The intelligence in his yellow eyes.

The man brought her back to the present. Did he smell like the wolf? Or did the animal scent simply linger in the wet air?

"We have to get you out of here."

"How?"

"I'll lift the branch. You pull your leg out."

She sighed. "I tried. It's too heavy."

"Of course it is," he said, and she wondered if she'd made a mistake by revealing her attempt at escape. Without her telekinetic powers, lifting the thing would have been clearly impossible.

He played his flashlight beam over the bough, inspecting it. "If I can't get the branch off you, I'll go back for a chain saw. But that will mean you'll be out here for a lot longer."

Bending over the limb, he wrapped his hands around the circumference, giving an experimental tug before looking back at her. "Get ready to pull your foot out if I can lift this damn thing."

"Okay," she said.

"My name is Talon Marshall."

An exchange of names. Another test.

"Kenna," she said, then remembered an important fact from her training. People here had more than one name. The last name told what family you belonged to. Vandar's men had picked a last name for her that was very common, in case anyone started trying to figure out where she had come from. "Kenna Thomas," she supplied.

"Sorry to be meeting you like this."

With a murmur of agreement, she braced for more questions. Instead, he silently grasped the branch again. As he strained to pull upward, she sent her telekinetic energy to the tree limb, giving him a jolt of assistance.

Feeling the pressure ease off her ankle, she kept up her energy burst while she yanked her foot out, then tumbled backwards at her sudden release.

He made a startled exclamation, his voice uncertain as he said, "It suddenly got lighter, then heavier again."

She only shook her head, unable to tell him that it had been her lifting and that the extra weight had piled on the branch when she'd run out of energy.

She was free! *Finally.*

He was talking again, and she struggled to focus on his words.

"Can you stand?"

"I think so." Quickly, she pulled off the blanket he'd draped over her and pushed herself up. But she had been in one cramped position for too long, and when she stood on wobbly legs, one knee gave way and she started to fall back into the tangle of branches where she'd been lying.

Talon Marshall darted forward, catching her before she could go down. As the two of them swayed on the uneven surface, she came to rest in his arms with her head on his shoulder and her wobbly legs wedged against his solid ones.

She felt herself trembling, from the cold and from her reaction to him.

"Are you all right?"

"Yes. I'm lucky you found me."

"You're lucky the trunk, or a major branch, didn't smack you in the back or hit you on the head."

His arms were strong. And his body was warm and comforting. She'd been virtually alone in a crowd of people for months. It was hard to remember a time when anyone had held her, comforted her. Unable to stop herself, she let her head nestle against his shoulder as she raised her arms to grip him.

He cradled her in his embrace, and she wanted to burrow further into his warmth.

"How did you get here?" he asked as his hands stroked over her back and shoulders.

The question brought a knot of tension back to her middle. This was the real start of her assignment. The story she would have to tell. She wanted to confess everything to him and get herself out of the terrible situation she'd been thrust into. But confession was not an option. Not when she was under Vandar's compulsion.

"I guess I got lost," she managed to say.

He could have let her go, but instead, he kept his arms around her. "You were very brave. With the tree and the fire."

"What else could I do?"

"Yeah." He laughed. Then his voice turned sober again. "You're wet and cold. We'd better get you inside."

"Inside where?"

"My lodge."

The assurance in his voice brought back the enormity of her situation. This man had found her trapped under a tree limb. He'd freed her. Now she was going to repay him with lies.

To her horror, she began to cry.

In response, his arms tightened around her. "It's okay. You've been through a lot."

She shook her head against his shoulder. She wasn't crying about what had happened with the tree. Instead, her thoughts were racing forward into the future and the situation that had already spun out of her control.

CHAPTER
SIX

MILES AWAY, A man named Ramsay Gallagher brushed back a lock of dark hair from his forehead as he stared out the reinforced glass window of his mountain chalet. He was searching for something he was pretty sure he wasn't going to see. Not yet.

From a distance his house looked like the vacation home of a millionaire who enjoyed indulging his whims.

In reality, it was a well-fortified stronghold, perched at the top of a Colorado mountain that he'd had the foresight to purchase years ago. It was an excellent location for a man who valued his privacy.

Only one winding gravel track led up from the highway. There were no guardrails, and a driver required nerves of steel to make it to the top of his mountain, where access to the house was blocked by a stout metal gate and sheer cliffs.

You had to want to come here. And you had to know how to get past the barriers he'd erected—unless, of course, you could fly.

He smiled as he thought of a helicopter circling his property, the pilot trying to figure out where to land. He'd be out of luck. And if men came down a rope ladder, Ramsay could nail them before they reached the patio outside his bedroom.

He grimaced. *Don't go looking for problems. You're not expecting an attack. Not today.*

Yet a change in the fabric of the universe had put him on alert, and he had learned to trust his instincts.

Some major element had shifted in a way that he didn't understand yet, but he would. And if trouble came his way, he was prepared to deal with it.

His fingers played over the leather of his easy chair, appreciating the soft, smooth texture. He liked his comfort, and he valued fine things, but now he was distracted by the sensations drifting toward him from far away.

Too restless to sit, he climbed out of the chair, strode to the window, and studied the mountain scenery. He could have lived anywhere in the world, but he had chosen this place because it suited him so well. Not just the grandeur of the craggy peaks, the pine forests, and the animals that inhabited them. He liked the isolation.

He had other houses, as well. One along the California coast where he could watch the waves crashing on the rocks twenty yards below. Another outside Washington, D.C., in Potomac, Maryland, where he was close to the center of world power. One on Lake Como in Italy. He was rich enough to own property around the world. And he traveled to his other abodes when he wanted a change of scenery.

But he always felt safest here. And for now, he would stay in this mountain retreat and watch for what might come.

TALON could feel the woman in his arms struggling to contain her tears. He didn't have much experience comforting women, but he gave it his best shot as he patted her back reassuringly and spoke softly.

"Everything's okay. Come on. Let's go inside where you can get warm and dry."

"Okay," she whispered as though the word was from a foreign language.

"How's your leg? Can you walk?" As he spoke, he stooped to pick up his gear.

"I think so."

Slinging his arm around her waist, he played his light along the ground in front of them, guiding her through the branches of the massive tree sprawled at the edge of the forest.

She was limping, he noticed. But her leg wasn't broken. That was the important thing. Not the feel of her soft breast pressing against his side. To distract himself, he went back over his finding her and the rescue. There was something strange about the way the branch had lifted off her. He'd been pulling up, and it had rotated slightly as it rose. Had he done that, or had some other force been operating?

The speculation brought him up short. What other force would that be? The branch must have conveniently shifted when he'd pulled on it.

He wanted to go back and have a look at it. But that was out of the question now. He had to get her dry and warm, or she could go into hypothermia, even in late summer.

They made their slow way out of the branches, and he breathed out a sigh as they reached open ground.

"This way." Turning to the left, he led her to the lodge.

As they walked, he could feel her trembling. A natural response to her narrow escape. And to getting drenched.

After she got out of her wet clothes, he'd put her in one of the bedrooms. He imagined her lying under the covers, and an erotic picture leaped into his mind. Of her reaching out naked arms to him and pulling him down to the bed with her.

Sternly, he ordered himself not to go down that road. She was simply a woman who had had the misfortune to get clobbered by a tree in the storm. On his property.

They reached the porch, and he helped her slowly up the two steps, then into the front hall. He'd given her a quick once-over outside, but it had been dark. Now, standing under the overhead light, he took in more details, starting with the light brown hair that hung in wet strands around her ears.

Her skin was paper white, making her look like she'd been living in a cave for months.

She was about average height. Too thin, he thought. Because she was dieting like so many women, or because she hadn't had enough food recently? Her large blue eyes were set wide apart, above high cheekbones, a small nose, and temptingly full lips.

Dropping his gaze, he noted the way her wet shirt clung to her breasts. Quickly, he lowered his eyes, taking in the soaked jeans and the leather sandals that looked like they'd been made on a hippie commune. Strange footwear for a tramp through the woods.

"Did you lose your pack or your purse?" he asked.

"My knapsack," she answered, her voice shaky.

"We can look for your stuff in the morning."

"Thanks," she murmured.

"Come on." He led her down the hall to one of the guest suites and sat her on the closed toilet seat in the bathroom while he thought about what she could wear.

KENNA sat where he'd left her, trying to make her fogged brain function. She was sitting on a toilet seat. In a bathroom. She had seen pictures of bathrooms in this world. She hadn't really understood how foreign they were.

Her mind skittered back to something Talon Marshall had said—about her purse?

What was that, exactly?

She'd learned so many facts about this world, but she didn't remember being told about a purse.

Lifting her head, she looked toward the door. He'd gone off to get her some clothing. While he was away, she could run out of the house.

And go where?

She shook her head. She was still wet and cold. There was nowhere to go, and she might as well make the best of this situation. This was what she was supposed to do!

Again, she forced herself to focus on her surroundings. The bathroom was strange and the house was just as confounding. She'd only gotten a quick look as Talon Marshall had ushered her down a hall, but she sensed that the structure was huge, like the residence of a noble back home. Yet the man was dressed too casually to be a noble.

She stopped herself, struggling to rearrange her thinking. There were no nobles in this world, so he couldn't be one. But it looked like he was rich, if he lived in a place this large.

Did he share this dwelling with anyone? A wife? Children? She had no clue. But it seemed impossible that he would be the only occupant.

Just from their brief meeting, she liked him. More than liked him. He'd gone out of his way to help a stranger. He could have gotten hurt climbing around the fallen tree, but he hadn't hesitated. And when he'd held her in his arms, she'd felt a spurt of attraction to him. Or had that just been gratitude that he'd rescued her?

She didn't want to feel either of those things.

Hating the prospect of spinning him her story, she turned her mind to the clammy fabric of her shirt pressing against her skin. It was warm inside the house, but the shirt was making her cold, and she should take it off. Then she'd feel better. She was fumbling with the buttons and had gotten a few of them opened when she heard footsteps in the hall.

"All right to come in?" he called.

"Yes."

He stepped into the little room, filling the small space. Outside, she hadn't taken in his size. Now she saw he was tall and well muscled, with a decisive jaw covered by dark stubble.

"Who lives here with you?" she blurted.

"No one." He shifted his weight from one foot to the other. "Well, not on a regular basis. I lead wilderness expeditions. Sometimes clients spend the night at the beginning or end of a trip."

She nodded, wondering what he meant by a "wilderness expedition."

Briskly, he changed the subject. "You need a hot shower.

Then you can put these on." As he spoke, he set down a pile of soft clothing on a square table beside the sink.

A hot shower? She'd been thinking of a bath, and her dulled brain scrambled to process what he was suggesting.

As he spoke, he pulled aside a curtain and reached to turn a lever. Water came spraying out of . . . The word eluded her.

As he fiddled with the dial, she continued to open her shirt, still struggling with the wet buttonholes. Finally, she got it off and dropped it on the floor, then stood and wrestled with the snap at the top of the pants. The zipper came down more easily, and she was just stepping out of the pants when he turned—and made a choked sound.

She'd been automatically getting out of her wet clothes. Now she blinked as she realized she was standing in front of him clad in nothing more than the unfamiliar underwear she'd put on a few hours ago. The revealing underwear.

"Oh!"

Taking a quick step back, she hit the toilet with her legs, throwing herself off balance.

She would have fallen if his hand hadn't whipped out and grabbed her arms, steadying her, drawing her closer, so that her breasts came to rest against his chest.

Neither of them moved.

"Sorry. I'm . . ."—a phrase she'd learned came to her— "a little out of it."

"It's okay."

She clenched and unclenched her fists. Maybe she could tell him the truth—right now. And everything would be all right. He could help her. Really help her, and she wouldn't have to keep up the lie that she'd already started.

The moment those thoughts stole into her mind, a stab of pain knifed through her head. She knew it was from Vandar, from what he'd done to her before she'd started her training for this assignment.

"What?"

"I . . ." Unable to stay erect, she sagged against him.

"What?" he asked again, his voice more urgent. "Did a branch hit your head?"

"I don't . . . know. Maybe," she managed to whisper, thinking that hitting her head would give her an excuse for her shaky behavior.

"Maybe I shouldn't leave you alone," he said in a husky voice.

She wanted to cling to him, and the sympathetic tone she heard in his voice.

No, don't leave me alone. Help me. You've got to help me get out of this trap.

That thought brought another stab of pain, but she was ready for it this time, and for the despair that filled her, because she understood there was nothing he or anyone else could do for her, not on the very basic level where she desperately needed help.

"I'll be fine," she whispered, pushing away from him.

He studied her face. "You're sure?"

"Yes."

The doubtful look he gave her made her heart turn over.

"I'll be here, if you need me."

"Thank you."

When he stepped away and closed the door behind him, she breathed out a small sigh.

The room was filling with steam, and she marveled at the torrent pouring from the . . . showerhead. She had better wash before she used up his supply of hot water.

She fumbled with the unfamiliar catch on the bra. Why in the name of Carfolian hell was it in the center of her back where it was almost impossible to reach?

As she finally got it open, she glanced toward the door. She was alone with a man in a house that was isolated in the woods. He could take advantage of her, if he wanted.

She struggled to put that thought out of her mind as she pulled off her panties, then climbed into the shower and stuck her hand under the water. It felt wonderful, and she pulled the curtain closed behind her, as much to shield herself as to keep from getting the pounding water on the floor.

TALON listened to the sounds of the woman moving around in the bathroom. When he heard the shower curtain rustle, an image of her naked body leaped into his mind. Annoyed with himself, he made a snorting sound, then turned away and strode down the hall, cursing the male imperative to respond to an attractive woman.

When she'd started getting undressed, he'd had a very nice view of her body. And even as he'd been comforting her, he'd registered the weight of her breasts against his chest.

She'd acted spacey. Not seductive. Unless she was a good actress, pretending to be out of it while she worked her feminine wiles on him.

He clenched his jaw. That last thought was another over-reaction, he told himself. Yet there had been something strange about her. Something he didn't understand. And didn't trust, to be more specific.

She had an unfamiliar accent. Where did she come from?

With narrowed eyes, he examined the circumstances under which they'd met. She'd been trapped by a massive tree limb as a fire threatened her. Apparently, she'd been out in the storm and gotten into trouble.

And maybe . . .

What? Someone had sent her to spy on him?

He deliberately relaxed his tense shoulders. He'd been off balance since the cops had stopped by, which was damn annoying.

Back at the front door, he grabbed the flashlight he'd set down. Slipping out into the night, he headed for the lightning strike that had started the fire.

The rain had finished putting out the flames, and his nose told him that the embers were no longer smoldering. But he gave the area a thorough inspection before heading back to the house.

One problem solved, but his mind was still churning as he strode back inside. To distract himself, he stopped in the living room and turned on the flat-screen television set, tuning to a cable news channel. He could see the picture from the kitchen, and with his excellent hearing, he could also follow the commentary.

THE hot water beating down on Kenna felt like a trip to heaven. Looking around the shower enclosure, she found a bar of spicy-smelling soap resting in a niche in the wall. She picked it up, sniffing it before lathering her body. There was also a bottle of something called shampoo, and when she read the directions, she found it was for washing hair. Again, she liked the fragrance as she lathered and rinsed.

She wanted to stay under the pounding water, as much to postpone her inevitable reunion with Talon Marshall as for the warmth. She had been living in a chilly cave for months, and the heat of the water made her sigh with pleasure. At the same time, she knew she couldn't stay hidden there. So she peered at the lever—which said "hot" on one side and "cold" on the other.

Guessing at what she should do, she turned it all the way to the cold side, and the water went off.

After pulling a towel off a bar fastened to the wall, she marveled at the soft texture as she rubbed it over her skin. It was like nothing she had ever felt, not even when she had lived in Cardon's household.

When her body was dry, she worked on her hair, getting out as much of the moisture as she could, knowing she was spending so much time on it because she didn't want to go out and face the man who had rescued her.

But if she didn't emerge soon, she knew he was going to come back and ask if she was all right.

Suddenly self-conscious again, she turned to the pile of clothing on the little table. The soft pants would have been too long, but some kind of stretchy band at the bottom held them at her ankles. The long-sleeved shirt was also soft. Both of them carried the scent of Talon Marshall, and she knew they must belong to him.

She didn't want to wear his clothing, especially against her bare skin, but she saw no alternative since her underthings were still wet.

After dressing, she turned back to the sink. Above it hung a looking glass, which was covered with moisture from the steam. After she'd wiped it with a towel, she stared at herself. The image that stared back was startlingly clear. She inspected her curly brown hair, still damp from the shower. Peering more closely at her eyes, she saw that they looked blue. She'd never been quite sure of the color until this moment. She took in the shape of her lips, then opened her mouth, looking at her teeth, glad that they were straight and even. Next to the sink were two things she recognized from her prep sessions. A toothbrush in a clear package. And a tube of toothpaste. After unwrapping the brush, she carefully squeezed the toothpaste on the bristles, then scrubbed the brush across her front teeth. The minty flavor was a surprise, but after a few moments, she decided she liked it.

When she'd finished scrubbing her teeth, she set the brush next to the package, washed out her mouth with water from the tap, then gave her face one more inspection. In this world, she knew that women might wear makeup. She didn't have any. Would she be attractive enough to Talon Marshall? Would he . . .

Let her stay here?

That was the end of the thought, but she hardly dared to hope for that much.

Unable to keep looking herself in the eye, she whirled away from the mirror.

"Don't think about it," she ordered herself. "You don't have any choice about what you have to do."

Almost against her will, she exited the bathroom and started down the hall.

When she'd been wet and cold, Talon had hurried her

toward the shower. Now she walked more slowly, glancing into the rooms. Most of them had wide beds and chests with drawers. But all of the beds were neatly made, and no personal possessions were lying around, which made it look like nobody was actually sleeping in the rooms.

On the chests were more of the magazines she had looked at back in her own world. She wanted to page through them, but not now.

Another chamber had a desk, a chair, and equipment that she had never seen before, but she knew from her research that the thing on the desk was a computer.

A voice came from the end of the hall. Someone talking. Not Talon Marshall. Did he have a visitor? Had he called the authorities to come take her away?

The police! She'd seen pictures of them. They were like soldiers or guards back home. But they had guns that could kill you from yards away.

She wanted to run to the back of the house and hide, but that would do her little good. Instead, she tiptoed down the hall and stopped short when she saw a picture sitting on a chest. A picture of a man talking. Only she could see his mouth moving and hear his voice.

Astonished, she stood and watched. Was this the television that she had learned about? She'd thought the adepts were exaggerating to impress her. Now she saw it for herself. The picture switched abruptly to a mass of people running down a street, with flashes of smoke landing among them.

What did that mean?

The people looked angry, and a voice came from the television, telling her that they were protesters in India.

The scene switched again to a peaceful-looking forest with shafts of light breaking through the trees—the same picture she had seen in one of the magazines. Only this scene moved. And a woman walked into the picture, talking about something called deodorant. Something you put in your armpits, she remembered. Only the woman rubbed it on the back of her hand as she spoke.

Kenna watched transfixed, thinking the television thing would be a wonderful source of information about this world.

If Talon Marshall let her stay and watch it.

A noise at the end of the hall told her his probable location. Knowing she had to get the meeting over with, she hurried in that direction and found him in a room that she knew was a kitchen.

His back was to her, but he must have been listening for her, because he turned, an expectant look on his face.

"How are you feeling?"

"Good," she whispered automatically, then took a step into the room, just as a high-pitched shrieking noise filled the air and she couldn't hold back a scream.

CHAPTER
SEVEN

TALON MOVED WITH the lightning speed of his were-wolf reflexes. Although it registered that Kenna's reaction wasn't normal, he knew the whistling kettle he'd put on to boil water had terrified her. Snatching it off the burner, he slammed it down again onto the surface of the stove before sprinting across the room toward her.

"What?" she gasped, looking wildly around as though she thought the house was under attack.

He kept his voice low and calm as he folded her into his arms. "It's all right. It was just the kettle. It's all right," he repeated, feeling her quiver in his embrace.

"The kettle?" she asked in a shaky voice, her gaze shooting to the thing that had made the noise. It was still making a feeble sound, but nothing like the high-pitched shriek that had frightened her moments before.

"It whistles to tell you when the water's heated. You've never heard that before?"

"No." Her voice was faint and apologetic, edging on tears again.

He held on to her, because he didn't know what else to do. For a long moment, she pressed her cheek against his shoulder. Finally, she raised her head and looked up at him, her blue eyes wide and helpless.

That look undid him, even when he tried to cling to logic.

He barely knew her. He didn't trust her. He should ease away from her before it was too late.

Too late for what? The question flickered somewhere in the depths of his brain.

Instead of answering the question, he tightened his embrace.

The last time he had held her, she'd been wet and cold. Now she was dressed in his sweatpants and shirt. The knit fabric clung to every sweet curve of her body—her breasts, the feminine roundness of her hips, the indentation at her waist.

He pictured himself lowering his hand to her bottom, so he could press her more firmly against himself. Somehow he maintained enough control to keep his hands above her waist.

But control was slipping fast as every one of his senses responded to her. He heard her breath turn ragged, inhaled the fresh scent of the shampoo in her hair and the soap on her skin.

She didn't have to stay in his arms. She could have pulled away, but she didn't move, didn't stir. When she raised her face to his, her skin was flushed a delicate pink.

Their gazes locked. Her mouth was mere inches from his, and he caught the warmth of her breath and the scent of mint toothpaste. That tempting flavor drew his head down, so that his mouth touched hers. She'd been frightened, and he'd leaped to comfort her. Perhaps he was trying to fool himself into thinking that comfort was still his motive. But at the moment of their first mouth-to-mouth contact, something wild and unexpected flared between them, a mutual kindling of emotion.

As his lips moved against hers, she did the same, tasting him, sipping from him, consuming him.

His hands roved restlessly over her back, her shoulders, frantic to take in as much of her as he could. He felt no bra under the knit fabric. When his hands drifted downward, he couldn't detect a panty line. Lord, she was naked under the sweatpants and shirt. *His* sweatpants and shirt!

The thought drove him mad. All he would have to do was pull the shirt over her head and shuck down the pants—and she would be nude.

But somewhere in his fogged brain he knew that would be too fast. He didn't know her well enough for this.

With an effort he tried to hang on to that lie.

They clung together as though they'd both been caught in another storm, rocking a little, while the kiss turned more frantic and blood pooled in the lower part of his body.

This was his own damn fault. He had stayed away from women for months, telling himself that he had work to do. But deep down he knew that fear had been one of his motives. He was close to thirty, close to the age when the men of the Marshall family bonded with their life mates. But he liked his life the way it was. He liked going out into the wild whenever he wanted. Liked living alone. Liked making decisions without answering to anyone else.

Being tied down to a wife and kids had no appeal, so he had made that scenario impossible.

Then the thunderstorm had broken, and Kenna had cried out to him from the depths of the tempest. Through a chain of events outside his control, she was in his arms, stirring feelings he had worked hard to suppress.

As he kissed her, he silently acknowledged that he needed more, a lot more.

More than she was willing to give?

No. She was warm and willing in his arms, as caught up in the emotions of the moment as he was himself.

Through two layers of fabric, he could feel the points of her nipples stabbing into his chest, and he wanted to ease far enough away so that he could slide one hand between them.

His fingers ached with the need to stroke back and forth against those tight points. Or better yet, pulling up the sweatshirt and lowering his head so that he could suck her into his mouth and circle one of the tempting nubs with his tongue.

Somehow he kept from going that far, but he couldn't stop himself from bringing his hands inward to press against the side of her breast through the fabric of the sweatshirt.

The world had contracted to a small space with room for only himself and the woman in his arms. When she made a strangled sound, he reached a whole new level of arousal.

The disparity in their heights meant his cock was pressed against her middle. Wanting it in the cleft between her legs, he moved back, bracing his hips against the kitchen counter. Taking her with him, he splayed his legs to equalize their heights. She leaned in closer, moving her center against him. That had been his goal, but the intimate contact was close to driving him mad.

More images flashed into his mind. The two of them in his bed, arms and legs tangled together. Bodies fused.

No. The bed was too far away. Maybe they could make it to the rug in the living room.

"Kenna," he growled into her mouth as he knit his fingers with hers.

"Talon Marshall," she answered.

And the strangeness of that response brought him up short. *Talon Marshall?* That was a curious way to address a man when you were getting ready to make love to him.

He raised his head, staring down at her.

She must have seen the question on his face.

"What?" she whispered.

"I think you know me well enough to call me Talon."

"Talon," she repeated.

He wasn't sure why he asked his next question. "Where do you come from?"

The sudden fear that flashed in her eyes was like a punch in the gut. She broke away from him, exited the kitchen, and hurried down the hall. Unwilling to let her simply escape, he caught up and grabbed her arm.

Her gasp was another sucker punch. What was he doing? Forcing her into intimacy? *No!* He was trying to get to the bottom of a mystery.

"Don't run away."

She stood with her face averted.

"What are you afraid of?"

Her body jerked as though she'd been struck. "Everything."

"You don't have to be afraid of me," he said, wondering if it was true.

She stretched out her arm, then let it fall back against her side. "You . . . we . . . were just . . ."

"Yeah. I got kind of carried away. I apologize."

She swallowed. "It was as much my fault. I shouldn't have let you . . ."

He wasn't sure if that was true. He had overstepped the bounds, certainly broken one of his own rules about bringing a strange woman back to the lodge to have . . . He cut off the thought. He hadn't brought her here to have sex. He had freed her from a fallen tree and rescued her from a storm.

"I'm . . . not myself," she murmured.

He could say the same thing. Maybe the unlikely circumstances had overtaken them both. Instead of continuing the personal discussion, he changed the subject abruptly. "I was going to make you some hot chocolate. That's why the kettle was on."

"What is it?"

"Hot chocolate?"

She gave him that frightened look again, and he wondered why something so innocuous could set her off.

"A warm drink," he answered. "Haven't you had it before?"

"I . . . don't think so."

He tipped his head to the side and asked the question that had been circling in his mind, "What are you doing here?"

KENNA took a deep breath. So far, she'd made a mess out of this encounter. She didn't even know about the name part. He'd called her "Kenna," and she'd responded because that was the name she used, until Vandar's adepts had added the "Thomas" part. So she hadn't even thought about what she was saying when she'd called him Talon Marshall. It was right. But it was wrong, too. She hadn't learned that in her endless lessons. If you kissed a man, you didn't use both names.

She'd spent two weeks getting ready for this assignment, but a little thing like that had snared her. How many more mistakes was she going to make?

She glanced toward the wall and took a deep breath, letting it out before turning back to him. "I'm running away."

"From where?"

She gestured vaguely with her arm. "Up in the hills."

"Why?"

Her fingers curled and she fell back on a phrase she'd learned. "I'd rather not say."

He gave her a long look, and she prepared to hear him tell her to leave. To her surprise, he answered, "Okay."

Did that mean he accepted her explanation? Or was he only waiting to ask more questions?

He confused her again by turning and heading back to the kitchen. With no other choice, she followed.

The kettle thing that had scared her was sitting on the stove, mocking her.

"The water should still be hot enough," he said as he opened a cabinet above the counter and brought down two mugs. A flat envelope with some writing on the side was lying on the counter.

She watched everything he was doing, trying to memorize the actions so she could repeat them if she had to.

Methodically, he tore off the top of the packet, dumped the contents into one of the mugs, and added water from the kettle. Then he stirred the mixture with a spoon.

As soon as the water and the powder combined, a delicious aroma drifted toward her.

Hot chocolate, he had said.

After passing her the mug, he opened another cabinet and took out a small rectangular box with a picture of vegetation on the side. From it he removed a smaller packet, which he put into the other mug, then added water.

None of this was like any food preparation she'd ever seen, and her throat tightened as she tried to absorb the details. Vandar's men had had no idea of what she would face here.

Talon Marshall stirred his own drink, and she caught a mixture of spicy flavors.

"Why are you having something different?" she asked.

"I don't eat many sweets."

"Oh."

After taking the packet out of the mug, he opened a door under the sink and tossed the wet thing into a tall, square bucket thing.

When he carried his cup to the table, she followed.

Sitting across from him, she took a cautious sip of the hot chocolate. It was rich and sweet and delicious.

"This is wonderful," she murmured. "You really don't like it?"

"Family trait," he clipped out.

She nodded and took another sip.

"How did you get here?" he asked.

She almost choked on the drink and fought to recover. "I hitched a ride . . . from a truck driver," she said, repeating the story she'd been given. "Then I got out and walked."

He kept his gaze on her. "Why are you running away?"

"Do I have to talk about it?" she asked in a small voice.

"Not if it makes you uncomfortable."

"I have to figure out what to do," she said.

When he didn't comment, she went on. "If you let me stay here for a few days, I could earn my keep." As soon as she'd said it, her face flamed, because she realized how he might take that. "I . . . I mean doing work for you. Things around the house."

As she watched him considering the suggestion, she held her breath. He could let her stay, or he could send her away.

THE storm was over, and from the darkness of the forest, Mitch Sutton cautiously approached the old hunting lodge.

He'd tracked the cocksucker here, and now he was going to figure out how to get even with the guy.

Not that anything he could do was going to make up for the missing million bucks. But at least he could make the bastard sorry that he'd ever stuck his shovel where it didn't belong.

It was dumb luck that Mitch had seen the guy. He'd been about to do a quick check on the stash when he'd spotted two cars coming up the rutted road and stopping. His pulse had started pounding as he'd watched the civilian and the two cops get out.

From what he caught of the conversation, he'd been pretty sure the fucking money was gone. Mitch had circled around and used his binoculars to read the civilian's license plate. Then he'd faded back into the woods and waited until the coast was clear to check the hiding place, hoping against hope that he was wrong.

No such luck!

He'd planned the gig, and he'd killed Jim Edison to keep that dumb fuck from throwing around wads of cash and drawing attention to himself.

Now . . . it was all gone.

He'd made friends with a chick at the DMV who'd done some favors for him off and on. His first step in his revenge plans had been to take her out to lunch and sweet-talk her into giving him a reading on the license plate.

The vehicle belonged to a guy named Talon Marshall, and when Mitch had looked him up, he'd found where he lived. Right next to the park where Mitch had buried the money.

Well, screw him!

Mitch stayed in the shadows of the trees, watching the house. A few lights were on, which meant Marshall was probably still up.

He'd done some research on the guy and found out that he made his living leading tree-hugger trips for city types who wanted to get back to nature. And apparently he went for long walks in the woods where he'd somehow discovered the damn box.

He was going to end up dead pretty soon. But first Mitch had some plans for him.

CHAPTER
EIGHT

TALON LEANED BACK in his seat, keeping his gaze fixed on Kenna. "What can you do?" he asked.

At first, it looked like her mind had drawn a blank. Then she began to speak. "Keep the house clean. Weed the garden. Carry wood. Carry water. You don't have to pay me. It can be an exchange."

Well, that was an interesting set of skills. "How are you at MS Word?" he asked, watching her carefully.

"What?"

"A computer word processing program."

She seemed to shrink into herself. "I'm not familiar with that."

Another thought struck him. "Do you have a driver's license?"

She swallowed. "No."

From the panic in her eyes, he wondered if she knew what a driver's license was. Where the hell did she come from, really? With her odd accent and her out-of-kilter fears. She'd made a vague reference to "the hills." He knew there were rural areas of Pennsylvania where people lived in isolated communities. Maybe she belonged to one of those crazy religious cults where one guy ran the whole show. Or maybe there was a bunch of elders telling everyone else what to do. Was she being forced to marry one of the old men? Was that why she'd run away? Or had she been abducted by aliens and just escaped from the mother ship? *Yeah, sure.*

"How old are you?" he asked.

"Twenty-two," she answered in a quavery voice.

He nodded.

"Can you cook?"

She looked toward the stove. "You could teach me."

"It's not my best skill."

She jumped back in with more suggestions. "I can sew. And . . . make beds. And I know how to make soap and preserve books."

"Preserve books?"

She flushed. "Well, I guess you don't do that here."

The almost desperate expression on her face made his stomach clench. He didn't know her background. He wasn't sure he could trust her, and he was worried about his wild, out-of-control response to her. *Yeah, let's not forget about that.*

Or was that part of the reason he was willing to keep her close? He hated questioning his own motives. But even if he'd have to watch himself around her, he wasn't going to toss her out. At least not without proof that she was up to something underhanded.

Before he could talk himself out of it, he said, "We can give it a try."

The look of relief that flooded her face was almost too much to take. She wanted this. More than she was letting on.

"Thank you," she murmured.

Because he was having trouble coping with his own emotions, he asked, "Do you want something to eat?"

She hesitated, her tongue flicking out to stroke her lower lip.

"You're hungry, right? But you don't want to ask for food."

"Yes," she admitted in a low voice.

"You don't have to second-guess everything with me," he said, wondering if it was true.

He thought about his larder. He had a lot of meat in the freezer and the food he took on camping trips. There was also a stock of canned goods for when he had clients staying over.

"Canned beef soup all right?" he asked.

She nodded.

"I guess you're not a vegetarian."

"A what?"

"You eat meat."

"Doesn't everybody?"

"No."

While he opened a can from the pantry, he noted that she was watching him carefully, as though she had never seen a can opener and wanted to learn how to do it.

He stirred the soup, put some in another mug, and set it in the microwave. This time her expression was wide-eyed, and he was sure she had never seen the appliance before.

"You cook it in there? In the cup?"

"It's already cooked. The microwave heats it up."

"Oh."

When the timer rang after a couple of minutes, she took her lower lip between her teeth. "It does it so fast?"

"Well, it depends on how much you have. With more food, it takes longer."

"Oh," she said again, like he was explaining Einstein's theory of relativity.

He took out the mug with a potholder and set it on the counter, along with a couple of spoons. "Be careful. The mug's hotter than the soup. Use the handle."

"Okay."

After carrying her soup to the table, he poured the rest of the can into another mug. It wasn't his favorite meal, but he could handle it.

She sipped cautiously. "It's good."

"Probably, you're used to homemade."

"Yes."

"You know how to slaughter cattle?"

"I've never done it."

When she didn't offer any more comments, he leaned back and watched her eat. She was trying not to gulp the simple meal, but he could see she was hungry, and he felt guilty about taking part of the soup when he was only sipping it to keep her company.

Getting up, he found a box of crackers in the pantry, took out half a dozen, and put them on a plate, which he passed to her.

She ate them quickly.

"Finish up. Then you should get to bed."

Obediently, she spooned up the meat and vegetables at the bottom of the mug.

When she'd finished and looked up, he stood and reached for the crockery.

"I've made extra work for you. Let me wash those," she said.

"No need. I'll just put them in the dishwasher."

"The dishwasher. Right," she said, and he had the feeling again that she'd come from another universe. Or at least an environment without modern conveniences.

Staying matter-of-fact, he showed her how to stack the mugs in the appliance. Then he escorted her to a bedroom next to the bathroom where she'd showered.

She tensed and he wondered what she thought he was going to do—grab her? He took a step back, but because he didn't want her to stumble around in the dark if she got up in the middle of the night, he pointed out the overhead light switch, as well as the lamp on the bedside table.

Then he left, because he couldn't help feeling awkward standing in a bedroom with her.

WHEN she'd closed the door, Kenna breathed out a little sigh. He'd left her alone, when he could have continued the heated scene they'd started in the kitchen. But since then, it was obvious that he was working hard to distance himself from the intimacy.

She might have thanked him for that—if she'd felt comfortable bringing up the subject.

There was a door from her bedroom into the bathroom.

After stepping through, she used the toilet, marveling at the way she could flush it when she was finished.

Back in her bedroom, she switched the lamp on and off, enchanted by the way the warm light flooded from under the shade at the press of a button. Then she turned off the overhead light at the switch and slipped into the bed. It was wide and comfortable, more comfortable than any bed she had ever slept in. And the coverings and pillows felt soft next to her skin.

She lay there for several minutes, staring around at the room, hardly able to believe that she was really here. In a lodge. In another universe. Then she pressed the switch on the lamp, plunging the room into darkness. Well, not quite darkness. A little light came in around the covering over the window.

Wriggling down under the covers, she lay with her eyes closed, trying to come to grips with everything that had happened. She'd fooled Talon Marshall into believing her story about escaping from the hills. No, she should call him Talon. And *had* she fooled him? Certainly he knew there was something strange about her—at least from his point of view. Could she keep him on her side?

Even though she hated herself for lying to him, she wanted to stay here. Because she was attracted to him? Or because this was an ideal place to learn about this world?

Both things were true. But one thing she knew: she didn't understand him. They were alone in an isolated house where they had shared a passionate kiss, and in her world she was sure he would have taken advantage of that, taken advantage of her. She wouldn't be lying in this bed alone, or maybe she would, after he'd finished with her.

But it hadn't turned out that way. And now she had time to think about what she should do.

Using him made her stomach knot. The moral thing to do was leave, but she had connected with him. If she left, she'd have to start all over again and try to trick another man. Who might not be as chivalrous.

Was she rationalizing? Or was Vandar reaching out and controlling her?

She shuddered. Maybe he wasn't reaching out, but he'd planted compulsions in her mind, compulsions she couldn't ignore. Which meant that she didn't even know if her decisions were her own—or his.

IN his warm and comfortable office, Ramsay Gallagher disconnected from his online brokerage account and pushed his chair away from the desk. As he expected, his finances were in good shape, even with the recent economic downturn. He was a seasoned investor; he knew when to buy stocks and when to pull back and buy municipal bonds and CDs. Some of his money was in land that would only go up in value. And he had buried gold, if he needed it.

But an unaccustomed sense of anxiety had overtaken him, prompting him to take a financial inventory. And earlier, he'd checked his name through a private online database. As far as he could tell, nobody in cyberspace was checking up on him.

No surprise there, either. Over the years, he'd made himself difficult to find. None of his contacts had the address of this house. What mail he received was delivered to a post office box thirty miles away. And he was untraceable on the Internet.

The financial and privacy checks he'd just run should have put his doubts at rest, but the feeling of anxiety remained.

Standing up, he paced to the darkened window and looked out at the stars shining down on his mountaintop. In the cities, the ambient light dimmed the glory of the sky. Out here, the resplendency of the stars shone out as it had for thousands of years.

The window was large, and he could see many familiar constellations. Their names and stories came from mankind's superstitious past, but that didn't detract from his enjoyment of the familiar patterns.

He had studied the meaning of the star patterns and studied many ancient techniques for acquiring knowledge.

If a computer couldn't help him, there were other alternatives he could try.

Leaving his office, he walked down the hall to a door that was hidden in the paneling. When he pressed first at the top and then halfway down the flat surface, the door slid to the side, and he reached through to turn on a light switch. The outside door was wood. Behind it was a blast door that would withstand anything but a direct nuclear strike, and maybe even that.

After sealing the entrance, he descended a flight of steps, then another, into a set of secure rooms that he had carved out of the living rock below his chalet.

If need be, he could take refuge in this hidden apartment, waiting out any danger that threatened him from the world above. He had installed a computer connection, as well as feeds from video cameras that gave him a view of the chalet's exterior and the surrounding area.

He wasn't under siege, but this place was more than a stronghold in time of danger. It also isolated him from contact with the world.

One area was outfitted as a lounge. To its left was a bedroom. He walked through to another pocket door. Beyond it was a chamber with rock walls that looked like the cave of a primitive people. Before stepping inside, he stripped off his modern clothing and laid them on the bed, then untied the leather band that held his dark hair at the back of his neck.

After shaking out his hair so that it hung freely around his broad shoulders, he turned to a narrow closet beside the door and brought out a leather loincloth, leather shirt, and an old-fashioned hunting knife, which he donned.

He closed the door with a leather flap hanging from a pole, then walked barefoot into the primitive environment beyond. Inside the secret chamber, it looked like he had stepped back into the ancient past.

Fur rugs covered the stone floor, and a fire pit with a

hidden chimney occupied the center of the room. Fresh kindling and logs were already laid in the stone fire circle. Continuing with the illusion that he was in another time and place, he knelt on one of the buffalo robes and removed flint and steel from under one of the rocks.

Expertly, he began to strike the flint against the steel until he could drop a spark onto the kindling. The dry tinder flared up, and he leaned over to blow on the flame. When the fire was burning nicely, he removed a leather pouch from the same place where he'd gotten the flint and steel.

In it was a mixture he had learned about long ago from the elders of an Indian tribe. He had collected this batch of leaves, bark, and berries from the mountains, dried them on the screened porch at the back of the chalet, and pulverized them with an old-fashioned apothecary mortar and pestle.

He poured a heap of the powerful hallucinogen into the palm of his hand, judging the amount by eye. Then he slowly sprinkled the powder into the flames.

As the herbs hit the fire, pungent smoke flared up, and he leaned over the fire, taking several deep breaths.

The burning mixture made him light-headed, but he took in several more deep breaths before lying down on the buffalo robe and closing his eyes, chanting words from a Native American religious ceremony.

No longer able to speak coherently, he lay with his head swimming, bright colors dancing behind his closed lids. He appreciated the light show, and he let himself drift with it, knowing he couldn't speed up the process. Finally, the lights began to fade, and he saw an outdoor scene. Trees. A rural area.

He knew that it was night, yet in the vision he could see as well as if it were daylight.

As he watched, the figure of a woman winked into existence. One minute she wasn't there. In the next, she stepped from the shelter of some rocks into a woods.

She was small and slender, with curly brown hair and

light eyes. She was dressed in jeans and a jacket. And . . . sandals.

Had she stepped out of a cave?

No, it seemed as though she had come out of the rocks— from *somewhere else*.

He didn't know what that meant. *Somewhere else? Where else could there be?*

Before he could deal with that, another image assaulted him.

Lightning crackled in the sky above the woman, and he saw her running through the darkness—even though the scene came to him with unnatural light.

Wind whipped the branches of the trees around her. Then a massive oak wavered in the tempest. He tried to shout a warning, but his voice was carried away by the wind as the tree came crashing down on her.

When she disappeared in a sea of leaves, he thought she must be dead. Then, to his astonishment, he saw a pale hand emerge from the mass of green. As she struggled to free herself, he drew in a sigh of relief.

He didn't know who she was. He wasn't sure why he should care what happened to her. But his chest tightened as he looked at the massive tree that trapped her.

While the branches rocked, then settled down, she fell back into the leaves as though she had put out a massive effort to free herself.

An animal came speeding into the scene. It was a wolf that reached the tree before carefully picking his way to the woman, where he stood staring into her face before trotting away.

For a long moment after that, she lay still. Then, at the edge of the scene he saw the glow of fire.

He caught his breath, terrified that she was going to die.

As the glow increased, the smoke from the vision drifted toward Ramsay, mixing with the drugged smoke in the ceremonial room, and he started to cough. As his chest heaved, the vision began to waver. Though he tried to hold it fast, it dissolved in a shower of gold and silver sparks.

Another time he might have appreciated the twinkling display. Now it brought frustration and anger.

"Shit!"

His curse rang out through the darkened cave. When he tried to recapture the vision, more sparks flashed, this time setting off small explosions inside his head.

The vision could have been a fantasy, but he didn't think so. It had been too specific and too tied to some other reality.

He needed to find out more about what he had seen and what was going to happen next. Had the woman died in the fire? Had the wolf brought help?

He didn't know exactly when the incident had taken place. Was he seeing it in real time, or had it already happened? And where was it? Not around here. The trees were all wrong. And the terrain. He thought it was somewhere in the eastern United States, but he couldn't even be sure of that.

Were there wolves in the East?

His mind turned to the animal. Was it real? Or was it a symbol of something that was important to the vision but still hidden?

As he tried to put the pieces together, more pain welled inside his head, and his fingers clawed at the buffalo skin rug.

He knew that he couldn't push the vision, but he knew something else as well.

The woman was going to be important to him. In a way he didn't yet understand.

What would she be to him? A lover? A friend? An enemy? Or did she herald a shift, an entirely different direction in the journey that was his life?

It had happened before—abrupt changes in his biography.

He pushed himself up and looked around the cave. It was a deliberately primitive environment. But he lived in an age that was far from primitive. Perhaps there was some way to use modern search capabilities to track her down.

Could he find out where she was?

He longed to sprinkle more herbs on the fire and go into another vision. But he knew that the ceremony wasn't going to work twice in a row.

Still, he could speculate on how the relationship would play out. Would she be his ally? Or would he end up having to kill her to protect himself?

CHAPTER
NINE

TALON WALKED QUIETLY down the hall, then listened outside Kenna's door. When he heard nothing, he turned the knob and eased the door open. After allowing his eyes to adjust to the dim light, he saw her buried under the covers, lying with her eyes closed.

His chest tightened as he gazed at her. She was such a strange combination of traits. She seemed so innocent. She'd been upset by the things she didn't know, but she had determination.

To do what? Escape from her past or run a con on Talon Marshall? Long con or short? Well, he guessed that depended on how long she wanted to hang around.

He'd told her they would give her staying here "a try," when he knew that he was leaning toward keeping her close, even though it might be one of the biggest mistakes he ever made. She was a temptation. Did he want to let her stay to prove that he could keep his hands off of her?

An involuntary shudder went through him. Was it already too late to make a clean break? Had he already bonded with her?

A few weeks ago, that thought wouldn't have entered his mind; now the question made his throat tighten.

He didn't want it to be true. He wouldn't let it be true—if he had a choice. Which meant he should tell her to leave.

As the circular reasoning wheeled in his head, he kept his gaze fixed on her face. While she slept, he could do some prowling around—first on the Internet.

In his office, he went to Google and looked up "Kenna

Thomas." There were several women with that name. A jewelry designer. A financial expert. A psychologist. None of them sounded like they could be the woman sleeping down the hall. According to their biographies, all of them fit too well into the modern world, while the Kenna Thomas he knew was like a time traveler.

But he had another way to get some information. She'd had a backpack with her when he'd rescued her from the tree. He could go out there and get it and see what was inside.

After shutting off the computer, he walked to the front door and slipped outside.

The scent of the fire hung heavy in the air, but there was something else, too. Something that seemed familiar yet at the same time didn't belong in this part of the woods.

He stood for several moments, breathing in the foreign smell. Did it have something to do with Kenna? Had someone followed her here or come with her?

OUT in the darkness, Mitch tensed when he saw Marshall step onto the porch. *What the fuck is he doing now?*

Mitch froze, waiting to see what would happen. When the guy walked in the other direction, he breathed out a sigh. Maybe this wasn't the best time to stake out the bastard's place.

He took a step back, then another, thinking he'd get the hell out of there and come back another time.

AFTER stepping into the circle of pines, Talon stared up at the stars, thinking that his long-ago ancestor had viewed the same sky. The ancestor had asked the Druid gods for powers that no men possessed and gotten more than he had bargained for.

He'd gained the ability to change himself from a human to an animal of the forest. Gained it for himself and his sons—and all the Marshall men down through the ages.

But they'd paid a terrible price for the gift. Girl babies born to the clan died at birth. And half the boys died the first time they changed to wolf form.

Talon knew there was new hope for the Marshalls. His cousin Ross had married a doctor who specialized in genetics—and she had changed the equation.

Like all Marshall men who hadn't yet bonded, Talon didn't spend a lot of time with his relatives, but Mom had made sure he knew that Ross and Megan had a daughter, the first girl born to a Marshall since that long-ago Druid priest had changed the lives of his family.

The thought of Ross made him pause. He also knew from his infrequent conversations with Mom that a lot of the cousins were getting together. That is, the ones who were already settled down with their life mates.

He wasn't interested in joining that happy group, but he'd also heard that Ross had been very helpful to the clan, particularly in his private detective role. Maybe he could figure out who Kenna Thomas really was.

Yeah, he might give Ross a call, but obviously not in the middle of the night. That didn't stop him from doing some sniffing around on his own, starting with the knapsack, which might yield some clues to her background.

In a low voice, he began to say the chant that changed him from man to wolf. Once again, the muscle and sinew of his body changed. Thick fur sprang up on his skin, and when he came down on all fours, he was an animal of the night. Slipping through the pines, he started toward the place where the fire had been burning.

BEFORE Mitch could make a getaway, a huge sucker of a dog came bounding out of the darkness, heading right for him. Like it was going to have him for dinner.

Shit!

Just what he needed.

In a panic, he pulled out the revolver stuffed in his belt and fired at the beast.

                           *   *   *

A shot rang out in the darkness, the bullet whizzing by
Talon. As he dodged to the side, another report followed.

   What the hell?

   He slithered on his belly, working his way into the leaves
of the fallen tree, keeping down as he made his way in the
direction from which the slug had come.

   Had the shooter seen the wolf? Maybe. Or had he been
hoping to get Talon Marshall?

KENNA sat bolt upright in bed. A sharp sound had awak-
ened her. While she was deciding if it was part of a bad
dream, it came again.

   From outside?

   She was too off balance to know, and she wasn't sure
what she was hearing, although she suspected it might be
something dangerous. It had been loud, like a bolt of thunder, but different. Something that wasn't natural.

   She had gone to bed in her clothing, so she was fully
dressed when she leaped out of bed, except for her wet sandals, which were in the bathroom.

   "Talon?" she called out as she ran barefoot into the hall.
"Talon?"

   When he didn't answer, fear for him made her heart
thump inside her chest. In truth, she hardly knew him, yet
he had become important to her in a very short time.

   Standing stock-still, she listened. When she heard
nothing in the house, she hurried toward the front door and
threw it open. In the light from the moon, she saw the wolf
streaking across the open space between the house and the
woods.

   As the animal disappeared from view, she stepped onto
the porch, scanning the nighttime scene.

   From the woods, she heard the sound of pounding feet.
Still the wolf? Maybe. But something else, too?

Then a louder noise—like a giant clearing his throat—drowned out the other sounds.

Moments later, she heard the grinding of gravel under the wheels of . . . a cart with a heavy load? Then the night was still again.

Her heart was still pounding as she strained her eyes to find out what was happening.

"Talon?" she called, hearing the high-pitched sound of her own voice. "Talon, are you out here? Are you all right?"

He didn't answer, but the wolf came trotting toward her and stopped short when he saw her on the porch. For a long moment, they confronted each other from a dozen yards away before he turned and disappeared into the darkness again.

She was afraid to stay outside. Yet she couldn't move from the spot, either.

"Talon?"

This time he answered as he strode out of the woods, hurrying toward her. "Yes?"

She stared at him, taking in the details. His hair was mussed. And his shoes were missing.

"You're barefoot," she whispered.

He looked at her feet. "So are you."

She answered with a little nod. "Are you all right?"

"Yes."

Unable to stay where she was, she dashed down the steps and ran toward him. When she reached him, she threw her arms around him.

She had kissed him before, and she wanted to do that now, but she couldn't allow herself that pleasure—not after the way the two of them had burst into flames the last time. Still, because she didn't want to let him go, she held on tight, her arms around his waist and her face pressed to his broad chest as she leaned into the solid strength of his body and listened to the pounding of his heart.

When his arms came up to clasp her, she breathed out a sigh, absorbing his warmth.

"What are you doing out here?" he asked, his voice gritty.

"I heard . . ." Her voice trailed off, and she started again. "I don't know what it was. Then I saw the wolf. Did he go after you?"

"He's a friend of mine," he clipped out, his tone making clear that he didn't want to talk about the animal.

She nodded against his chest because Talon Marshall wasn't going to take advice from her. There was no point in protesting that having a wolf for a friend was dangerous. Instead she asked, "What were the loud noises I heard?"

"Shots."

"From a firearm?" she asked.

His hand tightened on her shoulder. "Yeah."

"Someone tried to kill you?" she asked.

"They tried to kill the wolf, I think. But I don't know for sure. I ran after the guy, but he drove away."

"You know it was a man?"

"I'm guessing."

"The other sound I heard," she murmured. "That was the vehicle?"

"Pickup truck. I saw it speeding down the road. Too bad I couldn't get the license number."

She nodded again, not understanding what "pickup truck" meant and wondering about the license number. Earlier, he'd asked if she had a driver's license. Did he think she would have a car or a truck? The only thing she knew for sure was that something dangerous had happened.

"You shouldn't have come outside," he said in a rough voice. "You could have gotten hurt."

She shivered and burrowed more tightly against him. "I was worried about you."

"I'm fine."

"Why were you out here?" she asked.

He paused for a moment before saying, "I was going to get your knapsack."

"My carry bag?"

"Yeah."

She stiffened in his arms as she thought about the bag. Someone had brought it back to Vandar's community from this world. But the contents were another matter. What would he think of them?

She did a quick inventory in her mind. She had a change of clothing. Bread and cheese wrapped in a tanned animal skin. A knife that would probably look primitive to anyone from this universe. A talisman that she had been ordered to keep with her. And some gold beads that she could use if she needed to pay for something.

As she tried to remember everything in the . . . knapsack, her hands clenched into fists. Why was that word so hard to remember?

She liked Talon Marshall—very much. She didn't like the idea of him seeing all the things she'd brought with her and wondering what they meant. She wanted to tell him, but as the words rose in her throat, pain shimmered inside her head and she knew it would get worse, much worse if she tried to reveal her secret.

Was there some way she could get around the pain? She wanted to, but she'd have to figure out how to do it.

CHAPTER
TEN

TALON WATCHED KENNA'S face. He was sure she had started to say something, then changed her mind.

"I'd better go back to bed," she said.

"Yes."

She turned and walked quickly back to the house. With the warmth of her body gone from the front of him, he felt suddenly cold.

He wanted to run after her and pull her into his embrace again, but he stayed where he was. At the same time, he wanted to go back and pick up the knapsack he'd come out here to get.

But he knew that could be dangerous—with someone out there armed and reckless.

Who? They'd driven away, but they could come sneaking back.

Talon walked to the front door, staring out into the night before stepping back into the house and closing the door. Standing in the darkened living room, he considered what had happened.

For a werewolf, he was pretty good at dealing with people, but over the years, he'd inevitably had some run-ins with clients—men who had gone on various trips with him and hadn't fit into the group or followed directions.

He'd been on a rock-climbing expedition at the Breakneck Bridge area of McConnells Mill State Park a few months ago when one of the guys, Barry Montgomery, had insisted on going down the trail to urinate. The guy had tumbled partway down a cliff, and Talon and the rest of the men had kept him from breaking his neck. Montgomery had been mad as hell, and he'd threatened to sue because Talon had taken him to a dangerous location. Nothing had come of it, and Talon had written off the incident. Was Montgomery stupid enough to come here with a gun?

He'd thought the guy was more bluster than bite. Maybe it was worth checking up on him. And who else was mad enough to come here half-cocked?

Of course, there was a difference between a guy who would shoot at a man and one who would shoot at an animal.

As he turned that over in his mind, the recent incident with the box in the woods leaped into his mind.

Someone had buried that money. Did they know who had found it and turned it into the cops? If so, how?

Perhaps he should have asked the state police a few more questions. Or perhaps not. And did he want them out here investigating tonight's incident? Maybe a werewolf could take care of it on his own by identifying the shooter and ripping out his throat.

That route had a lot of appeal, although he'd better think about it before he let his savage nature take over.

He looked down the hall, toward the room where Kenna had disappeared. How would she react if he brought up the subject of the police? And what would it mean? That she was here to spy on him? Or that she didn't want to run into the authorities?

With a sigh, he headed for his room, determined to get up early and retrieve the knapsack.

FOR a while after Kenna woke, she had no idea where she was. Then it came back to her. The portal, the storm, Talon Marshall.

Her throat tightened. She was here, in the other universe, but she didn't know how she was going to carry out the impossible job Vandar had assigned her. Because even with his powers, he had no idea what this world was really like. He should come through the portal and find out for himself, but it was clear he would rather have a slave take the risk.

Closing her eyes, she said a little prayer to the Great Mother asking for strength.

"Help me," she whispered. Then she dared to say what was in her heart. "Help me break away from Vandar. Help me find a way not to betray Talon Marshall."

She waited with her heart pounding, waited for the pain inside her head. Apparently, she hadn't stepped over the line.

How far could she go? A wayward thought stole into her mind, and she dared consider the subversive idea. Perhaps, if she was careful, she could erect a wall in her mind, a wall that would keep Vandar out.

But this morning she had something else to do, if it wasn't too late.

Slipping out of bed, she hurried to the window and pulled the shade aside, noting that it was still early. Could she get to the knapsack before Talon Marshall found it?

After using the bathroom, she picked up her sandals and tiptoed down the hallway. Not until she was on the front porch did she put the sandals on.

She'd come here at night, and she'd been shaken up by her rude introduction to this world. This morning, she was seeing Talon's home in daylight. At the side of the house was something she hadn't noticed in the dark. One of the horseless carriages. She had seen pictures of them, but this was the first one she had encountered up close. They were called cars, but the simple word did nothing to convey the imposing appearance.

Bright silver, large and sleek, it was nothing like a horse-drawn wagon. She tiptoed over to it and ran her hand over the smooth surface. It was cool and hard to the touch, and the riding compartment was completely enclosed by doors and windows. Inside she saw comfortable seats and an array of dials and other mysterious instruments under the front window. There was a wheel in front of one of the seats, and she could only guess at its purpose.

Yesterday Talon Marshall had asked if she had a driver's license. A license to operate this thing? She guessed it would be hard to get one.

Looking away from the car, she saw a one-story building with no windows and a large bank of doors in front. After taking twenty steps toward it, she turned around and looked at the house.

It was made of stone and wood, and her breath caught as she stared at the long, low structure with the large windows that brought the outside in. The style was nothing like any dwelling she'd ever seen in Breezewood, but she admired the simplicity and the beauty of the design.

She drank in the sight, marveling that this home sat alone in the middle of the woods. Apparently, Talon wasn't worried about soldiers or the police attacking. Of course, there had been the shots in the dark last night. But Talon had seemed surprised by the incident.

Sighing, she turned away from the house and hurried toward the woods, stopping when she reached the area where the giant tree had gone down. She didn't know what kind it was because she had encountered few trees in her life. She only saw that it was big and that it could easily have crushed her.

Beyond it was a blackened patch where the fire had burned. Thank the gods Talon Marshall had put it out before it had reached the place where she was pinned.

After contemplating her narrow escape, she took a deep breath and clambered into the branches. But she was coming at the tree from a different angle, and she wasn't sure where she'd been when the monster had pinned her.

Frantically, she began to search among the branches, looking for the place where she'd been lying, but there were so many leaves that she couldn't find the right spot.

The need to hurry made her clumsy, and she tripped over a bough, sprawling in a tangle of leaves. Picking herself up, she wormed her way farther into the mass of limbs and leaves, sweeping debris aside as she searched for the knapsack.

"Looking for something?"

She jumped, losing her balance. She would have fallen off the branch she was on if a strong male hand hadn't whipped out and caught her arm. As the hand steadied her, she twisted around to stare into Talon Marshall's face. Although his expression gave nothing away, she was sure that he was wondering why she had come out here so early in the morning.

"I was looking for my carry bag."

"Why?"

"I wanted to change my clothes."

He tipped his head to one side, regarding her. "The clothes you had on are still wet?"

She hadn't even checked the jeans and shirt in the bathroom, so she raised one shoulder.

"Let me help you find the knapsack."

"You don't have to."

"You seem to be having trouble."

"Yes."

He let go of her arm, sat down on a bough, and closed his eyes. She watched as he breathed deeply. After about a minute, he looked to his right.

Without speaking, he stood up and worked his way to a dense section of foliage. Reaching down into the leaves, he moved his hand around. When he brought it up again, he was holding the knapsack.

"How did you find it?" she asked.

"I followed the scent," he answered, as if there was nothing unusual about the talent. Was that true—here?

She could only stare at him. "You smelled it?"

As she had done before, he shrugged. "One of my woodsman talents."

"Oh."

"Let's take it back to the house and get those clothes."

Her nerves were jumping as he helped her clamber back through the foliage to solid ground.

She wanted to run into the woods and disappear, but she knew he'd simply catch up with her and haul her back.

With no other option, she walked beside him, stealing glances at the carry bag slung over his shoulder.

In the dining room, he dumped the contents of the main compartment onto a large table. Then he riffled through the small pockets, taking out the objects he found there.

"What is it you didn't want me to see?" he asked in a conversational voice.

"Nothing," she managed to answer as she watched him emptying the bag.

When everything was on the table, he began sorting through the items. He picked up the clothes first, shaking out the shirt and pants before pushing them toward her.

She clutched the fabric of the shirt and stood with her pulse pounding, watching as he inspected the contents of the knapsack.

He unwrapped the bread and cheese and stared at it. "Your mother bakes bread?" he asked.

Her throat tightened. She hadn't seen her mother in months. And Mama had bought her family's bread from the baker up the street. But Kenna nodded because that seemed to be the answer Talon Marshall expected when he saw the rough slices.

He continued to stare at her, and she wondered what her expression had given away.

"You don't have plastic sandwich bags?"

She swallowed. "I guess not."

He rummaged through her possessions and found the talisman—a green polished stone disk about an inch in diameter, mounted in a gold setting.

"What's this?"

"A keepsake," she said.

"It looks expensive. Did you steal it?"

Outrage bubbled inside her. "Of course not!"

He gave her a long look, then picked up the leather pouch with the gold beads. Opening the drawstring, he poured some of the beads into his palm, moving his hand so that the beads clanked together. "Gold?"

"Yes," she whispered.

"Also keepsakes?"

"They're in case I need . . . custom."

"Custom?"

She flapped her arm. "Need to pay for something."

"Ah."

"That's not the right word?" she asked in a low voice.

"Most people around here carry money issued by the U.S. Treasury."

"I don't have any."

"Apparently." He kept his gaze on her as he shifted his weight from one foot to the other. "Your background is . . . out of the ordinary."

"Yes," she replied.

"Are you going to tell me why?"

She wanted to—so much. But she knew it wasn't possible. Not yet.

"Can you give me some time?" she asked, her breath freezing in her lungs as she waited for his answer.

CHAPTER
ELEVEN

TALON LOOKED AT Kenna's pinched features. She was afraid to tell him the truth about herself.

Fighting to keep his voice even, he asked, "I don't suppose you know anything about a box buried in the woods?"

The quick change of subject left her looking genuinely confused. She had secrets she wasn't willing to share, but from her reaction he was pretty sure they didn't have anything to do with the money he'd turned over to the state police.

Relief flooded through him. She wasn't here to spy on him. Or was he seeing what he wanted to see on her face?

Remembering why they were standing in the dining room, he looked down at the table where her belongings were spread out. Quietly, he began to stuff everything back into the knapsack. When he was finished, he said, "Let's go have breakfast."

She scuffed her sandal against the rug. "Does that mean you're going to let me stay?"

"Yeah," he answered, watching the hope bloom on her face. "We'll work out a barter system. Room and board in exchange for work." He didn't mention that the gold beads could easily have paid for her room and board. *What the hell would he do with gold beads?*

"Yes. I want to pay my way."

"After breakfast, you can help me do some laundry. I had a group here last week, and I left the sheets and towels for later."

"Just show me where to find the washtub," she answered, then looked toward the window. "And I didn't see your clotheslines. Do you put it out each time?"

"Washing machine and clothes dryer," he corrected, struck once again by her lack of familiarity with the simplest accoutrements of the modern world. What the hell kind of community did she come from? Apparently, one where cheap manual labor took the place of modern conveniences. When was she going to tell him about it? He started for the kitchen, weighing the advantages of turning the meal preparation into a cooking lesson.

TRYING not to be too greedy, Kenna ate scrambled eggs, bacon, and the toasted bread that Vandar had asked her about. Back then she'd thought the idea was weird. Now she realized you could get used to the stuff, particularly when it was slathered with butter and something called blackberry jam.

Talon had taken the slices out of the freezer and put them into the toaster thing.

He'd showed her how to do everything, and she was hoping she could accomplish it by herself next time.

He ate only a bit of eggs and a lot of the bacon, but she didn't ask about his expensive dietary habits.

Then he took her to the laundry room and showed her how to use the washing machine and the dryer. If machines like that had existed in her world, an adept with psychic talent would have run them with mind power. Here, the power came from electricity.

It could do a lot of things. But it was dangerous, too. Talon had showed her where the metal prongs on the end of the cords plugged into the wall and warned her not to poke anything in there.

The morning set the pattern for the next few days. Polite interactions, work assignments, lessons on life in his world, and more leisure time than she'd expected.

She'd pictured herself sweeping his floors with a broom.

Instead, he pulled a vacuum cleaner out of a closet. Another machine. It picked up a lot of dirt, but it was clumsy to drag around.

He had a special brush to scrub the toilets. And another brush for the shower and the sink. And cleaner that came out of a bottle when you pumped the top.

When she wasn't working, Kenna spent hours watching and learning from the television and reading the magazines that were stacked around the house.

And Talon—she was getting comfortable calling him "Talon"—didn't confine her to the house. In the afternoons, she started taking long walks in the woods where she discovered there were several other dwellings within a mile of Talon's lodge, although none was as nice as his.

Their days settled into a routine. Talon was outside most mornings, using a loud kind of saw to cut up the fallen tree and maybe going off in his pickup truck for food or other supplies. He brought back frozen food he thought she'd like. Something called twice-baked potatoes was wonderful. So were pizza and apple pie with vanilla ice cream. You baked the pie, then put the ice cream on top.

In the afternoons, he did office work at his computer and on the telephone, ordering supplies and talking to clients. She gathered that he had a trip coming up, and he was finalizing the details.

TALON stepped out of his office and walked down the hall, checking the rooms. He'd thought he heard Kenna go out half an hour ago, but he wanted to make sure she wasn't around.

When he established that he was alone in the house, he consulted his phone book and found the name of Ross Marshall. He hardly knew the guy, but he'd decided it was time for a call.

Still, his chest tightened as his fingers hovered over the phone buttons.

"Either make the call or forget it," he muttered to himself. Finally, he pressed the buttons, then stood up and looked out the window so he'd see Kenna if she came back. Because the back door was locked, the only way she could get in was through the front door. Which meant he'd have plenty of time to terminate the call if he needed to.

"Hello?"

He took a breath and said, "This is your cousin, Talon Marshall."

The voice on the other end of the line was enthusiastic. "It's good to hear from you!"

"You're probably wondering why I'm calling out of the blue."

Ross waited a beat before saying, "No. I figure you're looking for a private detective who will understand your unique situation."

"Yeah. Something like that."

"You live up in Pennsylvania, right? Bedford County."

"Yeah," Talon answered, thinking that his cousin probably knew exactly where to find his den.

"What can I do for you?"

"A woman showed up at my house last week, and I can't figure out who she is."

Ross was silent on the other end of the line.

"She may be hiding out from a closed community up in the hills. She doesn't have a driver's license. She doesn't know much about modern conveniences, like washing machines and toasters."

"You looked her up on the Internet?"

"Yeah, but I can't even be sure she gave me her real name."

"What is it?"

"Kenna Thomas."

"How did you meet her?"

"Under rather strange circumstances." Talon recounted his meeting with Kenna in the storm, pretty sure that Ross was taking notes.

"You may know my wife owns a medical lab. I'd like her to do a DNA test."

"On what?"

"Can you mail me a sample of Kenna's hair? Preferably with a hair follicle attached."

"I can do that," he said thinking about the comb Kenna had left on the bathroom sink.

Ross gave the address of the lab, then asked, "Does she show any psychic abilities?"

The question took him by surprise, but he thought back over the time he'd spent with Kenna. "I . . . don't think so," he murmured. "Why do you ask?"

"You made me wonder about her," Ross answered.

Talon hadn't said much, and he waited for his cousin to make some crack about werewolves and bonding. When Ross remained silent, Talon asked carefully, "Wondered about what?"

"I'd rather not speculate until I have more information."

"You like being mysterious?"

"There are some cases that have come up," his cousin said. "And she could fit the pattern. But I don't want to suggest anything that turns out to be leading in the wrong direction."

"Okay."

Talon didn't press.

"Anything else I can do for you?" Ross asked.

Talon thought about it for a moment, then told him about the box of money he'd found in the woods, the visit from the cops, and the guy who'd taken a shot at him a week ago.

"Did you talk to the authorities about the shooting incident?"

"No."

"Why not?"

"First place, the guy was shooting at a wolf. Second, I don't want the cops messing in my business," he snapped, then wished he'd kept his voice under control.

They spoke for a few more minutes, with Ross asking more questions both about Kenna and the box of money.

When Talon hung up, he stood at the window, wondering if there was more to his houseguest than he'd imagined.

Ross had mentioned psychic abilities. Talon had said that Kenna didn't have them, but that had been a knee-jerk reaction. Had he spoken too quickly?

What abilities, exactly?

Staring off into space, he thought of the time he and Kenna had spent together. Had she read his mind?

He didn't think so. If she could, wouldn't she have picked up clues to modern life from him?

Could she predict the future?

Again, he couldn't find any evidence. She'd been worried about his letting her stay here, which meant she hadn't known what he was going to decide.

Another power was the ability to make someone follow a course of action that they hadn't thought of for themselves. That possibility made the back of his neck prickle. Was he keeping her here because she'd *compelled* him to do it?

He shook his head. He was acting out of character, all right. But he was pretty sure she wasn't *compelling* him to do it. Not by mind control.

He got off that track and focused on another psychic talent.

What about shape-shifting? She certainly hadn't changed to some other form, not in front of him. Of course, he hadn't done it in front of her, either.

She was going for long walks in the woods. Could she be turning into a bobcat when she was out of his sight?

Somehow, he didn't think so. *Okay, why?*

For one thing, she seemed to have only normal human senses while he had a heightened sense of smell, for example, even as a human.

As he stood staring through the window, he ran through other talents she might have, but he couldn't come up with anything that made sense.

KENNA walked through the woods near the lodge, thinking about Talon. As she'd watched him in his normal routine, her admiration for him had grown.

If she had to give him a familiar label, she'd say he was like someone who was highborn back in her own world. A man who was his own boss. A man who knew what he wanted and got it without asking permission from anyone else. And he had a confidence she'd rarely seen in Breezewood. When something went wrong, he fixed it on his own and moved briskly on to the next task.

If he had any doubts about a course of action he'd selected, she couldn't detect them. But he wasn't interested in power over other people. Back home, a man like him would have been on the city council, if only to protect his own interests. Here, Talon didn't worry about that kind of security.

One thing she'd noted was his self-control. On the surface, things between them seemed calm, but every moment they were alone in this house, she felt the tension between them. They were both being careful not to touch, not to delve into the deeply felt needs that had bloomed from a simple kiss.

But it wasn't just the physical relationship that he kept under control. He had to be curious about her background. Who wouldn't wonder about the strange woman who knew so little about ordinary life?

Even so, he didn't bombard her with questions. Instead, he seemed to be waiting until she trusted him enough to tell him the truth.

She wanted to do it. So much. Not just for him, but because living in this world had given her a taste of freedom she hadn't known in months.

But the freedom was just an illusion unless she could break away from the monster that held her captive.

She moved her arms, trying to dispel the restless feeling that tightened her chest. Her life had taken on the unreality of a waking dream, but she knew the dream had to end. She wanted to stay here. With Talon. She wanted to change the equation between them into something real. But the only way to do it was to free herself from the compulsion Vandar had laid on her.

If she had the courage to do it.

Her hands squeezed. She couldn't go on like this. And she had been trying to solve the problem.

Sitting down, she pressed her back against a tree trunk, breathing in the scents of the forest—the vegetation, the earth, and the dried leaves. And the air that now seemed normal to her.

Everything here was so different from any place in her own world, and the reality of this new environment helped separate her from the other universe.

Once she felt mentally grounded, she went back to what she'd been practicing over the past few days—putting up a wall in her mind to shield her from Vandar. If she could make the wall strong enough, she could get out from under the spell he'd placed on her.

In school, she'd taken classes in erecting a barrier against a strong psychic threat, usually provided by the instructor. She hadn't been the best student, but she'd been fairly successful, and she'd always had good feedback from her teachers.

She grimaced as she reminded herself that her biggest failure had been when Vandar had initiated her into his cadre of slaves, and her defenses against him had crumbled. But he'd been right there in the ceremonial chamber with her, his dark eyes boring into hers as his mind sent out its deadly tentacles.

She looked up at the tree branches above her. She was miles away from Vandar in another world. Surely, that gave her the separation she needed to break his hold on her.

Once again, she worked on a mental image of building a stone wall, block by block, like the solid walls of Talon's house.

Then she added layers to the back and front, so that it felt like her mind was inside a fortress so strong that nothing could crack through.

Was that an illusion? She hoped not. She wished she could practice with one of her teachers, but in this universe, there was only one way to test her mental handiwork.

Standing up, she looked at the shadows filtering through

the leaves above her. It was getting late, but her practice session had made her nervous. Instead of heading directly back to the house, she walked down to the small river that ran through the forest. She liked wandering along its banks, stopping at a place where the water ran deep. It looked like she could swim there if she knew how. But that was a skill they didn't teach in Breezewood.

She also liked looking at some of the other houses that backed on to it. None of them was as nice as Talon's lodge, but they were all large and sturdy compared to the average house back in her own world.

As she walked, she silently debated the course of action she was contemplating.

Could she really sever Vandar's control? Or was she going to end up with her mind fried and her body lying on the floor like a dead husk?

The image was all too real, and she shuddered. Feeling pulled in one direction and then the other, she kept walking. Finally, she knew she couldn't stay out any longer. She was usually home by now, and Talon would wonder why she was out so long.

Retracing her steps, she hurried back toward the lodge. When she stepped out of the woods, she spotted Talon. He was standing on the brick paved area that he called the patio, in front of some kind of round table that she'd seen out there. It had shiny metal legs and a black body. When she'd passed it before, it had been covered by a black dome with a handle in the center.

This afternoon, the dome was sitting by itself on a built-in bench.

Wondering what Talon was doing, she kept walking toward him. He had a rectangular can in his hand, and he pointed it downward, shooting a stream of liquid into the curved bottom of the table. Even at this distance, the liquid gave off a sharp smell that she didn't like.

Curious, she came closer, just as he pulled a box out of his pocket and dragged something across the edge. A small flame sprang up, and he held it toward the table.

As she stared in horror, a great mass of fire leaped into the air.

"Talon!"

At the sound of her voice, he spun toward her, but he was still so close to the flames that she knew his clothing was going to catch on fire.

CHAPTER
TWELVE

KENNA'S HEART BLOCKED her windpipe as she took in the terrifying scene. It flashed through her mind that she could use her talent to shove Talon away from the fire, but he was still fifty feet away, and at that distance, he was much too heavy for her to push him to safety.

The table was much lighter. Gathering her mental forces, she sent a wave of energy toward it, pitching it over so that the flames shot away from Talon. The table landed on its side, the black pieces scattering across the patio surface.

"What the hell?"

When she saw Talon's foot moving toward the still-burning pieces, she leaped at him, trying to throw him to the ground. But even with her arms around him, she couldn't bring him down.

Holding on to him, she struggled to speak. "Stay away from it."

"It's okay." His arms came up to cradle her reassuringly.

"Are you all right?" she whispered.

"Yes." He stayed where he was but looked over his shoulder at the overturned table. "What just happened?"

"I . . . I don't know," she answered in a shaky voice. "The fire was going to burn you."

He shook his head. "It was just the starter fluid for the barbecue grill." From the quizzical tone of his voice, she suspected that he hadn't been in danger at all. She'd simply misinterpreted another innocent event from his world.

He turned his head and stared at the barbecue grill where it lay on the ground.

Although desperation had made her throw the thing away from him and fling the burning black pieces across the patio, she couldn't admit that she had done it. All she could do was hold on to him, because it felt like the universe was tipping under her, and he was the only stable thing she could grasp.

Or maybe she just wanted the excuse for the close contact. She'd thought that she was grateful he was keeping his distance. Now she understood that she'd been lying to herself.

And lying to him by her silence. She wanted to change the rules between them, and the only way she could do it was by telling him the truth about herself. Maybe he would be angry. Maybe he would send her away, but at least that was better than the shame of lying to him.

Making a sudden decision, she said, "I have to tell you . . . something important."

"You're finally ready to come clean with me?"

"Yes." She swallowed hard. "I come from . . ." She was prepared to tell him the truth, but before she could finish the sentence, a bolt of lightning struck inside her head, sending a shock wave of pain through her skull.

She screamed, and her knees buckled. She thought she had built a fortress around her thoughts, walling her off from Vandar's reach. She had, and the pain came from inside the wall, reverberating off the insides of the safety zone she had built.

Another scream bubbled in her throat. As she gasped and jerked in his arms, he tightened his grip on her.

"Kenna?" Above the pain, she heard the urgency and the fear in his voice. "Kenna, what's happening to you? What's wrong?"

Her lips moved, but no words came out. She was incapable of speech. All she could do was fight the agonizing sensation of hot needles drilling into the fibers of her brain.

She had practiced protecting herself. She thought she

had put up barriers against the monster who held her in his grip. He was far away. Out of her sight. In a different universe. But she'd been wrong. He didn't need to be here to punish her act of rebellion. The trigger was already in her head, put there before she left home.

The pain held her captive, robbed her of speech, and crushed the air from her lungs. She was going to drown, like a fish tossed onto the deck of a boat.

Talon had laid her gently on the ground. Above her, through wide, staring eyes, she saw his face wavering in her vision. He looked frightened and confounded as he stared down at her. When she tried to force his name past her lips, she found her muscles were no longer under her command.

She heard him curse as he crouched over her. "I should get help. But I don't want to leave you," he muttered.

MILES away, Ramsay Gallagher was about to step through the doorway of his office when he felt a jolt of pain in his head. His vision wavered, and he had to grab the doorjamb to stay on his feet.

For a long moment he stood in the doorway, fighting the sudden stab of disorientation that was so different from anything he had ever experienced in his long life.

The feeling of disconnection and the pain were real, yet he couldn't relate to them in any normal way. Iron bands kept him from drawing air into his lungs, and sweat broke out on his forehead and the back of his neck.

Finally, as the pain began to ease, he drew in a full breath.

When he felt as though he could let go of the woodwork, he swiped his hand across his forehead and staggered to his desk chair, gripping the leather arms as he struggled to ground himself to reality.

He didn't know what had just happened, and he didn't like it. But he had always had a great deal of self-awareness, and he catalogued the sensations that had struck him.

The sudden pain in his head. The constriction of his chest. The cold sweat. The fuzzy sensation in his brain.

They had all struck at once, and he couldn't recall a similar incident in his long life.

He had fought long and hard to protect himself from harm. Was he dying after all these years?

What had he done recently that could have triggered this sudden attack? Nothing, he assured himself, until he remembered the ceremony a few days ago, when he had let his mind drift where it might and found the woman who had been caught in the storm, then trapped by the great tree.

A ripple of alarm went through him. Did she have powers he hadn't guessed at? Had she done this to him? Or were the two of them caught in something that neither of them understood?

He had thought he should try to find her. It had stopped being a choice. He *must* do it.

But first, he needed to get himself back to normal. After several deep breaths, he walked to the front door of the chalet, then out into the afternoon sunshine, dragging in a draft of the clean mountain air. A herd of deer was grazing in a sheltered meadow nearby. Although he couldn't see them, he knew where to find them, and he started through the pine forest, humming softly, telling them that he was coming.

WITH a terrible effort, Kenna managed to get out one word, "Stay."

"Okay," he murmured, his hand closing around hers. She felt her fingers twitch, but she couldn't grasp him.

She didn't know how long the awful spell lasted. But after a time, the pain in her head eased. Somehow she found she could move enough to press his hand and gasp in air.

His total focus was on her, and when he saw she was a little better, a look of relief flooded his face. "Kenna."

"I . . . I'm . . . fine," she managed to say before her voice died out again.

Tenderly, he scooped her up in his arms as though she weighed no more than a child and carried her to the house. Closing her eyes, she rested her head against his broad shoulder, feeling him climb the two steps to the porch, open the door, and kick it closed behind him as he carried her down the hall to her bedroom.

After laying her down, he sat on the side of the bed, his face drawn with concern. "What happened?"

She scrambled for an explanation, and a word popped into her head. "Migraine." She hadn't even known what it meant until she said it. But the knowledge came with the unfamiliar syllables. It was a kind of serious headache that some people got.

His brow wrinkled. "But you're better now?"

"Yes."

"Do you have medication for it?"

"It goes away by itself," she whispered.

"I should take you to a doctor."

"No!" A feeling of desperation welled inside her, and she didn't know if it came from her own mind, or if it had been triggered by Vandar's silent orders to her. But she knew she couldn't risk having a man with medical knowledge examining her. He might know she was lying, and he might find out her secrets. What if he could tell she was from another world?

"You're . . ."

"Fine now," she said, reaching for Talon, telling herself she had to distract him, but that was only part—a small part—of her reasoning.

When he stiffened, she tugged on his shoulders.

"Talon, please. Hold me."

As he hovered above her, the breath froze in her lungs. His face was taut, telling her that powerful forces warred inside him. She felt the same pull and push. But the pull was stronger. For her.

Was it stronger for him?

She searched his face, seeing the banked fire of desire in his eyes, certain that she had the key to breaking through his resolve.

She pulled him toward her, until she could feel his warm breath on her face. Then, finally, his lips touched hers, and she rejoiced at the emotion she felt surging between them.

The contact was heavenly, but she knew she needed more.

Opening her lips under his, she drank him in—the subtle combination of scents and taste that were uniquely his.

It was clear that he had stopped resisting, and she pulled him down to the surface of the bed so that he sprawled half on top of her. As his body settled onto hers, she clasped him more tightly, captivated by the weight of him—and by the way his hands roamed restlessly over her, moving from her shoulders to her ribs to her hips.

Boldly, her tongue met his to stroke and slide, the contact sending alternately hot then cold shivers over her skin.

"Talon," she murmured into his mouth, getting it right this time, but she wasn't even sure he heard her, because the syllables were lost in the pressure of her lips against his.

When he lifted his head a few inches, her breath caught as she saw the way he was looking down at her.

Fire burned in the depth of his gaze, a fire that sank into her soul.

He wanted her. And she wanted him. Because he could drive the terrible thoughts from her mind.

No. It had started like that. Now she was swept into a whirlpool of passion that threatened to drown her. But she *wanted* to drown in the passion.

In this charged moment, she knew that the only important thing in either universe was what was happening between the two of them.

Struggling to hang on to that truth, she tugged on his shoulder again. Resisting the pull, he shifted her in his arms, easing her to the side so that they lay facing each other on the bed.

As her hands traveled over his face, his broad shoulders, the corded muscles of his arms, her heart raced, the beat frantic, as frantic as her need to get closer to him. As close as a woman could get to a man.

Reaching for the placket of his shirt, she began to open the buttons, revealing the broad expanse of his chest. Without giving herself time to think, she swept the fabric aside, then plunged her fingers into the crinkly hair that fanned out across his chest. When her fingers slid over his flat nipples, he sighed his approval.

She wanted that same pleasure. Tossing away any pretense of propriety, she dragged his hands to the front of her shirt, cupping them around her breasts.

He made a sound of pleasure, shifting his lower body against hers so that she could feel the pressure of his stiff rod against her thigh.

She knew about this. From whispered conversations at school—about how a man's thing got hard when he was ready for sex.

In Breezewood, a decent woman must be married to get this close to a man. But she wasn't home, and the rules didn't apply. Certainly they didn't apply to a slave. Those rationalizations went through her head as she eased into a more intimate position so that his sex was pressed to hers, with only scant layers of fabric separating their heated flesh.

"Lord, Kenna" he groaned, his hips moving rhythmically against hers, his body like a furnace, heating her.

The hands at her breast stroked and pressed, skimming over her stiffened nipples, sending a quivering wave of need surging downward through her body.

"You're not wearing a bra," he said in a thick voice.

"I'm sorry. I know I'm supposed to, but it's not comfortable."

He muttered something that was a cross between a laugh and a curse. Then he found the hem of her shirt and dragged it up, exposing her breasts to the cool air.

"Beautiful," he murmured.

"Am I?"

"Don't you know?" Lowering his head, he took her breasts in his hands, pressing his face between them.

"Oh," she gasped.

She ran her hands through his thick hair, heard his breath coming hard and fast. Like hers.

Nothing in her life had ever felt this good, this intimate. And even in her inexperience, she knew that there was only one way this encounter could end.

But when he lifted his head, the words he spoke astonished her.

"We have to stop," he said between gasps of air.

"Why?"

"Because you just had a . . . migraine attack, and I'd be taking advantage of you now."

"You're not! I . . . I started this."

He eased away, flipping to his back and lying with his body rigid and his eyes closed, breathing hard.

What if she shifted herself so that she was lying on top of him? Would that change his mind? Probably. But he'd given her a moment to think, and she knew he was right, at least for him. If she forced him into something that he thought was wrong, she would regret it.

So she lay beside him, struggling to hold back the hot tears forming at the backs of her eyes.

She ached to tell him the truth about herself—so much. But that wasn't an option.

"After you have a migraine, what do you do?" he asked.

Scrambling for an answer, she answered, "Rest."

"Okay." He made a dismissive sound. "I guess you don't want steak for dinner."

"What?"

"I was going to grill steaks. That's what I was doing with the barbecue."

"I'm . . . sorry I didn't understand."

"Don't worry about it." As he spoke, he climbed off the bed.

She looked at the rigid set of his jaw, expecting him to

say something else, but he exited the room, leaving her alone.

Her hands clenched as she lay staring after him. She might have pushed herself off the bed and followed, but she wasn't sure what she would say. Or do.

CHAPTER
THIRTEEN

TALON WALKED DOWN the hall, trying to will his heart to stop pounding—and will away the trembling feeling in his arms and legs.

Christ!

One moment he had been comforting Kenna. In the next, he had been on the verge of making love to her, until a burst of sanity had swept over him.

He cursed again. He could be lying next to her, feeling totally content. Instead, his nerves were jumping. His feet carried him to the front door. Outside, he righted the barbeque grill, then used a shovel with a squared-off blade to scoop up the charcoal briquettes and dump them back into the grill. A few were still burning.

How had it tipped over? Had he caught one of the legs with his foot when he'd whirled around? He didn't think so. But maybe he hadn't felt it in the heat of the moment. *Heat, yeah.*

At dinner, he was going to tell Kenna about the upcoming canoe trip. He'd still have to take care of that.

Back inside, he headed to his office. At the computer, he Googled "migraine" and scrolled through the symptoms, which included throbbing or pounding pain in one temple. Interestingly, the temple afflicted usually changed sides from one attack to the other.

Kenna had been in severe pain. That was certain. But the attack didn't match what he was reading about migraines. Take the duration, for example. These headaches usually lasted for four to seventy-two hours, which didn't exactly square with what had happened to Kenna. The pain had come on her suddenly, when she'd been trying to tell him something.

What had she said? "I come from . . ."

That was as far as she'd gotten. Was the timing of the attack significant? Could it have something to do with her words? She wanted to tell him, but the pain stopped her.

But why?

Wishing he could consult someone, he thought of his cousin Ross again. But his major problem wasn't something he wanted to talk about with another werewolf.

He was afraid he was bonding with Kenna, and there was nothing he could do about it. He wasn't going to fool himself. Even if he'd managed to climb out of her bed, it was just a matter of time.

It flashed through his mind that he could still send her away. As soon as that thought entered his brain, a terrible feeling of desolation followed.

That was as frightening as anything else. If he managed to tell her she had to leave, he'd only end up on a desperate search for her.

He started to get up from the computer, then stopped and clicked back from the migraine article to the Google screen, where he cleared away the subject query, hating himself for feeling the need to erase the evidence of his search. He didn't think Kenna knew how to use the computer, but he still wasn't taking any chances on her discovering that he was checking up on her.

In the hall, he listened for sounds from her room but heard none. Was she sleeping? Or was she lying low because she wanted to avoid him after what had happened?

She'd wanted to make love with him. There was no doubt in his mind about that, but as he thought back over the encounter, he sensed an inexperience beneath her passion.

When he'd first encountered her, he'd wondered if she'd run away because she'd been abused. That was still a possibility because it could be true, even if she had no experience making love.

He cursed in frustration, thinking that he was fixated on the woman. Turning on his heel, he walked out of the house and toward a secluded circle of pine trees where he changed to wolf form and set off into the woods. He knew the run would feel good, but it wouldn't solve any of his problems.

ON the other side of the portal, Vandar sat very still, listening. Not with his ears, but with his mind. He had sensed something that disturbed him. His connection to the woman, Kenna, was much weaker than if she'd been in his universe. But he could tell that she had tried to break away from his control. As he'd felt her rebellion, his anger flared to fearsome proportions.

How dare the little bitch!

She thought that because she was out of his sight, she could defy him. Instead, the wards that he had wrapped around her mind had held her fast, with pain mechanisms and images that were already firmly in place.

At least he hoped so.

If he had been in his dragon form, his anger would have set his office on fire. Since he was still in the guise of a man, he had only his hands to work destruction. He picked up a priceless glass vase from his desk and hurled it across the room, where it crashed against the wall. Next to it was a pottery pitcher that came from a city in ancient Greece. When he had destroyed that, too, he was able to get some control over his anger.

Should he call the woman back to this world now and drain her blood? That would give him a few moments of satisfaction as he watched her die and fed on her fear, but it wouldn't serve his primary goal. He still needed to collect information about the other universe, and if she was the best instrument for his purposes, she could live a while longer.

He thought back over the centuries he had lived among mankind. At first he hadn't known how different he was from them.

He rarely pulled out his earliest recollections. But he did it now, going back to what he knew of his beginnings. A man and a woman had found him abandoned on a mountainside. A small boy wandering through the scrubby vegetation, lost and crying.

He'd had no memories of his own people, and no hint of what he might become.

Centuries later, he'd wondered if he came from another planet in the universe, a child born of aliens who had come to Earth long ago. That somehow he'd gotten lost, and they'd left without him. What kind of parents would have done that?

He'd cursed them. But back in his childhood, he'd had no clue about his beginnings. He still didn't know anything for sure.

The human couple who found him had taken him to their humble home. They'd fed him, clothed him, and treated him with a degree of kindness, but they had also made him work for his keep. He'd subsisted on human food, which had given him a tenuous hold on life. But he'd managed to survive.

When he was about twelve in human years, the crops had failed, and the man and woman had been on the verge of starvation. With regret, they had sold him to a neighbor who wanted a slave.

That had been the worst period of his early life. Halendor, his new master, had worked him to exhaustion and beaten him when he could barely stagger up the hill with a load of sticks on his back. He had thought he was going to die.

Then had come the fateful day when his anger and frustration had flared up, and he'd lashed out in anger against his oppressor. He hadn't struck Halendor with his fist or with a weapon, but the man had fallen to the ground, convulsing in pain. The young slave had thought he was lucky that his master was dead. He hadn't known that he was the one responsible for the man's destruction. But as he'd watched Halendor lying on the ground, something had compelled him to kneel beside him. He'd felt an unfamiliar sensation in his gums. Then he'd bent and sunk his teeth into the man's neck.

Blood had flowed into his mouth. It had tasted wonderful, and he had swallowed it eagerly, until there was no more to suck from the body.

Feeling better than he could ever remember, he'd stood and wiped his lips, then started searching the man's house and found his stash of gold. After stuffing it into a leather bag, he'd fled.

The money had helped transform his life. He'd found he was good at gambling games, often guessing what was in his opponent's mind. He'd doubled his original stake, then doubled it again. The new wealth allowed him to live comfortably and gave him the luxury of time to rest and educate himself about the world and about himself, as well.

As he'd matured, he'd found that he had strong psychic talents and the ability to change his shape as the mood struck him, his power fueled by the blood he now drank on a regular basis.

He could have used his gifts for the good of humanity. But every year he lived with them reinforced his conviction that they were unworthy of help. They were greedy and immoral. Below his regard. He had been lonely among them, but his special talents gave him satisfaction. Now they were his chief solace.

As he had perfected his techniques, he had assured himself that none of that inferior race could stand up to his might. Until the terrible time of the psychic change at the end of the nineteenth century when a group of humans had suddenly acquired powers equal to his own.

They had recognized him for what he was and joined together to fight him. He had barely escaped with his life and had vowed to never again let himself be vulnerable to any of the humans who infested this planet.

Since then, he had vanquished all his enemies. Not always easily. But in the end, he had increased his power so that no one could challenge him. Certainly, not a mere woman with some telekinetic powers.

From this world, he had little direct control over her. But he could reach the main trigger he had placed inside her head. He could send her a message to come back. When she did, she would feel his wrath for defying him.

KENNA heard the front door open and close again. Earlier, she'd gone to the window and watched Talon clean up the mess she'd made with the barbeque grill. This time, she watched him walk purposefully off into the forest. It looked like he wasn't coming back anytime soon, but she waited for several minutes to make sure. Then she got up and walked down the hall, stopping in his office because he'd left the light on, and she knew he had been there.

The computer was on, and she wondered what he'd been doing. Nothing that she could easily figure out. The machine was still a mystery to her, so she continued on to the kitchen.

She was hungry, but as she looked through the food that he'd bought since she arrived, she stopped herself before taking a small pizza out of the freezer.

Would he notice she'd eaten something? And would someone with a migraine headache want to eat? She didn't know. She didn't even know what a migraine was, exactly. But it had popped into her head, and it had seemed to satisfy Talon, or maybe he'd just let her think that he'd accepted the explanation.

Her jaw clenched. She hated going back over every little incident with him and trying to figure out if she had given too much away. But it seemed that she had no alternative.

After a few moments' hesitation, she got out the pizza, set it on a plate, and put it in the microwave. Progress in the ways of this world.

She wouldn't let herself think in terms of progress with Talon, because she knew she'd messed things up with him.

Because she was trying to tell him the truth—for all the good that had done her.

The bell on the microwave dinged, and she reached for the plate, testing the heat before picking it up.

As she chewed on the pizza, she listened for Talon. She was pretty sure he'd gone out because he didn't want to run into her. Which meant that she'd be better off eating in her room.

Hating herself for the way she was making decisions, she stood, wiped off the counter, and took her simple meal back to the bedroom, along with a glass of cold water from the refrigerator.

Sitting in the chair by the window, she ate, then put the plate and glass in the dishwasher before going through the bedtime routine that she'd gotten used to.

In this world, people washed and changed their clothes every day. She liked the feeling of being clean and knew she wouldn't like the reverse when she went back to Vandar's cave.

That thought jolted her. Going back? She didn't want to do that. But soon. She must do it soon.

Trying to put that idea out of her mind, she busied herself with brushing her teeth, washing her face, and changing into a fresh T-shirt.

Then she turned on the small television set on the bureau across from the bed. Flipping through the channels with the remote control, she came to *Swift River*, a television story about a town full of young people and their parents and grandparents.

The show came on every evening, and she was getting to know the characters, amazed that she was so involved in their lives when they weren't even real people.

They were just actors in a story someone was telling, like in a play.

But watching them told her a lot about life here.

"Space cadet," she repeated after one of the girls said it. Then "dumb blond joke."

Strangely, she could click to another channel and watch

an earlier time in their lives. Some days she did that. Tonight, the characters didn't hold her interest for more than one episode.

She was still listening for Talon when she finally turned off the television and lay down, thinking it would be impossible to sleep. But she drifted off quickly, and for a time she was lost in blessed oblivion.

Until she plunged into a nightmare where a huge hand with long pointed nails reached out and grabbed at her hair.

CHAPTER
FOURTEEN

AS KENNA WRENCHED away from the monster, she could feel her hair being torn out at the roots. Turning, she fled for her life. She was on a flat plain, littered with ruined buildings and dead trees, and she knew this was the badlands of her own universe. She had traveled through them with Vandar's warriors on her way to his cave.

Desperate to escape, she ran in the other direction. At least, she hoped it was the other direction. In the dream, she was wearing jeans and a T-shirt and the tennis shoes that Talon had brought home from the store for her.

The shoes helped her run across the dry ground, and for a time she thought she could get away.

Vandar was in his human shape, and she heard the sound of his breath, hissing in and out behind her, but it was getting farther away.

Then, suddenly, he was a huge dragon, flying in the air above her. He circled around her before arrowing down, making straight for her. Instead of catching her, he hit her with a blast of his fiery breath, searing her skin and making her cry out in pain.

As he flew lower, his great talons caught the skin of her back, ripping through her flesh. Blood dripped down her back and his tongue flicked out to lap at it. When she stumbled, he shoved her to the ground

"No!"

Again she screamed, then felt hands on her shoulders, holding her to the bed.

"Kenna!"

Desperately, she tried to break free, flailing out with her arms, hitting him with her fists.

"Kenna."

It filtered into her mind that it wasn't Vandar holding her or speaking. When her eyes blinked open, she found herself staring into Talon's tense face.

"Are you all right?" he asked, his voice urgent.

"Yes." She looked from him to her raised fists, knowing she had struck him. "I hurt you."

"It's okay. You were having a bad dream."

She nodded, remembering her terror. "He had me. He was tearing me apart."

"Who?"

Somehow, perhaps because she was still half awake, his name passed her lips. "Vandar."

Talon's hands tightened on her shoulders. "The man who hurt you?"

"He's not . . ." As she tried to explain, pain seared the inside of her head, and she clamped her lips together.

Talon's expression grew urgent. "What's happening? Another headache?"

"No. Just a nightmare."

He stared down at her, his dark eyes clouded with worry.

Panic gripped her. Panic and the knowledge that she must not let this moment pass. Talon was here again. In her bedroom.

She reached for him, pulling his head down.

"Don't."

Ignoring him, she kept up the pressure, and when his lips touched hers, she felt a jolt of sensation.

"Please," she murmured into his mouth. "I want the same thing you do. Don't run away this time," she managed to say, her lips moving against his, inviting him to take anything he desired from her.

"I didn't run away," he growled. "I thought it was best for you to stop."

She knew that was only part of the truth. "For me? Or

for you?" she asked, astonished at her own audacity. Or was it desperation?

Where she came from, no woman would challenge a man so boldly. But her short time in this world had changed her. Partly it was seeing the way the people on *Swift River* acted. And partly it was living with Talon. She had compared him to a noble back in Breezewood, but really she had never met anyone like him at home.

Yet he was a man, and she knew that women had ways of getting what they wanted from the opposite sex.

He didn't answer, but they were still mouth to mouth.

In invitation, her lips began to make little sliding, nibbling motions. He stayed where he was, and her heart began to pound as she waited for him to make a decision. Then a sound welled up from deep in his throat as his lips began to move over hers, like a starving man invited to a feast.

At the same time, his hands traveled over her, stroking down her arms to the backs of her hands, his palms pressing against her and his fingers knitting with hers, raising goose bumps on her skin.

It was what she wanted—so much. For this space of time, if that was all she was allowed. She was only a visitor in this world, and she couldn't have him to keep, but she longed for these moments with him, longed to make memories to warm her when she was alone again, and afraid.

She had gone to bed in only a T-shirt, and she had kicked the covers away when she'd struggled in the dream.

Talon stared down at her, his gaze traveling from her face, slowly down her body, and back up again.

"Come here," she whispered.

She smiled as he lay down beside her, gathering her close, rocking her in his arms, his hair-roughened leg sliding against hers, his body naked except for the thin shorts she knew were his underwear.

She sighed and stroked her hands over his strong arms and wide shoulders.

"You feel so good, especially after that dream."

"It was bad?"

"Mm-hmm."

"And you're using me to drive it out of your mind." When he started to pull away, she gripped him tighter. "I want to be here with you. That's the truth."

"Part of the truth. What's the rest of it?" he asked in a tight voice.

"This is the most important part." Clasping the back of his head, she brought his mouth back to hers and kissed him with a desperation that welled from deep inside her.

When he finally lifted his mouth, they were both breathing hard, yet his dark gaze questioned her.

"Tell me why we should do this."

"Because there's something between us that neither of us can explain."

"You sense that?" he asked, his voice rough.

"Yes. And you do, too."

Before he could challenge her or ask her any more questions, she kissed him again, feeling the intensity spiral between them.

Still, she was afraid that she must act quickly, before something happened and he changed his mind.

Although she had little experience with men, she was pretty sure she knew how to push him over the edge. With her eyes squeezed closed, she reached and found his hardened rod through his thin shorts and pressed her palm against him, rocking her hand.

When she felt him shudder, she breathed out a little sigh, stroking her fingers against the firm shaft, listening to his breath quicken. Gods, he was big. Would he fit inside her?

Well, she would find out soon, she knew, unable to keep a small shiver from going through her.

When his hand came down over hers, lifting it away, her eyes blinked open to find him staring at her.

She tried to drag her hand back, but he curled her arm inward, holding it against his chest.

His voice was gritty when he asked, "Have you done this before?"

She swallowed, astonished by the question. "Why do you ask?"

"Because I can tell you're nervous."

"I . . ."

"Have you done this before?" he asked again, more sharply.

She dipped her head. "No. But I don't want to stop."

"You always stopped before. With other men."

She couldn't hold back a nervous laugh. "I never got this far before."

"Why?"

There was too much to explain about the relations between men and women in her world, and if she tried to tell him any of that, she would get all tangled up in things she shouldn't talk about at all.

Raising her chin, she stared into his eyes. "Are you trying to come up with an excuse to stop?"

"Yeah. And it wouldn't be an excuse. It would be a perfectly logical course of action."

"Then stop being logical," she managed to say, knowing she had no other words to continue the argument. She could only bring her mouth back to his for a long, passionate kiss. In the middle of it, she knew she had won. He wasn't going to walk away this time.

She thought it would happen fast now. She wanted it that way, so she wouldn't have time to think—or worry.

When he rolled up her T-shirt, exposing her breasts, her breath caught.

He raised his hand, sliding his fingers across her tightened nipples. It was only the lightest of caresses, but it made her gasp.

When he closed his thumbs and fingers around the crests, she arched toward him.

And when he replaced one of his hands with his mouth, she thought she would go up in flames. He swirled his tongue around the erect point, then closed his mouth over her, sucking and mirroring the caress with his hand on her other breast.

She stared at him, sure her expression must be equal parts shock and sensuality. She had known about kissing and touching, but she hadn't known that a man might put his mouth on a woman's breast, or how wonderful it would be.

She felt her skin flush. Felt her breathing accelerate. Felt an unfamiliar heat gather between her legs. When she moved restlessly on the bed, he lifted his head, looking at her as he slid his hand down her body, playing with her navel, then the crinkly dark hair at the juncture of her legs. His touch in those places felt good. It was nothing compared to the burst of sensation when he dipped into the hidden folds below.

It shocked her that a man was touching her so intimately, and even more shocking when she felt slippery moisture gather there.

She should be embarrassed, but the heat smoldering in his eyes told her he liked her reaction.

She caught her breath when he lifted his hand and licked his fingers.

"That's good," he murmured as he kept his hot gaze fixed on her face. "I'd like a more direct taste, but I think that would be a little too much for you."

She swallowed. Surely he couldn't mean . . . She stopped trying to figure it out when his hand went back to work and one finger dipped inside her.

"What . . . are you doing?"

"Giving you pleasure."

"I want to pleasure . . . you," she managed to say. "Isn't that what a woman is supposed to do?"

"No more than the other way around. Unless the guy is a total jerk."

He bent to play with her breasts again, using his lips and tongue and teeth while he slid his hand up and down through her wet and swollen folds in long strokes that dipped inside her, then moved upward to a place that sent tingling sensations radiating outward through her whole body.

As he touched her with such skill, she realized that he must have a lot of experience pleasing women.

"I'm going to . . ." She didn't even know how to finish the sentence. But she felt like he was pushing her toward some point of pleasure that was too much to bear.

When she began to move her hips, he seemed to know what she needed. Increasing the pressure, he kept up the maddening stroking, until a kind of explosion quaked through her, starting at that point of sensation and making little spasms clamp her internal muscles around his finger.

He stayed with her, drawing out the pleasure of it, and when it was over, her eyes blinked open, and she stared at him.

"What happened to me?"

"You reached sexual climax."

"You can do that without . . ." She let the sentence trail off.

He answered with a shaky laugh. "Yeah."

She thought about what had just happened and what she knew about sexuality. "I reached sexual climax. You didn't."

"I will."

He began to kiss her again, caress her again, and she understood that this time it wouldn't be his finger inside her.

Now more than ever, she expected it to happen quickly, but he surprised her again, kissing and caressing her until she felt that tempting pressure building inside herself once more.

He kicked off his shorts and shifted on top of her, parting her legs with his knee as he kept kissing her, murmuring into her mouth. She felt the pressure of his rod against her and started to tense up. But he surged inside her, and she gasped as he broke through the barrier of her virginity.

He went very still above her. "Are you all right?"

"Yes."

"I hurt you."

"Only a little."

"Do you want me to stop?"

"Gods, no." Because she couldn't say more, she moved her hips a little, feeling him slide inside her.

He gazed down at her, watching her face as he began to move above her, slowly at first.

Shifting to his side, he took her with him, caressing her breasts, then reaching between them to find that spot with his fingers.

As he stroked her there, her pleasure built again so that she was soon moving against him as she had before.

He moved, too, stroking in and out of her as he caressed her—until the explosion came again, more powerful than the time before. And while the aftershocks were still vibrating through her, she felt him follow her over the invisible cliff.

She clung to him, pressing her face to his shoulder.

"I'm glad it was you," she whispered.

"Yeah." His hands slid over her back and shoulders, and she snuggled into his warmth. She had never imagined this contentment, this closeness, with another human being.

His lips nibbled against her cheek and her sweat-slick brow.

"Will you sleep with me?" she murmured.

"Yes."

She drifted on a gentle cloud, her body cushioned against his.

"It never would have been like that in my world," she murmured.

He lifted his head, staring down at her. "What do you mean, your world?" he asked.

CHAPTER
FIFTEEN

KENNA SWALLOWED. IN the afterglow of making love, the words had simply slipped out of her mouth, and now she scrambled for an explanation that would sound plausible.

"My . . . community," she managed to say.

Talon pushed himself up, giving her a long look. Moments ago she'd been relaxed and cozy in his arms. But no longer.

"Which is where?"

Her throat clogged. She longed to tell him, but she knew it wasn't possible.

"We just made love, and you still can't trust me enough to tell me where you come from?" he said in a rough voice.

She looked down, unable to meet his gaze. She ached to speak honestly, but she had learned that was impossible.

When she remained silent, he climbed out of bed, naked. As he stood looking down at her, she was suddenly very conscious that she was naked, too.

She wanted to ask him to come back. Instead, she sat up, found the covers, and pulled them over herself. At least she wasn't so exposed when she looked at him again. Making love had been magic. Then she had ruined everything. He had expected honesty from her, and she had denied it to him.

He was speaking again, and she struggled to take in what he was saying. "At dinner I was going to talk to you about something."

Before she could comment, he went on. "I have a trip

coming up. Day after tomorrow. I mean, I'll be away from home with a group of men on a canoe trip. I'll be meeting them at a parking area along the Clarion River, and I won't be back for four days."

"You want me to leave?" she whispered, unable to keep her voice from quavering, or her body from trembling.

"You can stay here while I'm gone, if you want." He shifted his weight from one foot to the other. "But there's a complication. That gunshot last week. The guy who did it could be watching the house, and he might get bolder if I'm gone." He shrugged. "So you could be in danger."

"Maybe your being away won't make me less safe."

"Maybe."

Before she could answer, he turned and walked out of the room. Tears stung her eyes, and holding them back was too much effort. The beauty of making love with Talon was shredded around her. Because of the compulsion Vandar had placed on her.

As she lay in bed confronting her misery, she told herself this was for the best. She wanted to stay with Talon forever. But that was impossible. Instead, she would complete her assignment and go back where she belonged.

FOR the next day, as he prepared for his trip, Talon stayed out of Kenna's way. Was he hoping that she'd tell him the truth about herself? Or hoping that when he came home she'd be gone?

And was that what he really wanted? Did he *want* her to disappear from his life?

"Up to her," he muttered.

Making love with her had been . . . He couldn't finish the sentence because there were really no words to describe how good it had been.

But what did that matter? If she couldn't trust him enough to be honest, there was no future for the two of them. Or was he kidding himself about that? Was he stuck with her no matter what? Did the life mate of a werewolf feel the same compulsion he felt? Would it be impossible for her to leave?

He should be worried about the shooter. In his present mood, this was the least of his concerns. Perhaps that meant he wasn't acting rationally.

He took a breath and tried to think through his options. Was there someone who could stay with Kenna? Keep her safe while he was gone?

Could he send her to Ross?

Yes. That might be the solution.

Shit! He'd have to explain why she was so important to him. But he'd do it, because he wasn't going to leave her here alone.

Unable to deal with his roiling emotions, he doggedly checked his supplies and equipment for the trip and made sure everything was ready.

Often he met his party at the lodge, but this time they were meeting at a parking lot in Ridgeway, one of the places where you could put boats into the Clarion River. He wasn't sure why he'd made those arrangements. To keep Kenna's presence at the lodge secret—for her sake? Or because he didn't want to explain what she was to him?

One thing he knew: after the confrontation in the bedroom, she'd been avoiding him, just as he was avoiding her.

But he kept turning over that last conversation with her. She'd said "gods," not "God." Had he heard her right? And what did she mean about "her world"?

Could Ross answer those questions?

Maybe, but how the hell was he going to talk to another werewolf about it?

While he dealt with his own anxieties, he couldn't stop listening for her, even as he lay awake at night. Which was why he heard her tiptoe down the hall at two in the morning, then slip out of the house.

Now what? Was she running away?

His throat closed as he climbed out of bed and opened

the sliding glass door that served as his bedroom window. After pulling off his shorts, he rushed through the chant that changed him from man to wolf. As soon as he came down on all fours, he was out of the house, sniffing the air. It took only moments to locate Kenna. Silently, he followed her into the forest, where she walked rapidly, using a flashlight. Over her shoulder she carried a backpack.

She seemed to know where she was going. To meet the guy who'd buried the money? Had that been her intention all along? And now she was proving her duplicity?

He kept expecting her to rendezvous with the man. Instead, she walked toward a house that was used as a vacation residence by a couple from Philadelphia, Mr. and Mrs. Winslow.

Staying well back, he watched her climb the two steps to the porch and pause at the front door.

He had thought the Winslows would have locked up the cabin, but after a few seconds, Kenna opened the door and stepped inside.

The wolf moved closer, slipping from tree to tree in the darkness. He thought about climbing the front steps. But he decided it was better to wait until she came out and see what developed.

KENNA knew she had to go home. But she had one more thing to do before she left. Teeth clenched, she closed the door. She'd used her telekinetic powers to open the lock, but she hated being in here, and she was going to get out as soon as possible. Still, she had to bring some artifacts from this world back with her, and she would rather steal them from the people who owned this house than from Talon.

Walking quickly through the rooms, she took in the details. The house was much smaller than Talon's, yet it was still luxurious by the standards of her world. She recognized the appliances in the kitchen: the stove, the refrigerator, and the dishwasher. The living room had comfortable furniture, in a much different style than Talon favored. The fabrics had flowers, and there were lots of pillows and knit blankets. In front of the fireplace was a fancy brass screen.

The two bedrooms were furnished in the style of the living room. One looked like adults slept there. The other had a couple of dolls leaning against the pillows, and toy animals on the dresser. Opening the closet, she found small dresses on hangers. She might have taken one, but they were too pretty to steal, so she stepped back into the hall.

She had thought the bathrooms in Talon's house were luxurious. They were nothing compared to the bathroom connected to the bedroom where the adults slept.

It was huge—larger than her bedroom back in Breezewood. The tub was enormous, big enough for two people, and there were two sinks, set in a stone top with a cabinet that looked like expensive furniture.

Trying to select things that weren't too valuable, she riffled through the drawers and took a package of soap. In the kitchen, she took a knife, fork, and spoon from another drawer. Then she plucked a book from the shelves beside the fireplace and picked up an old guide to the television programs.

Was that enough? Quickly, she returned to the kitchen and took a can of soup and an old can opener. In the closet by the front door, she took one of the folded-up umbrellas. And from a jar on a shelf, she scooped up some of the coins that they used in this world.

After putting everything into the knapsack she'd brought along, she hurried out the front door, locking it behind her.

TALON waited in the darkness. Kenna was in the house less than fifteen minutes. When she came out again, she hefted the knapsack onto her shoulder, and it looked like it was a lot heavier than when she'd gone in. She turned back to the door for a moment, then started rapidly into the forest.

Again he waited to find out what the hell Kenna was doing. She headed back toward the lodge but stopped several yards from the structure, near the garage where he'd piled up wood chips to use as mulch. As he watched from behind the trunk of a tree, she looked around, then scooped out a hole in the center of the mulch, set the knapsack inside, and covered it back up again.

Once more she checked to see if she was being observed, then headed rapidly back to the house.

Talon waited in the woods until she had gone back inside the lodge. When the coast was clear, he trotted to the circle of trees where he liked to change. Dressed in sweatpants and a shirt from the box, he went directly to the pile of wood chips, where he scooped away the top layer, uncovered the knapsack, and pulled it out. After brushing the chips back into place, he carried the knapsack back to his room and dumped the contents on the desk.

Kenna had taken a number of items from the Winslow house. A stainless steel knife, fork, and spoon. A paperback mystery novel. An old TV guide. Canned soup. A can opener. A compact umbrella. A few random coins. A bar of soap. Nothing of any real value.

He shook his head as he looked at the collection. What the hell did she want with this stuff?

Was she planning to take it away when she left? Or—

As another possibility struck him, he shuddered. He'd thought she might be a con artist. What if this was part of a plan to help the bank robber? The guy could alert the cops to this cache and claim that Talon had taken it.

Did that make sense? He wasn't sure, not in his present state of mind. But he did know that he wasn't putting the knapsack back.

He'd like to find out what happened when Kenna discovered it was missing. But probably she was going to make her move while he was gone, and he couldn't change his plans to be there.

He wanted to stride down the hall and confront her, but he was sure nothing had changed. He'd only get the same old bullshit she'd been giving him all along.

He was angry with her. Angry with himself for making

love with her. In a way, he was glad he was leaving in the morning, because that got him away from her for a while.

And what about his plan to call Ross? He'd be saddling his cousin with a thief, and he sure as hell wasn't going to do that. Besides, if Kenna was friends with the bank robber, she didn't need protection.

Again, he wasn't sure about his logic. All he wanted to do was get away from Kenna so he could think clearly. If that was possible.

He left for his trip in the morning, without saying good-bye to her. If she was here when he got back, maybe they could finally get some things straight.

WHEN Kenna heard Talon leave, she felt a mixture of sadness and relief. He was gone. Probably, she would never see him again, because she was going where he couldn't follow her.

For the last time, she took one of the wonderful hot showers that she loved so much. Then she made herself scrambled eggs with ketchup, which had become her favorite breakfast, and cleaned up carefully after herself.

After dressing in the clothing she'd worn here, she went out to the pile of wood chips to retrieve the knapsack. When she began to dig, she found the carry bag was gone.

Frantically, she dug in other parts of the loose pile of chips, but as far as she could tell, the spoils of her robbery had vanished.

Great Mother. What had happened?

She couldn't imagine how the items had disappeared, but she knew she had to make other plans. She couldn't go back to the house of the people where she'd stolen the objects. Not in broad daylight. Not when someone could see her.

Talon was gone. She could wait until dark, but now that she had made up her mind to leave, she felt an overwhelming need to return through the portal.

Was that her own will? Or was Vandar calling her?

She had no way of knowing.

With a tight feeling in her chest, she went back into Talon's lodge. She had tried to avoid stealing from him. Now she gathered up some of the same things she'd taken from the other house. *Nothing valuable,* she reminded herself. Ordinary items that would interest Vandar.

Simply saying his name made a wave of sickness rise in her throat. If she could have run from him, she would have. But the compulsions in her head limited her choices. She had to go back and face whatever happened.

After taking a few things from the lodge and putting them into another carry bag, she walked rapidly into the woods again, going back to the place she had avoided since her arrival: the portal. Perhaps she was heading for her own destruction, but she hardly cared.

With a feeling of resignation, she pressed her hand against the trigger point that mirrored the one on the other side.

When she touched the cold rock, she felt a vibration under her palm. As the solid surface thinned in front of her, she felt her heart leap into her throat. Even though she'd been through it and was prepared, she wanted to turn and run. Instead, she stepped back into her universe.

SHE was gone. One moment Ramsay Gallagher had sensed the woman—somewhere far away. In the eastern part of the United States, he thought. He'd decided to travel east and try to find her. Now that was impossible.

Thinking he might be wrong, he put on a burst of energy, trying to reestablish the connection. But he knew it was no good. She simply wasn't there anymore.

Was she dead?

It felt like her consciousness had winked out of existence. Like she'd been shot in the heart, and her life had snuffed out.

Should he be relieved?

Or alarmed?

It was a long time since he had been so uncertain, and he didn't like the feeling.

KENNA took a deep breath and let it out. Now the air on her own side of the portal smelled strange, and the landscape made her chest tighten.

She had been living among beautiful, natural surroundings. The gray landscape here was like a jolt of horror.

Six of Vandar's men were waiting for her. As soon as she stepped out of the cave that hid the portal, they surrounded her.

Three were guards, and three were the adepts who had brought her to this place.

All of them kept their distance from her, as though she might have some power that could harm them. Or maybe they thought she had picked up some disease from the other world, and she would contaminate them.

"You're back," Wendon said, looking her up and down with a critical eye.

She answered with a tight nod. Had he thought she could escape? Had he been assessing his own chances to break free from their master?

"Vandar wants to see you right away."

"Yes." She had come back because she was compelled to do it. Did he know she'd tried to break away?

If so, would she survive the meeting with her master?

Trying to keep her fear from showing, she said a silent prayer in her head as they marched her over the burnt ground to the cave.

CHAPTER
SIXTEEN

KENNA'S HEART WAS pounding so wildly that she was surprised it didn't break through the wall of her chest. Struggling to keep her expression composed, she entered the great cave that housed Vandar and his slaves.

As she walked down the corridors, people glanced at her, then quickly away, and she wondered what they'd been whispering about her. Did they know where she'd gone? Or did they just know Vandar had sent for her, and maybe she was going to be his next meal?

That might still be true. She had no way of knowing.

She shuddered, then tried to make her mind blank as she followed Wendon toward the master's private quarters.

Her terror flared when they stopped at the door of his lair.

"Come in," a harsh voice called in answer to the adept's knock.

As he had done before, Wendon opened the door and pushed Kenna inside, then closed the barrier behind her, trapping her.

All at once she was facing Vandar, struggling to catch her breath.

In his guise as a handsome man, the master was sitting in the same easy chair, staring at her.

For a long moment he simply sat where he was, his dark eyes glittering as he looked her up and down, making her want to turn and run. But she knew that route was folly. He had superhuman speed, and he could grab her before she reached the door.

"I've lived among humans for a long time," he said, and she was surprised by the words, because she hadn't expected him to speak about himself. "A man and a woman found me abandoned on a mountainside. A small boy wandering through the scrubby vegetation, crying."

She wanted to ask why he was telling her his story, but she knew that if he wanted to, he would explain.

"I had no memories of my own people. And no hint of what I might become. The year their crops failed and they had nothing to eat, they sold me to a neighbor who wanted a slave. My new master, a man named Halendor, worked me to exhaustion and beat me so badly I could barely do the backbreaking labor he expected. But one day, I lashed out in anger with my mind and he fell to the ground, convulsing in pain. Do you think that was fair?" he asked.

She tried to swallow, but her mouth was too dry to speak.

"You tried to break away from me."

When she still said nothing, he continued, "Tell me why I shouldn't kill you."

She raised her chin and found enough moisture to answer. "Because I know more about the world on the other side of the portal than anyone else. And if you want the information, you need me."

A smile flickered at the corners of his lips. "Well said. You have spirit."

She waited for him to ask a question; instead, he stood and glided toward her in a way that was so nonhuman.

Despite her resolve, she backed away. Then, suddenly, she was unable to take another step, as Vandar clamped his hand over her shoulder. As he held her in place, his other hand rose and pressed against her forehead.

She felt a jolt of pain, like the jolt when she had tried to tell Talon the truth about herself. The pain resolved into a sucking sensation, as though everything she knew was being pulled out of her brain.

"Don't," she whispered.

The terrible process went on and on, dragging the life out of her. Then, in blessed relief, the world went black.

"GOOD meal. I didn't think you could make a decent stew from a package of dehydrated ingredients."

"Technology is amazing," Talon told one of the five men who had hired him to take them down the Clarion River from Ridgway to Cooksburg, a forty-five-mile stretch of easy-to-navigate water. It wasn't a remote area. Several bridges crossed the river that had once been in danger of dying. Fortunately, careful management had brought the waterway back. Now he was gratified to see all kinds of wildlife. He'd pointed out warblers, ducks, and geese, and even an osprey and two eagles. And they'd also seen a mother raccoon with two youngsters, wading in the shallows looking for food.

The night before, they'd eaten fish they'd caught. Today Talon had seen the men were tired after a long day of paddling, so he'd gone for a quicker option for tonight's dinner.

Ed Bangle finished washing the dishes. Peter Welsh crawled into his dome tent and brought out his dopp kit, then headed for the place where Talon had set out a container of purified water.

Welsh and James Fitzgerald had taken canoe trips before. Bangle, Trent Dalton, and Jake Presley were all newcomers to the sport. But they were taking to it with enthusiasm.

"We want to get an early start," Talon advised as he checked the stove.

"I guess we should turn in," Dalton said. "I'm beat."

The others agreed.

Talon crawled into his own tent, listening to the sounds of the men getting ready for bed.

When the camp had settled down, he climbed out and stretched, looking at the darkened silhouettes of the other tents. Standing in the quiet of the night, he listened to the familiar sounds of the forest. The insects. The animals who were drawn by the smell of food. But none of them had invaded the campsite.

Talon was doing his job, but his heart wasn't in the trip. He hoped he was giving this group of men the experience they deserved, the experience they'd paid for.

He couldn't be sure because he was functioning on automatic pilot. Half his mind was on Kenna. No, more than half.

He'd been angry when he left, and putting some distance between them had seemed like an excellent idea. Now that he could think more clearly, he knew he should have made sure she was safe before he walked out. And he should have given her his cell phone number, in case anything happened at the lodge.

Or would she even be there when he got back? When he considered the possibility that she might have walked away while he was gone, he had trouble breathing, and he admitted what he'd known for days. He had bonded with her.

With a woman he couldn't trust!

Because she had secrets she was afraid to reveal. Or couldn't reveal. He wasn't even sure which was true.

He clenched his fists, fighting the impulse to tell the guys he had to cut the trip short. That there was an emergency at home.

But he couldn't do it, not when he prided himself on giving his clients more than they'd paid for. And cutting the trip short wasn't that easy. There weren't that many road-accessible places to put boats into the water and take them out again. He'd arranged to have his van driven to Cooksburg. If they got off the river early, there would be no transportation for them.

But should he do it anyway?

Cursing under his breath, he slipped into the woods thinking he could change to wolf form and run off his frustration. He stopped when he was only a few yards from the campsite. The safety of these men was his responsibility, and he couldn't just disappear into the night.

Too bad he couldn't free himself from the agony coursing through his veins.

"Damn you," he muttered, speaking to Kenna, because she was the source of his misery.

He had made love with her, and it had been different from his experience with any other woman.

More intense. More emotion-charged.

He'd been sure it had changed everything between them. Then the disappointment of discovering she still didn't trust him had been like a knife plunged into his heart. So he'd fled. Now that he was alone, he knew he couldn't run away from her. Instead he had to transform the terms of their relationship. Because there was no question about it. He had to make her trust him, or he was doomed to a life of agony.

SOME time later, Kenna woke. She was lying on a narrow bed, not in her old dormitory, but in the room where she had lived while she was being trained for her mission.

As she remembered the moments before she'd blacked out, she shuddered.

"You're awake."

She focused on the speaker, a woman she had seen around the compound who sat on a chair in the corner.

"He wants to speak to you again."

"Can you give me a few minutes?" she asked, struggling for calm.

Instead of answering, the woman exited the room.

Kenna's chest tightened. She didn't want to be anywhere near Vandar, but at least she was still alive. That must mean something.

When she pushed herself up, she had to fight a wave of dizziness. But the pressure inside her bladder made her climb out of bed and stagger across the sleeping chamber to what passed as a bathroom in the cave. There was a kind of toilet with a collection pot underneath. She used it and grimaced as she thought how primitive it was, compared to the other universe. Well, she'd better get used to it, because this was her world again.

Feeling grimy, she glanced toward the door, then took off her clothes and washed quickly, using a cloth and the bowl of cool water on the washstand. A change of clothes hung on a rack at one side of the room, similar to what she'd just taken off.

Her brow wrinkled. Why was she supposed to dress like a woman from the other world?

At least she didn't have to put on her slave's white tunic—yet.

After pulling on her clothes, she slicked back her hair and inspected herself. There were dark circles under her eyes, and her skin looked pasty.

When the door opened, she tensed, expecting Vandar to walk in, but it was only her guard, returning with a covered tray. "You must eat."

As the woman spoke, Kenna's stomach growled, and she realized she was starving. "How long have I been sleeping?" she asked.

"Three days."

Kenna tried to absorb the information. *Three days!* That seemed impossible, but she assumed the woman wasn't lying to her. What would be the point?

The guard set down the tray on the table across from the bed. When Kenna pulled off the cover, she found roast chicken, some cooked vegetables, and a mug of water. Because she knew the woman was watching her, she tried to eat slowly. But once she started, it was almost impossible not to gobble the food—not that she tasted much of anything as she ate.

When she finished, she wiped her mouth with the cloth.

"Come with me," the guard said.

With no other option, she stood and followed her escort out of the room. She thought she was going back to Vandar's private residence.

Instead, they walked into another part of the cave. As she

stepped through a doorway, she gasped, feeling a wave of sadness and wonder. She was standing in Talon's kitchen.

"How?" she whispered as she hurried toward the counter. As she approached the stove, she realized that it wasn't real. It looked like the appliance she remembered, but on closer inspection, it seemed to be a wooden box with painted controls and burners.

There was a drawer next to the stove, and she pulled it open to find knives, forks, and spoons. When she picked them up, they felt real.

In the cabinet underneath were pots and pans but not exactly like Talon's. Above the counter were plates, cups, and bowls, similar to his.

Moving to her right, she came to the sink. When she turned the faucet, no water came out. The refrigerator was similar. Although the door did open, the interior was not cold. And the "food" on the shelves was only a representation of the expected packages.

Taking out a loaf of bread, Kenna held it up to the light and saw that it was made of some kind of composite that she guessed wasn't even edible. She had just put it back when she heard a noise behind her. She whirled around.

Vandar was standing in the doorway, dressed like a man from the other universe: he wore jeans, a button-down shirt, and running shoes. Although she wanted to cringe and turn away, she straightened her shoulders.

He tipped his head to the side, studying her. "You're looking well."

"Thank you."

"What is this place?" he asked.

"The kitchen in Talon Marshall's lodge." She pressed her hands to her sides, then said, "If you don't know what it is, how did you build it?"

"From your memories. I know it's his kitchen. I want you to tell me about it."

She dragged in a breath as she remembered the terrible sucking sensation before she'd blacked out. He had dragged this picture from out of her. Not just a picture. It was more like . . . She thought for a moment and came up with the words: "stage set." And workmen must have scrambled feverishly to construct it.

Before she could think more about it, he went back to asking questions.

"What is a lodge?"

She struggled to put the word into context. "It's like a house, but bigger. He has a lot of spare bedrooms because he has guests," she answered, thinking that he had gone off on an expedition without the guests assembling at his headquarters.

Had her presence altered his behavior?

Before she could ponder any more about Talon, Vandar made another demand. "Tell me the functions of the furnishings of this room."

She looking around. "Everything?"

"Yes."

As she thought about the daunting task, he crossed to the sink and pulled the lever up, then pointed to the spigot. "Water comes out of here?"

"Yes."

"How?"

"There are pipes under the sink. They bring the water. I don't know where it comes from."

"I suppose not. Long ago there was something like that in this universe. In the houses of the rich."

"There was?"

"Yes. And toilets that flushed. Like the ones at Talon Marshall's house."

She nodded, wanting to ask about the past of her own world but knowing that Vandar wasn't here to give her information. Instead, she went around the kitchen showing him the various appliances and smaller things like the packages of food and cans of soup.

She fumbled to explain the microwave. And the dishwasher.

Finally, Vandar waved a hand to cut her off. "I wanted to see the kitchen for myself. As I thought, the other universe is a better place to live. Much more comfortable, with all sorts of conveniences like running water, central heat, and air-conditioning."

He continued, sounding like he was speaking to himself, not her. "And the population will be completely unprepared for anyone like me."

She couldn't stop herself from asking, "How do you know?"

"It's obvious the other universe developed differently. With machinery instead of people with paranormal powers."

Kenna nodded. There were a few psychics in Talon's world. Occasionally, she'd seen TV shows about them, but they seemed to have no revered place in the society. They might try to help the police find a missing child or solve a murder, but they were as likely to be wrong as right.

As she thought about that, Vandar turned to her. "You'll be going back there."

She went very still, suddenly filled with hope and at the same time with despair. "I thought . . ."

He waved her to silence. "I'll want some more artifacts from you. Not random objects. Things that will be useful for the invasion. I have my powers, but it will be better if my men are armed. With some of those guns."

She swallowed. "Guns?"

"You saw them on television programs. Talon Marshall has a lot of magazines that feature them. And someone shot at him one night."

"How . . . how . . . would I get guns?" she asked, hearing the quaver in her own voice.

"You'll figure it out. I want fifty of them. The small ones. Handguns, they're called. And the bullets."

"Fifty."

"You'll get Talon Marshall to buy them for you."

She was about to tell him that wasn't possible, when the coldly calculating look on his face stopped her.

"You fucked him."

Kenna felt her cheeks heat as she lowered her gaze. That certainly wasn't how she'd put it. But Vandar must have pulled that from her mind, too. Did she have no privacy from this monster?

He was speaking, his voice a buzzing in her head. "Fucking with a man is a good way to control him. If he questions you about where you have been, take him back to your bed."

She wanted to refuse, but there was no way to defy Vandar's wishes. Not if she wanted to survive.

He laughed, obviously enjoying her discomfort. "You called his member his 'rod.' Probably, he calls it his 'cock' or his 'dick.' When it gets hard, that's called a hard-on. Use the right words."

He had stopped speaking, yet she felt information pouring into her head—the reverse of what he had done before. He was giving her more orders. Orders that would destroy her relationship with Talon—if she still had a relationship with him.

Yet she must obey.

TALON and his group finished stowing the canoes on the top of the van in the Cooksburg parking lot.

"Fantastic trip," Trent Dalton said. "You know the river like the back of your hand, and you know a lot about the wildlife in the area."

The others voiced their agreement.

"I'm glad you enjoyed it."

"When's the next time you're running this trip?"

"Probably in the fall."

"I'll definitely be coming back—with my son," Jake Presley said.

"That's a good idea," James Fitzgerald said. "Maybe Billy and I can do it with you all."

He and Dalton began discussing times they might get together with their sons.

The group of men had bonded on the expedition, and Talon had promised to provide them all with an e-mail list so they could keep in touch. He knew they were savoring the last few minutes together, but his own anxiety was reaching critical levels. He had to get home.

To make sure Kenna was still there—and make sure that everything was okay. Because he couldn't fight the bad feeling that something had gone terribly wrong.

Struggling not to transmit his anxiety, he cleared his throat. "We'd better get back to Ridgway." That was the town where the men had left their cars. Too bad they weren't parked at his house because then he wouldn't be facing a three-hour drive.

CHAPTER
SEVENTEEN

THAT AFTERNOON, AFTER answering more questions about things like television programs, Kenna stepped through the portal, this time with a mixture of eagerness and sadness. She wanted to come back to Talon's world. She longed to repair the breach between them. But she was under orders from her master, and there was no way to stop herself from following them.

Although she had been anxious about her last trip here, this time would be far worse. This time she was supposed to get Talon to buy her guns, although she was sure he wasn't going to do it. Vandar had a long history of people following his commands, but he didn't know what he was dealing with now. Talon was a man who took orders from no one.

She shuddered. Unless Vandar got control of his mind. Gods! She couldn't let that happen. Not to Talon. She had to figure out a way to stop it.

As she started down the hill toward the lodge, she wondered what she would find there. Talon had been about to leave on a trip. Was he back home, or was he still away? And what would she say to him when they saw each other again?

She fretted about that as she walked toward the lodge, her pace slowing as she approached.

Just as she was about to step out from under the trees, something brushed against her—something powerful—and she gasped. Jumping behind a tree, she pressed tightly against the bark and peered into the woods, probing the shadows with her gaze, half expecting to see Vandar come swooping down out of the sky.

She saw nothing.

Closing her eyes, she went very still, trying to calm herself and figure out what had happened. Something had reached out toward her, but it was far away.

Vandar? She didn't think he could actually reach through the portal so directly. Unless the deeper contact with her mind had made it possible.

Goose bumps rose on her flesh, and she went very still, listening. But she heard nothing with her ears. It was like the presence had been waiting for her and found her almost as soon as she'd stepped through the portal.

As suddenly as it had touched her, it was gone, leaving her standing with her pulse pounding.

Had she imagined it, because she was so off-kilter? Or was it something real?

She looked back over her shoulder, toward the portal which was now hidden by the trees. Going back to her world wasn't an option. So she dragged in a breath and let it out before starting down the hill again.

When she peered into the open space around the lodge, she thought she saw a male figure standing in front of the building, and a surge of joy went through her.

Talon!

Unable to contain her feelings, she ran forward, drinking in the details. He wore the kind of clothing Talon favored: running shoes, jeans, and a T-shirt. And his hair was dark like Talon's. But as she drew closer, she saw that it was longer and greasier. And his body was shorter and chunkier.

It wasn't him.

Should she stop before he saw her?

But it was already too late for that. He'd heard her coming and jerked around to confront her.

As they faced each other, she saw that the look in his blue eyes was wary.

"Who are you?" he demanded.

Wondering what kind of response he expected, she answered, "A friend of Talon's."

"Oh yeah? Where did you come from?"

"The woods."

"You're just dropping in on him?"

She nodded, thinking this was a very strange conversation, and not just on her part. Studying him, she asked, "Who are you?"

"A friend of Talon's," he answered. But the way he said it sent a shiver down her spine.

"What's your name?" she asked.

"You don't need to know."

A large rounded can with a spout sat a few yards away on the ground. When she looked at it, she recognized the kind of can that Talon used to fill his chain saw and other equipment. With . . . gasoline. He had told her it was dangerous, that it could catch on fire. And she was supposed to stay away from it.

"What are you doing?" she asked, keeping her voice even when her heart had started to pound.

"Nothing you need to worry about. Talon's not home. This isn't a good time to visit."

"He'll be home soon."

"Oh yeah?" As he spoke, he lunged toward her, but she reacted instantly, using her mind to put up a stumbling block near his feet. He tripped, sprawling on the ground. "What the hell?"

Her breath came fast and hard as she stared at him. She hadn't intended to use her power so openly, but when he'd attacked, she simply reacted.

"Stay away from me," she whispered, hoping he wouldn't realize she had tripped him. She'd had no real plan when she'd stopped him, but now she was thinking that she would run back into the woods and hide—with the gas can that was still on the ground.

Snatching up the can, she turned and sprinted toward the trees. But before she had gotten more than a few feet, something hit her square in the back, and she went down, knocking the breath from her lungs.

Seconds later, the man was on top of her, grabbing her by the hair and slamming her head against the ground.

She saw bright splotches in front of her eyes. Then everything went dark.

KENNA'S eyes blinked open. For a long moment, she struggled to figure out where she was. She was lying on her side, on a bed. Facing a wall.

She closed her eyes, letting herself drift. Her head hurt. And . . . and, when she tried to push herself up, she realized that her hands were tied behind her back. Looking down, she saw that her legs were also tied at the ankles with thick cord.

Gods! Had Vandar brought her back to her world to sacrifice her?

Her heart started to pound as she stared at the wall. It was smoother than any wall in the cave.

"Calm down," she muttered to herself. "It's not the cave. It's not that."

Swiveling around, she saw a chest of drawers that she recognized.

She was inside Talon's lodge. But she didn't remember coming inside. How had she gotten in here?

Teeth gritted, she struggled to dredge up her most recent memories. Vandar had sent her back. She'd come down the hill from the portal and found a man at Talon's house. A man with a gas can.

They'd talked. Then . . .

The last part was fuzzy, but she knew he'd lunged at her, and she'd tripped him before turning and running toward the woods.

But she'd never gotten there. Moving her shoulders, she felt a renewal of the pain. She hadn't been facing him, but she was pretty sure he'd hit her with something hard.

Lying on her back hurt her arms, and she eased to her side again. But she knew she couldn't stay in the bed. The man was here to do something bad. She was sure of that, and she was the only one who could stop him. Except that she was tied up, and he was probably the one who had done it.

Closing her eyes, she focused on her wrists. They were held together with some kind of restraint, but she couldn't see what it was. And she didn't think it was the same stuff as the rope that bound her ankles.

Could she manipulate the wrist cords without seeing them?

She'd never done anything like that before. How could you move something when you had no idea what it looked like?

She didn't know, but she had to try.

Moving her arms, she felt the way the restraints rested against her skin. There wasn't much play in the stuff, which made it hard to figure out what she needed to do.

Her mind spun as she lay with her fists clenched. Then she swung back to the chest. A mirror hung above it. If she could get to it, maybe she could see her wrists.

By wiggling her body, she inched to the edge of the bed, careful not to dump herself onto the floor. Sitting up, she swung her legs over the side, then eased her feet onto the floor.

Now came the hard part. Carefully, she stood up, fighting a wave of pain as she changed the angle of her head.

Thrown off balance, she flopped back onto the mattress and sat breathing heavily. She longed to lie down again, but she didn't have that luxury. More carefully this time, she stood. When she felt steady on her feet, she took short, hopping steps to the dresser, where she braced her hips against the front. Then she slowly turned so that her hands were facing the mirror.

Twisting around, she got a look at the restraints. As she'd thought, it wasn't the same thing that tied her ankles. That rope looked like it was made of fiber. The cord on her wrists was from a telephone.

Apparently, the man had scrambled around for something to secure her and he'd used whatever he could find quickly.

Working slowly and methodically, she tried to get her mind inside the telephone cord, but it was disorienting seeing it in the mirror instead of straight on.

Still, millimeter by millimeter she began to stretch it.

When she found she could move her wrists, she felt a spurt of victory. But it wasn't enough. So she kept up the mental pressure, pulling her wrists apart until finally, finally she was able to slip her hands out of the binding.

It dropped to the floor.

With a sigh, she flopped back down onto the bed resting from the effort. In a moment, she'd tackle the rope around her ankles.

She was just starting to sit up when she heard footsteps coming rapidly down the hall.

CHAPTER

EIGHTEEN

KENNA SLUNG HER hands behind her, in the same position they'd been in when the phone cord had held them fast. Rolling to her back, she turned her head toward the door.

The man from outside stepped into the room, his gaze zeroing in on her where she lay on the bed.

"You're awake."

As she stared at him, a terrible thought closed her throat. She'd dropped the cord when she'd freed her hands. Where was it now? What if he saw it?

When her breath turned ragged, he smiled at her. "Too bad you came along. But I can't leave any witnesses."

"What happened to me?" she whispered.

"I brought you down with a rock."

So that was it! "Please, let me go," she whispered, because that was what she thought he expected.

"Sorry." He stayed where he was, and she prayed to the Great Mother that he wouldn't come any farther into the room. When he took a step toward her, she clenched her teeth, ready to spring up at him if he found she'd freed herself.

"How did you trip me?" he asked, his voice hard.

She widened her eyes. "I don't know what you mean."

"I think you do."

"No."

He clenched his fists. "Too bad I don't have time to beat the truth out of you. But I've got to burn the house down and split."

As she tried to digest his words, he turned and disappeared down the hall again. When she was alone, she let out the breath she'd been holding, listening intently for the sound of footsteps coming back.

TALON was about to turn into the driveway that led to the lodge when he saw something that stopped him in his tracks. A pickup truck pulled into a little break in the woods.

Who was parked on his property? A stranded motorist?

Easing his van onto the gravel shoulder, he got out and cautiously approached the truck. No one was inside. There was no white handkerchief or anything else tied to the door handle, indicating that the motorist was in trouble. And the vehicle was almost hidden from view. He wouldn't have seen it in the shadows if he hadn't been scanning the woods the way he often did when he came home from one of his trips.

A shiver slithered down his spine. He didn't like this. First he memorized the license tag. Then he strode farther into the woods where he ducked behind the massive trunk of an oak and started taking off his clothes as he said the chant that changed him from man to wolf, pushing through the transformation.

Coming down on all fours, he started up the hill toward the lodge, speeding through the forest. When he broke from the cover of the trees, he saw something that raised the hairs on his back.

A stranger with a gas can in his hand.

But where was Kenna?

KENNA listened intently. Was the man really gone? Or was he waiting to trick her?

Finally, she sat up and began to untie the rope that bound her ankles.

As she worked, her mind scrambled for a plan. He'd told

her he was going to burn down the lodge. She had to stop him.

Vandar had asked her to bring guns to her world, and she knew Talon had some, locked in a cabinet in one of the rooms. She had seen them, but she didn't know how to use them. So she couldn't shoot the man.

Could she throw something at him—and give the missile extra weight with her hidden power?

AS the man began to pour the gas around the foundation of the lodge, Talon crept silently closer, preparing to spring. Then, around the corner on the other side of the house, he saw something that froze the blood in his veins.

Kenna. She was here. With a can of something from the pantry, raised high in her hand. Lord, did she think she was going to stop the guy with that?

He wanted to shout, "No! Get back."

But he couldn't speak in his wolf form. All he could do was spring forward, trying to get to the guy before Kenna reached him.

The man heard the wolf and whirled, gasping as he saw the charging animal.

Talon followed, snarling as he closed in on his quarry, preparing to bring the bastard down and rip out his miserable throat—until he heard footsteps behind him.

Jesus! It could only be Kenna, following them.

He stopped in his tracks. The guy made a moaning sound and sprinted onward, toward the truck hidden in the woods.

Torn, Talon hesitated. But the idea of Kenna seeing him tear someone to shreds made his stomach curdle.

Turning, he stepped into Kenna's path, and she screeched to a halt on the leaves that covered the forest floor. They stood facing each other long enough for him to hear the car engine start and know that the would-be arsonist had gotten away.

Shit!

He snarled in frustration, and she took a step back.

"Who are you?" she gasped.

He couldn't answer, so he turned and trotted deeper into the woods, stopping behind a tree where he could watch Kenna.

She scanned the landscape, looking for him.

"Come back!" she called.

Long seconds passed and he wondered if she was going to plunge into the darkened forest. Finally, shoulders slumped, she turned and headed back toward the house.

Once he knew she was out of danger, Talon circled back toward the place where he had left his clothing. After confirming that the invader was gone, he silently said the chant that transformed him back to human form, then climbed into his clothing before running back to his van and climbing in.

Minutes later, he was speeding up the driveway toward the lodge. When he climbed out, the gasoline-saturated air made him cough.

"Kenna?" he called. "Kenna, where are you?"

When she didn't answer, he started toward the woods, toward the spot where he'd last seen her.

As he reached the trees, he caught sight of her, trudging back the way she'd come. She stopped short when she saw him, then ran forward, straight into his embrace.

He wrapped his arms around her and held on tight.

KENNA clung to Talon, hardly able to believe that he was holding her in his arms. He had come back, just when she needed him.

"How did you know . . . ?" she managed to say.

She heard him swallow. "I was coming up the road toward my driveway when a truck pulled out from a hiding place in the woods and peeled rubber down the highway." He gripped her more tightly. "Was he here?"

"Someone was here."

"Someone you knew?"

"No." She pushed far enough away so she could look into Talon's eyes. "But the wolf chased him away. Who is he? I mean . . . the wolf."

He gave her the same line he had before. "A friend of mine." He changed the subject back to the intruder. "What was the guy doing?"

"I found him outside when . . ." She had been about to say, *when I came back from my world*, but she stopped and started again. "He had a gas can. When I asked him what he was doing, he hit me and knocked me out. I woke up in the lodge, tied up. Then he told me he had to hurry because he was going to burn the lodge."

Talon winced. "Are you all right?"

"Yes."

"How did you get free?"

She knew then that she had made a mistake. "I guess he did a sloppy job of tying the knots. But I knew I had to stop him."

"You could have gotten hurt. You should have called the police."

"I . . ."

"Okay. Right. You're trying to stay away from the cops," he clipped out.

"But I would have called them, if I'd thought of it." She watched his face, knowing that he was thinking the incident through.

"You said you were outside. Where?"

"The woods," she replied. "Lucky I was."

He looked like he was going to ask another question, and she couldn't let him do that. Cupping the back of his head, she brought his mouth down to hers.

He could have pulled away, but the moment his lips touched hers, emotions exploded between them. It was like a jolt of molten energy that sent a wave of heat through her blood.

They had parted on bad terms, and she hadn't been sure that she would ever see him again. Now he was back in her arms, and her feelings for him surged. Later, she would have to deal with the pain of betraying him. But not now.

Now she would give him everything that was in her power to give.

She was trembling in his arms, and at the same time, she couldn't stop herself from running her hands over his broad back, his wide shoulders. And he was doing the same thing, his touch telling her how relieved he was that the man hadn't hurt her.

The urge to show him how she felt was like a primal need, wiping everything else away, sealing her to him.

She clasped him tighter, feeling his rod—no, his cock—wedged between them like an exclamation point. And she was just as aroused.

She had thought of him while she'd been in her own world, but she hadn't dared let herself take the longing to a sexual level. Now it felt like she had been aroused for days but hadn't been able to admit it. And she was free to give him anything he wanted.

As his mouth plundered hers, she drank in the familiar woodsy taste of him, sure that no other man could taste as good.

She made a needy sound, her mouth opening to give him better access, telling him that if he didn't make love with her, she would lose her sanity.

In the conscious part of her brain, she knew she should warn him to run for his life. Run as far from her as he could get, but he was beyond warning—not when his hand was sliding down to her hips, pulling her more tightly against himself.

Under the protective canopy of the tree branches, she stepped back far enough to start tearing off her clothing. He did the same, both of them kicking off their shoes, then throwing shirts and pants onto the leaves to make a bed.

Gods, he was magnificent, standing naked in the forest, his body all hard muscles and flat planes, his hard-on standing straight up against his body.

With a whimpering sound, she came back into his arms, rubbing against him, feeling like her body was going to ignite and set the woods on fire.

He reached up to take her breasts in his hands, his thumbs stroking over the hardened tips, bringing another whimper to her lips.

She needed him on top of her. Inside her. Here. Now.

Grabbing his arm, she pulled him down to the make-shift bed under the tree boughs.

Hot and hard, he clasped her to him, murmuring her name as he slid his lips over hers, caressing her breasts with his face, then turned his head so he could take one pebble-hard nipple into his mouth, sucking on her, teasing her with his tongue and teeth while he used his thumb and finger on the other nipple.

She arched into the caress, her fingers sliding through his dark hair. He shifted so he could trail one hand down her body, finding the hot, slick core of her.

When he dipped his finger between the silken folds, she made a low, needy sound.

"Now. Please, now."

As he covered her body with his, she braced for the pain of their joining. But this time, when he slid into her, there was only pleasure that made her cry out in mingled sur-prise and joy.

On a sob, she circled his shoulders with her arms, hold-ing him close as he began to move within her in a fast, hard rhythm.

Nothing so vivid could last for long, and the intensity quickly built to flash point.

Her inner muscles tightened around him, sending waves of shattering sensation through her body.

"Oh!" she gasped as the heat of it blotted out the world.

Feeling her climax, he began to move with more urgency, crying out as he followed her into the heat of the explosion.

She was shaken to the depths of her soul as he col-lapsed against her, because she knew that the two of them belonged together for all time, and she must find a way to make things right between them.

Turning her head, she slid her lips against his cheek, trying to hold back the tears that threatened to burst forth. Because now that she had had this moment, she knew the reckoning was coming.

CHAPTER
NINETEEN

TALON STIRRED BESIDE Kenna.

"We should go back," he said.

"Yes," she whispered, still waiting for him to start asking questions. When he didn't do it, she felt some of the weight lifted off her chest.

An idea was starting to form in her mind. A desperate idea. She didn't even know if it would work. But she had to try it.

They both stood. Picking up her shirt, she turned slightly away, shook off the leaves, then pulled her arms through the sleeves. Talon was also shaking off leaves and getting dressed.

"Are you going to call the police?" she asked.

"I got here too late to tell them what happened." He gave her a long look. "And I doubt that you want to talk to them. That would bring up a whole bunch of problems for you, wouldn't it?"

The question hung between them.

"Yes," she finally managed to say.

"He hit you on the head. You don't want to get checked out, right?".

This time she could only answer with a small nod.

"We *will* work this out," he said.

The way he spoke made hope leap inside her. It was followed by despair. How could they ever work it out?

As they approached the lodge, she could still smell the gasoline.

Talon made a face. "I'd better check the foundation," he said in a tight voice.

"Yes." She speeded up, hurrying inside, glad that he was holding back from pressing her and wondering why. Last time he'd been angry. This time he was . . . she didn't know what to call it. But she knew that they couldn't go on the way they were. She had to change things. And maybe there was a way to do it.

Inside, she hurried down the hall to the office where she stopped short. It was a mess, and she gasped.

Papers were all over the room.

And she knew what the man must have been doing after he'd hit her. He'd come in here and started searching through Talon's records. Which was lucky for her. Because if he hadn't taken the time to do it, he would have set the fire earlier, and she'd probably be dead.

Gods!

She looked toward the door. She should tell Talon. But he'd find out soon enough. And she had to do something more important, before she lost her nerve.

Quickly, she pulled some papers out of the printer tray and found a black marker the man had thrown on the floor.

Leaning over the desk, her heart pounding, she quickly wrote one word on the top sheet.

SLAVE.

When lightning didn't strike her, she breathed out a small sigh.

On the next sheet she wrote: PORTAL.

When a dart of pain stabbed her in the head, she stood up on shaky legs and grabbed the papers and pen. Down the hall in the kitchen, she set down the stack of papers and shuffled the words she'd written to the back. On the top sheet she wrote: SPY.

This time, the stab of pain was worse, and she dropped the papers on the counter. Backing away, she took several deep breaths.

After waiting half a minute, she grabbed another sheet and wrote: ANOTHER. She would have added WORLD, but that was all she could do now. The pain was starting to build up too far.

Scrabbling the notes into a pile, she carried them down the hall. But now the sheets of paper burned her hands.

All she could do was throw them on the dresser and back away.

Her breath coming in gasps, she staggered out of the bedroom, struggling not to pass out. It felt like the atmosphere in the lodge was thickening in her lungs, and she knew she had to get out of the house.

Since Talon was out front, she slipped out the back door, heading for the big rocks along the river where she sometimes sat by herself.

TALON stopped to wipe his sleeve across his forehead, then added another shovelful of dirt to the wheelbarrow he'd brought from the storage building. Luckily, the guy hadn't gotten too far with spreading the gasoline. A lot of it had evaporated. But some had sunk into the soil, and Talon knew that it would eventually get to the water table and contaminate the river down the hill. So he was digging it up and storing the dirt—until he could get it to a toxic waste dump.

He clenched his hands around the shovel handle and uttered a low curse. Fouling the environment was a sin, as far as he was concerned. But, of course, that thought hadn't entered the bastard's mind when he'd been trying to burn down the house.

Until Kenna had stopped him.

As her name leaped into his mind, he looked up at the lodge, wondering what she was doing in there. After they'd made love in the woods, he'd been more sure than ever that she was his life mate. He'd have to explain that to her, if they could ever have an honest conversation. *Dammit.*

Kenna was still lying to him. Lies of omission, if nothing else, and he had to figure out how to make her stop without making things worse. *Yeah.* And maybe she'd explain to him why she'd stolen a bunch of stuff from their neighbor. They hadn't even gotten around to that yet.

"Shit!"

He shoveled furiously, then picked up the shafts of the wheelbarrow and trundled it into the storage building, where he spread a large tarp.

When they made love, it was fantastic. Then . . . she kept shutting him out.

Or maybe . . .

What?

He thought about the times she'd tried to speak to him and the pain that had struck her so suddenly.

Was that it? Something was in her head that kept her from speaking?

What the hell could that be?

A phrase came to him. "Posthypnotic suggestion."

Jesus. Was that what was wrong with her? She'd been ordered not to reveal her background, and if she did, pain made it impossible for her to speak?

He cursed again.

Who would have done it to her? Was she part of some secret government project? Or did she belong to a cult that used hypnosis to keep their members from breaking away and revealing their secrets?

He had just started toward the lodge when his cell phone rang. Pulling the instrument from his pocket, he saw that the caller was Ross Marshall.

Did he want to talk to Ross now? He was about to put the phone back into his pocket when he changed his mind and flipped the cover open.

"Talon, this is your cousin Ross."

"Yes?"

"I'd like to talk to you about Kenna."

"You are talking to me!" he snapped.

"I'd like to have this conversation in person."

His stress level made him growl, "Why don't you start talking—and I'll decide whether we need to have a face-to-face."

"Because there are things I can't say over the phone."

"Fine!" Talon pressed the "off" button, then shoved the

phone back into his pocket. He didn't want to talk to Ross. He wanted to talk to Kenna.

Jaw clenched, he stomped up the front steps and into the lodge.

"Kenna," he shouted.

When she didn't answer, his chest tightened. First he looked in the kitchen and the living room. Then he started down the hall. When he saw his office, his breath caught. His files were all over the goddamn room.

What the hell! Had she been tearing the place apart while he was outside?

Or was it the guy looking for information?

Jesus!

Confounded and burning to confront Kenna, he sped down the hall, searching the bedrooms.

When he found the rope and the phone cord in one room, he cursed low under his breath.

His alarm grew when he couldn't find her anywhere. But on her dresser, he found a pile of printer papers and a marking pen.

She'd been writing on the papers in big block letters. One word per page. SPY. SLAVE. PORTAL. ANOTHER. What in the name of God did any of that mean? And why had she used so many sheets?

Was she a spy for a foreign country? Was that it? And that's why she had a strange accent? *Sure!* A foreign spy in Bedford, Pennsylvania.

"Kenna!" he called again, but the lodge remained silent.

Anger, confusion, and panic warred inside him. Taking a deep breath, he tried to follow the trail of her scent. When it led to the back door, the hairs on his arms prickled. She'd gone!

Alarm bolted through him. Without giving himself time to think, he opened the back door and tore off his clothing, then began to say the chant that would transform him.

When he came down on all fours, he howled, then charged through the door, pausing to pick up Kenna's scent.

She had gone into the woods. Was she leaving because she couldn't bring herself to reveal her secret? Was she going to steal stuff from another neighbor? Or had she taken something from the office? He couldn't discount that. Maybe the mess was a smoke screen so he wouldn't see what was missing.

If he had been a man, he would have shouted his curses aloud. Instead, he only howled them silently in his head as he trotted along the trail she'd made. It was as plain to him as if she'd sprayed dye along the ground. He knew her unique scent. It had sunk into the pores of his skin, the fibers of his heart, and it would lead him to her. And then what? Was he going to change to human form and confront her?

He didn't know. But he did understand one thing in the fevered depths of his brain. He couldn't allow her to leave him, no matter what was going on with her.

Stepping into the woods, he wound his way down a trail through the hardwood forest toward the river that ran through his property.

His heart stopped, then started up again in double-time when he spotted her through the foliage. She was sitting on a rock, her shoulders hunched, and her arms slung around her knees. She was rocking back and forth, and as he approached, he heard her moaning.

The sound propelled him forward.

When she looked up in alarm, he stopped in his tracks as the realization struck him. He was a wolf, not a man. What the hell was he going to do now?

And what would she do?

She had seen the wolf before. Now it was facing her, only a few feet away.

He tensed, expecting her to jump up and run. Instead, she stared at him with reddened eyes, her features taking on a look of wonder.

"Talon?"

The fur on his back bristled as he heard her speak his name. She recognized him?

"Talon, it's you, isn't it? The wolf is you. I should have figured it out. But I just couldn't see it until now. Is it because I know you better?"

He had no way to answer. Maybe she'd realized who he was because she was his life mate. Was that the way it worked?

Her voice drew him forward until he stood inches from her knee. When she reached for him, he crept forward, laying his head in her lap.

She stroked his head tenderly, scratched the soft places at the base of his ears.

"I didn't know they had werewolves here," she whispered. "How is that possible?"

He couldn't ask what she meant by "here." For the time being, all he could do was keep up the contact with her, marveling that she had accepted him as a wolf.

Never in a million years would he have imagined this situation. It sounded like she came from a place where werewolves were part of the landscape.

Where the hell would that be?

She bent to gently stroke her lips against the top of his head, and he made a low sound of pleasure.

"A wolf can't talk," she murmured.

He nodded against her lap.

"That first time, when I was caught by the tree, you came and found me."

Again he nodded.

"And when that man tried to burn down the lodge, you chased him away."

Once more he acknowledged the truth of her words.

She started speaking again in a voice so low that he had to strain to catch the words.

"Now I know your secret. And you don't know mine."

When she hitched a little sob, he raised his head so that he could meet her gaze.

He could see tears glistening in her eyes. "I'm so sorry."

He felt as though he were poised on the edge of a sharp blade.

"I want to tell you, so much. I tried to tell you. I can't say it, but I tried to write it down," she whispered.

He nodded, thinking about the sheets of paper on her dresser. She had written some words. But he had no way of connecting them. Not unless she gave him some clues.

She continued to stroke him, and now he felt her hand shaking.

"Vandar won't let me," she said, her voice thick with the tears.

Vandar. She had said that name before.

He saw the track of moisture slipping down her cheeks.

Delicately, he stretched out his tongue and wiped them away.

"Oh, Talon. Oh. You're so strong, and yet you can be so gentle."

He stood before her, wishing he could ask the question that burned in his throat. Vandar? Was he the leader of the group where she lived? Or the head of a secret project? He wanted to tell her she was his life mate, and they would get through this together, but speech was denied him.

"He . . ."

Every cell of his body strained to catch the rest of what she was poised to say.

But before she could utter another syllable, her whole body began to shake.

Kenna, what is it? Kenna, he shouted inside his head, the words emerging from his mouth as a series of strangled growls.

She grabbed her head with both hands and screamed, "Gods!"

As he watched in horror, she fell off the rock and lay shaking on the ground.

CHAPTER
TWENTY

A THICK, CHOKING fear engulfed Talon as he crouched beside Kenna. *Oh God, it's happening again.* The same thing that he'd seen before. She'd said she was having a migraine to cover the truth—that an attack seized her whenever she tried to talk to him about herself.

Kenna, I'm so sorry, he silently shouted, then moaned in frustration. This time he was getting her to the hospital. But he couldn't do it as a wolf.

He had to change, then get her into the car.

Or would she die while he was making the transformation?

Whatever happened, he couldn't stay a wolf. He was about to say the chant when he heard footsteps pounding down the trail he'd just taken.

Christ! Was the guy with the gas back? This time with his gun? He'd thought he'd scared the bastard away for a while.

Stopping in his tracks, he turned to face the enemy and blinked as he tried to make sense of what he was seeing: a dark-haired man, a wolf, and a petite woman running toward him.

He'd seen the man a long time ago. It was his cousin Ross Marshall, who had come to tell him that the Marshalls had started getting together—and would he like to join them for a family gathering? He hadn't wanted to hear about it then. He didn't want to hear it now.

The wolf must be another Marshall.

If he could have spoken he would have shouted at them.

Ross must have understood the look on his face because he stopped to catch his breath. "Sorry. When I phoned you, I wasn't far away," he called out. "Logan changed and tracked you. I can't let this go. I have to talk to you about Kenna."

The woman gasped when she saw Kenna lying on the ground. "She's hurt." Sprinting around him, she knelt beside the crumpled figure.

"What happened to her?"

I don't fucking know! Talon shouted inside his head.

Ross kept his voice even. "I've brought your cousin Logan and his wife, Rinna. Rinna is from the same place as Kenna. I think she can help you."

Talon goggled at the man.

When Ross pulled a knapsack off his shoulder, Talon growled and bared his teeth.

Ross held up his free hand, palm out. "Okay, I know we invaded your territory. I know that's a breach of werewolf protocol as far as you're concerned. But I'm hoping you won't attack us. This is urgent. You need to hear me out. Rinna and Kenna are from an alternate universe, and we need to know the reason why she's here. It's not an accident. Something's going on."

He felt as though the ground had tipped under him, and he had to fight to stay on his feet.

He wanted to shout that Ross was talking garbage, yet too many strange things had happened with Kenna for him to simply dismiss his cousin's words.

"There's a world that runs parallel to this one. It's similar but different. Rinna came through a portal to this universe a couple of years ago."

The word "portal" stopped him. It was one of the words Kenna had written on the pieces of paper.

"She's having some kind of attack," Rinna called out. "She needs help."

Talon swung toward his life mate, pawing the ground in frustration. What the hell could he do in wolf form?

"I carry clothes with me," Ross said, leaning over so that

he could toss the pack gently on the ground. "Go change
and put them on, so you can help her."

Talon hesitated, then snatched up the pack in his teeth
and dashed into the underbrush, where he silently pushed
through the chant of transformation. As soon as he had
hands to do it, he pulled out a pair of sweatpants and dragged
them on along with a T-shirt, then ran barefoot back to the
stream. While he'd changed, the other wolf had, too.

They eyed each other with barely checked hostility.

Talon pushed through the crowd and knelt beside his
life mate. Her eyes were open and fixed on him.

"Thank God. Are you all right?"

"Yes, now," she whispered.

Rinna was holding her hand. "It's okay," she said in a
steady voice. "My name is Rinna. I'm from your world."

Kenna's eyes widened in shock. "How?"

"It's a long story. I was running away from a man who
was a strong adept, a man who wanted to control me. He'd
come through the portal and set a trap that would catch a
shape-shifter. It caught Logan. That's how I met him. He's
my life mate and my husband now."

Talon was still struggling with the concept of another
universe. He wanted to demand proof, but for the time
being he'd just have to accept this crazy situation.

Kenna's gaze darted from Rinna to Talon and back
again. "I saw Talon as a wolf. You are, too?"

"Yes. And Logan and Ross. They're Talon's cousins. All
the men in the Marshall family are werewolves."

"I thought that here—" She stopped abruptly and winced.

"I can sense that you have your own talent. What is it?"
Rinna asked Kenna.

Fear and pain clouded Kenna's eyes.

"But you can't talk about it," Rinna said.

"I want to," Kenna answered, then cried out as her face
contorted.

"Someone's preventing it?"

"Y-yes," Kenna gasped.

"It hurts her," Talon shouted. "Leave her alone."

He scooped her up in his arms and started back toward the lodge. Without looking over his shoulder, he knew the others were following.

He could send them away. That was his right, but he knew he was facing something that he couldn't deal with on his own. Questions swirled in his mind. Questions and things that Kenna had said and done. He'd already started thinking something pretty strange was going on with her. It sounded like it was worse than he could have imagined. So he let the others follow him up the trail.

They stopped outside the lodge, and he bent to open the door, then stepped inside with Kenna in his arms, leaving them standing in the driveway.

Quickly, he strode down the hall, where he laid Kenna on her bed, then eased down so he was sitting beside her.

"How are you?" he whispered.

"Okay."

He knew it was a lie. Taking her in his arms, he held her as tightly as he dared and whispered, "Sweetheart, I'm so sorry."

"For what?"

"For not trusting you."

She moved her head against his shoulder. "You . . . shouldn't."

"We can talk about it . . ."

"No." She reached to press her fingers against his mouth. "Finally, there's a way out of this for me." Her gaze shot to the pile of papers. "I couldn't tell you . . ." She stopped and started again. "But I figured out that maybe I could write it down. One word at a time. Then I could fill in the little words and put the whole thing in order."

"That was clever of you."

"We'll see," she said in a thin voice. "Take them to . . . to Rinna."

"What?"

"Take them to her," she repeated. "Please. Talk to her. I think she might understand. But you can't do it here."

"I don't want to leave you."

"I don't want you to leave," she said in a thin voice. "But you have to go. I . . . I can't do it."

As she spoke, she gave him a look that twisted his heart, and he understood that if they tried to discuss this with her, he'd only trigger the pain in her head again. With a low sound, he swept the papers into a pile, picked them up, and went back down the hall. Outside, he found his visitors still standing awkwardly in the driveway.

ALONE in the bedroom, Kenna tried to calm the jumble of emotions surging through her. In the space of a few minutes, everything had changed.

Talon was a werewolf!

His cousins were werewolves. One was married to a werewolf—from Kenna's world.

She wanted to leap up and run back to the group of people who had come here without Talon's asking.

Would he send them away? Or would he let them help? And what could they do?

Hardly daring to hope, she turned on her side and hugged her knees, waiting to learn the outcome of the discussion they would be having.

Talon had been so tender with her. She'd wanted to stay in his arms. But she knew they had to settle this. And she knew that when he understood the full extent of her lies, he might end up hating her.

TALON studied the three people standing awkwardly outside. Ross seemed pretty calm. Logan, the other cousin, folded his arms across his chest.

Talon sensed that he was a hothead. Could he send him away? Maybe, but then the woman would leave, too. And Kenna needed her.

After a long moment, he muttered, "I guess you can come in." He probably didn't sound like a gracious host.

But that had never been the way with the men in the Marshall family. They were each the alpha male of their own pack, and that created problems with werewolf social relations.

When they followed him inside, he led them to the living room, then turned to Rinna. "Kenna sent me to you," he said, "because it hurts her to talk about it. Whatever 'it' is."

"Yes."

"You might as well sit down," Talon said.

They sat, and he continued to study them as he rolled up the papers Kenna had given him into a tube and twisted them in his hand. None of his visitors looked exactly comfortable. *Good.*

He swung back toward the hall, wishing that Kenna were part of this conversation because it felt like they were going to talk behind her back, but he understood that she couldn't be here. With a low sound, he took a seat facing the three people who had invaded his property without being invited.

"Okay, I want some answers," he growled.

Ross nodded. "Of course."

"How do you know that Kenna was from an . . . uh . . . alternate universe?" he asked.

"You were trying to figure out who she was, and you gave me genetic material," Ross replied.

"Yes, I mailed it to you week before last when I was in town getting supplies."

"My wife, Megan, is a physician who owns a bio lab in the D.C. area. When she tested it, she recognized a marker that she had seen in Rinna's DNA."

"What kind of marker?"

"It's a long story. But the short version is that their universe was like ours until the World's Fair of 1893, when a man named Eric Carfoli set up an exhibit. He claimed he could give people psychic powers."

"And?"

"And over there, it worked. A lot of people can tell the

future, read minds, change to an animal shape, do remote viewing, speak to the dead, move objects with their minds."

"You expect me to believe that?" Talon snapped.

"It's true," Rinna answered. "In our world, we culti-vate those talents. We send children to special schools to increase their powers." As she spoke, she reached for her husband's hand and gripped it tightly, then closed her eyes. Over on the side of the room, a circle began to waver in the air, shimmering with a light that came from within.

Talon stared at the shimmering air, then at the strained look on Rinna's face. "What the hell are you doing?"

The air abruptly returned to normal, and Rinna opened her eyes, looking like she'd just run a long race.

"That's the beginning of a portal between the worlds," she said between deep drafts of air. "I can't open one by myself or even with Logan's help. But if there were more people with talents, we could do it." She kept her gaze on Talon. "I could change to the form of a white bird, if you want to see me do that. But we'd just be wasting time."

"You can do that?"

"Yeah," Logan answered for his wife. "Like she said, there are a lot of people with special talents in the other universe. And their DNA is different because Eric Carfoli changed it."

Talon tensed as another question popped into his head. "What about religion in the other universe?" he asked, addressing Rinna.

"We have many religions. Many gods,"

He nodded, remembering that Kenna had said "gods," not "God."

Ross gestured toward the papers that Talon had rolled into a tube and was twisting in his hand. "What are those?"

He looked down at them, feeling like he was holding a bomb that was about to explode. "Something Kenna wrote. Just a few words. One of them was 'portal.' "

Talon looked at Rinna. "She told me to give them to you."

Slowly, he unrolled the papers, then reached across the coffee table and laid them down, smoothing them out.

His gaze stayed on Rinna. As she shuffled through them, she gasped.

"What?"

"She wrote 'slave.'"

"Which means what?"

She shifted in her seat. "In my world, we have slaves. I was born one. I think she was trying to tell you that is her status."

"No!"

"I understand why you don't want to believe it," she said gently. "But life is different there. You have fewer choices. Less freedom."

"And no modern conveniences," he said, reluctantly bolstering their case.

"Yes. I guess you noticed that she didn't know how things worked here."

"I thought she came from some primitive community up in the hills."

"Yes." Rinna shuffled the papers. When she came to the last page, she looked up at him with rounded eyes. "She's telling you her master sent her here as a spy. And I think she was trying to say 'another universe.' But she didn't get that far."

He stood up, reached across the table, and snatched the pages away. Because he simply didn't want to believe how bad the news was, he shouted, "I don't have to listen to this."

"Yeah, you do," Ross said in a hard voice.

Outrage bubbled from the depths of Talon's werewolf soul.

"This is my den," he answered in a dangerously calm voice, reaching for the hem of the borrowed shirt he was wearing.

If Ross wanted to fight, they would do it in wolf form.

Rinna's voice reached him through the anger simmering in his gut.

"And your life mate is going to die or go insane unless you let us help you," she said.

He felt as though she'd punched him in the chest.

"No!" he gasped.

He saw Rinna's gaze had shifted from him to the hallway. With a feeling of dread, he turned so he could see what she was looking at.

It was Kenna, standing there, white-faced, her hand on the wall to steady herself.

When she saw he'd discovered her, she fixed her gaze on him. "If you care for me, let them help me, please."

"Care for you?" Rushing to her, he gathered her close.

CHAPTER
TWENTY-ONE

THE PLEADING LOOK on Kenna's face almost ripped his heart out.

Lifting her into his arms, he carried her to a big leather chair and sat down, cradling her against himself.

Since he'd clashed with his father and left the family home, he'd been making decisions for himself. The right decisions. In this situation, he was utterly lost. When he looked up and saw the others watching him with sympathy, he wanted to take out his frustration on them. But he had come around to the opinion that they were his best hope.

Bending toward Kenna, he whispered, "We'll figure it out."

"I'm going to need help," Rinna said. "From the other life mates. A lot of them have powers."

"Are they from the other universe?" Talon asked.

"No. They come from this one. But they were born with talents most people here don't have." She looked at Ross. "Can you call Renata and Antonia, Jacob's and Grant's life mates?" she asked. "They're the closest. And also Sara, if she can get here in time. Renata is the reincarnation of a goddess," Rinna added in a hushed voice.

"Oh yeah?" Talon asked.

"A goddess!" Kenna breathed. "And she's willing to help me?"

"She's mortal—now," Rinna said. "And of course she's willing to help you. You're Talon's life mate."

"His what?"

Talon gave Rinna a fierce scowl. It wasn't for her to

give Kenna that piece of information. That should be his privilege.

She caught the expression on his face. "You haven't talked about that?"

"No," he snapped.

"I'm sorry. I should have . . ."

"It's okay," he said, wondering what he'd gotten himself into.

Ross gave him a direct look. "They'll come with their werewolf life mates. Is that okay with you?"

"You're asking permission?"

"Yeah."

He thought about it for a few seconds, wondering how he was going to stand so many of his cousins in one place. But he knew he was going to have to do it, because he had no choice. Still, there was something else he had to say.

"That money I found in the woods. I'm pretty sure the guy who buried it tried to burn down the lodge today. There's some danger in being here."

"With extra werewolves patrolling the area, he shouldn't be a problem."

"Let's hope."

Kenna turned toward Ross. "Thank you."

He nodded and stood, pulling his cell phone from its holster. "I'll go make those calls."

"And check the guy's license number while you're at it." Talon gave the tag number to Ross, who wrote it down and stepped outside.

Rinna stood and walked toward Kenna. "I think I can help you sleep. That might be the best thing for you now."

"Yes."

"Let's go back to the bedroom."

Talon stood with Kenna in his arms and carried her down the hall where he laid her down once again.

Then he stepped away and let Rinna take a seat on the bed.

"I'm not a healer, but I have some skill with going into

another person's mind." She swallowed. "My master tried to take that skill away from me."

Kenna was hanging on her words.

"Can you open yourself to me?"

"What do I have to do?"

"Don't resist me."

When Kenna nodded, Rinna pressed her fingers to Kenna's forehead. She closed her eyes, but opened them again after a few moments.

"I'm having trouble reaching you."

Kenna's lower lip trembled. "I'm sorry."

"I don't think it's your fault, but I can't break through. Not by myself."

Kenna nodded.

"I'll have to wait for the others."

"Okay."

WHEN Rinna left, Kenna took her lower lip between her teeth.

"Don't." Talon slipped onto the bed and gathered her close. "I know this is hard for you."

"And you."

When he stroked his lips against her cheek, she felt compelled to warn him, "It's not over. I mean the thing that's wrong with me."

"I understand."

She wanted to say so much more, but she knew that if she did, the pain would come zinging back.

"We'll fix it," he said again, but she thought he didn't sound as confident as usual.

"Maybe this will defeat even you."

"We'll do it!" he insisted, and she prayed to the Great Mother that it was true. She had found this man who had become everything to her, but there was no future for the two of them unless . . .

Even that wayward thought sent a dart of pain into her head, and she winced.

He raised his head, looking at her in alarm.

"I just have to keep my thoughts away from . . . my problem," she whispered.

"Yeah."

He pulled her closer, and she snuggled in his arms. She wasn't free yet, but she could see how it would be for the two of them, if Rinna and the others could help her.

The shimmering promise of what the future could be made her want to weep, but she kept from shedding any tears, because she knew that Talon would think she was sad, not happy.

"What's a 'life mate'?" she asked in a voice that was barely above a whisper.

She heard him swallow. "Wolves mate for life. So do werewolves. When one of the men in my family finds the right woman, they bond." He dragged in a breath and let it out in a rush. "I knew it was you, almost as soon as I met you. But I fought it."

"Because you couldn't trust me," she managed to say.

"Partly. And partly because I couldn't see myself settling down."

"And now you can?" she dared to ask.

"Yes. With you."

"It might not work out."

"We'll make it work," he said fiercely.

She wanted to spell out her doubts, but she knew that wouldn't help either one of them, so she asked, "And one of your cousins has a life mate who . . . who is the reincarnation of a goddess."

"Apparently. I haven't spent much time with my family, so I didn't know about it."

"Why not?"

"Because of the way things have been for centuries. There's only one alpha male in every wolf pack. Each of us has his own pack."

Family had been important to her, and being alone like that sounded sad to her, but she didn't want to say it. Instead, she murmured, "But it seems like Ross and the others have gotten together."

"The guys who are mated," he said.

Was that something she could give him—a connection with his family? She hardly dared to hope for so much.

She had been without hope for so long that it was impossible to believe in a real future for herself, for the two of them. But for now, it was wonderful to simply lie here in the arms of the man she loved. She wanted to tell him how she felt, but she wasn't free to do it, not yet.

Instead, she shifted against him. "I know how we could . . . distract me. Would you kiss me?"

"If I did, you know where it would lead. I want you too badly for just a kiss."

She nodded against his shoulder. "You have more willpower than I do."

"I'm trying."

She saw his fist clench and knew she shouldn't push him any further.

Determined not to start anything they couldn't finish, she closed her eyes and stroked his arm, amazed that his presence could give her so much comfort.

This was what it was like to belong to someone. Not the way she belonged to her master. To someone who cared about her—and whom she cared about.

As she lay in his arms, he did what Rinna hadn't been able to accomplish. While he stroked her and murmured reassurances to her, she felt herself relaxing.

Some time later, the sound of voices made her eyes blink open.

Rinna was back with two other women. Two more life mates, she guessed.

"I've brought Antonia and Renata," she said, gesturing toward the newcomers.

"Good to meet you," they said.

"Yes," she answered, even as she felt herself blush.

She was an unmarried woman lying on a bed with a

man, and there were three other people in the room, watching. In her world, that would be the height of scandal.

Well, maybe one of the women wasn't watching. As Kenna tried to meet Antonia's eyes, she realized with a start that the other woman was blind.

The knowledge that these people had dropped everything in order to help her was overwhelming.

"Thank you for coming," she said, hearing how thin her voice sounded. "On such short notice. I know I must be interrupting your lives."

"This is important," Renata answered.

Talon sat up. "Should I leave?"

Rinna looked toward Renata, and Kenna got the feeling that she was the one who was going to take charge. *The goddess.*

She hadn't realized she'd spoken aloud until Renata answered. "I'm not a goddess. I'm human. But I'm her reincarnation, which gives me powers I wouldn't ordinarily have."

"I . . ."

"Please . . . just think of me as a friend and . . . your sister-in-law. I didn't even know I had any special powers until a few months ago."

Kenna answered with a tiny nod, overwhelmed at the word "sister-in-law."

Renata turned to Talon. "You should stay," she said. "You may be of help."

"What should we do?" Antonia asked.

Renata stepped forward. "We need to find out what the problem is."

Talon moved awkwardly out of the way, and Renata sat down on the bed. "Will you let us connect with your mind?"

"If you can," Kenna whispered.

Renata looked at Rinna, and she was sure they had talked about what Rinna had tried and failed to do.

Well, why not? She had known this wasn't going to be easy. Maybe getting through the barrier was impossible.

"Relax," Renata said, reaching out toward her, both with her hand and with her mind.

The other women moved to the far side of the bed and sat down, each of them putting a hand on her. Their touch was reassuring.

"We're just going to see what's going on," Renata murmured.

Kenna felt her mental touch. It was strong—stronger than Rinna's had been, and she thought that this woman might have a chance of getting through to her.

She could feel Renata directing the process, feel the probing touch.

"Don't fight me," she murmured.

"I'm not."

Struggling to open herself, she felt some kind of barrier waver, then crack.

When the goddess sucked in a sharp breath, Kenna's eyes flew open.

"It's not a man. It's a monster," Renata whispered.

"Yes. Vandar."

When she said his name, she felt a jolt of pain digging into the cells of her brain. Struggling against the pain, she fought to send them a picture of the beast. More than one picture. Vandar in his winged incarnation. Vandar as a man. Vandar feeding.

Her vision had turned black, but she heard more gasps around the room.

"Jesus!" That was Talon. He must have somehow picked up the pictures along with the three women. "That's what's been holding you captive?"

"Yes," she managed to say that much before she felt a blast of hot, blinding pain.

"No!" she screamed, but she didn't even know if the word passed her lips.

From far away, she heard Talon bellow a curse. "What the hell have you done to her?"

"Not us," Renata answered. "It's the wards inside her head."

That was the last thing she heard before a terrible blackness sucked her down.

For a long moment, she saw nothing, heard nothing. Then the blackness turned to a dim gray light, shrouded in mist. Through the fog, she saw Vandar hovering in front of her. He had his human face, but his dragon body, so that his features were five times the size of a man's.

His mouth opened and a stream of fire shot out, enveloping her whole body in flames. But her flesh did not turn black. Instead, she continued to burn.

"You think you can defy me?" he asked, his voice rising up in the middle of the flames. "I'll show you what happens to mortals who try to escape from me."

She screamed and screamed again. Then, for a moment, she felt a spurt of hope, when the flames diminished a little.

Turning, she started to run, down an endless dark tunnel. At the end, she could see a light, and she knew that if she could reach it, she would be free.

She was almost there when something grabbed her from behind, a huge hand with sharp nails that dug into her flesh.

"Not so fast."

He pulled her back and spun her around, and she saw that he had changed his form again. He was a man, dressed in the black tunic that he wore for his ceremonies.

They were in a cave. Not the cave where she had lived with the other slaves. This was a rounded chamber with rock walls and a shaft of light coming down from the ceiling, shining on a wooden post with a cross bar at the top. The air smelled like rotting flesh, and a roaring sound rose all around her.

Vandar dragged her toward the cross, then clawed at her clothing with his free hand, shredding the shirt and pants she wore.

When she was naked, she tried to cover her breasts with her hand, but he pulled her arm roughly up, attaching it to the crossbar at the top of the post. He did the same with the other hand, so that she was standing with her arms out-stretched and secured above her head.

When she was trussed to his satisfaction, he stepped back looking at her.

"You and I are going to spend some time here together," he said in a satisfied voice. "And before I'm through with you, you're going to beg me to drain your blood."

CHAPTER
TWENTY-TWO

TALON SHOVED THE goddess aside and grabbed Kenna. She was limp as a rag doll. Her skin had turned the color of porcelain, and her breathing was so shallow that he had to press his hand to her chest to make sure it was rising and falling.

"What the hell have you done?" he repeated.

"Nothing!"

"What do you mean, nothing? Look at her."

The woman's voice turned hard. "It wasn't me," she said, punching out the words. "It came from within her."

"Christ!"

The other two life mates moved to the far side of the bed. All three of them put their hands on Kenna.

"She's gone deep inside herself," the one named Antonia whispered.

"Bring her back!"

He wanted to throttle them for coming here and doing this. He might have leaped at them except that three of his cousins charged into the room. The only one he knew was Logan, the hothead. But the others must be the husbands of the two other women.

"Something wrong?" Logan asked.

"Something's happened to Kenna."

Renata stood and faced the men, putting herself between them and Talon.

"He's upset," she said. "Kenna's life is in danger. I think we can help him bring her back, but we need to be alone."

"I'm not leaving," Logan said.

One of the other men put a hand on his arm. "Come on," he said. "Remember how you felt when Rinna was kidnapped?"

Logan nodded, but he kept his gaze on Talon. "If anything happens to Rinna, you'll be sorry."

"We're wasting time," Renata said. "Go."

Logan turned and marched out of the room. The others followed.

Talon focused on Renata. He'd been angry, but he knew deep down that she was his only hope to save his life mate.

"What should I do?" he asked.

"Lie down beside her. Hold her. You're the only one who can bring her back." *Not her. Him.*

He felt a spurt of hope, until she added, "If the bond between you is strong enough."

Was it? It had to be!

He might have been embarrassed. But he knew he was past that as he lay down and gathered Kenna's limp body in his arms, folding her close and squeezing his eyes shut.

The women closed in around them, each of them with a hand on him and a hand on Kenna, and he could feel them sending energy into him, energy that he then sent to Kenna. It was a strange sensation. He didn't know how he was doing it.

"Speak to her," Renata whispered. "Tell her how much you love her. How much you need her."

Could he do that? In front of these women?

Yes, because it was the only way to bring Kenna back, and he would die without her.

VANDAR reached out a hand and touched Kenna's shoulder. Digging in one nail, he scraped his way down her chest, across her breast, and down to the thatch of hair at the juncture of her legs. After admiring his handiwork, he leaned toward her and pressed his mouth to her breast, sucking the blood that had welled up there.

She clenched her teeth, determined not to scream,

because she knew he wanted to feel her fear, and denying him that was the only thing she had left.

When she heard footsteps in back of her, she stiffened. Someone else was here in this chamber.

As Vandar looked over her shoulder, his face contorted in anger.

"Get out of here."

"No."

It was Talon. He was here! But how could that be?

"Kenna is mine," Vandar shouted. "Go back to your own world."

"Make me."

She couldn't see Talon, and when she tried to twist around, Vandar reached out a clawed hand and held her fast.

"Get the hell off of her," Talon shouted.

"Make me," the beast snarled, repeating what Talon had said.

Behind her, Talon reached up and worked at the ropes holding her hands. As they loosened, the monster shot out a stream of fire from his mouth, and she heard Talon groan in pain, but he kept working.

"Get away. Before he kills you," she gasped.

"Not a chance."

He freed her hands, and she found that she could take a step back.

"Stop!" Vandar commanded, and she went rigid again.

Then Talon began to speak in her ear. "Kenna, I love you. So much. I should have told you, but I was afraid to say the words. I need you. I'm nothing without you beside me. Please, you have to come back."

"I can't," she said, hearing her voice crack.

"You have to."

"I'm his slave."

"Not anymore. You're in a different world. He isn't here."

"Yes, he is!"

"He put these images in your head to control you. They're not real, and they're not as strong as our love."

Was he right? When he said it, she felt a bubble of hope.

"Help me," Talon pleaded. "I can't do it alone. We have to fight him together."

FAR away, Ramsay Gallagher was in his garage, working on the 1933 Pierce Arrow that he had restored, when he caught a series of confusing images.

He knew they were coming from the woman—the woman he had first sensed in the smoke ceremony.

Days ago, he had thought she was gone. Dead. Or in some place that he couldn't penetrate. Then, from one moment to the next, he'd sensed the link with her again, as though she had stepped through a door from another place to this universe.

Was that possible? He didn't know.

Yet it fit the circumstances in some way that he couldn't articulate.

Now he went rigid, caught by the scene in his mind. The woman. And two men. But he knew as he looked at one of them that the guy wasn't human.

He sucked in a sharp breath.

Where the hell was all that coming from?

The scene was disturbing. The nonhuman creature was the most disturbing of all, because it brought back too many memories from his own past.

It was like the monster he had fought long ago—and won. At the time, he had been sure that there wasn't another like it on Earth. Could he have been wrong?

If he was, where had the damn thing come from? And where was it lurking now?

TEARS streamed down Kenna's face as she thought of what she longed for with Talon. And what she could have—if she fought for it.

Perhaps he felt the change in her. "Sweetheart, we can do it! Together."

Feeling her own resolve strengthen, she took a step away from her fearsome master.

"That's it! You can do it. *We* can do it." Talon's voice filled with hope as he guided her back, out of the rock-bound cave where Vandar had brought her.

As they reached an opening at the back of the cave, the monster shot out his fiery breath again, but it barely reached them. He was too far away, and the fire diminished as he receded into the background.

He was screaming at her, "Fuck you! You're mine. Fuck both of you. Come back." But she could hardly hear him now.

Then, all at once, she stepped backwards through a barrier that was something like a portal, only it felt more solid as her body jolted from a shadow world into reality.

Her eyes snapped open, and she dragged in a breath of sweet-smelling air. Blinking her eyes, she realized she was lying on the bed again, with Talon's face hovering over hers. It was wet with tears, and she realized she was crying, too.

"You brought me back," she said, hearing the wonder in her own voice. "You went into that horrible place and pulled me free."

"You had the courage to come with me," he answered.

"You did it together," a woman said, and Kenna's gaze snapped to Renata, then the other two women who had come to help her.

Suddenly, she realized that she and Talon weren't alone. The adepts were still in her bedroom, where they'd come to break the hold of . . .

"Vandar had me tied to a . . . cross," she said, bracing for pain as she said the forbidden name. To her amazement, nothing happened.

"Great Mother," she marveled, looking down at her body. In the dream, she had been naked. Now she was wearing the clothing she'd had on when the women had come in.

"How long was I . . . away?" she asked.

"Only a few minutes."

"It seemed like hours."

"He wanted it to. Do you understand that it was just his illusion?"

She nodded, trying to absorb what had happened.

Talon tightened his hold on her arm. "You're free of him. Forever."

"Vandar planted those images in your head before you left home," Renata said. "They were his last hope, if you tried to crack his hold on you. But your will was strong enough to break the compulsion he placed on your mind."

She marveled at that—at the difference in how she felt. The burden she had carried around was suddenly gone. She wanted to simply enjoy her wonderful freedom.

Yet as she absorbed the new truth, a jolt of panic zinged through her. "I . . . I have to tell you about him. About what he has planned."

"Yes. But not now. You've been through an ordeal, and you need to rest. We'll be here when you're ready."

The three women withdrew from the room.

When they had closed the door, she ducked her head away from Talon, but he tipped her chin up so that she had to meet his eyes.

"I'm so ashamed," she whispered.

"About what?"

"I was a spy. And a liar."

"Not because you wanted to be."

"But I feel awful. I felt awful the whole time I was doing it. I . . . I tried to tell you the truth, but I couldn't."

"I understand that now. It wasn't your fault. I saw how horrible he was."

She sucked in a sharp breath. "You saw him?"

"Yes. In your vision."

She ached to cover her face. Instead, she found Talon's hand and held on tight.

"He's surrounded by slaves who are all terrified of him—and all under his power."

"We can talk about that later."

"But . . . I have to tell you all of it."

"Later."

Before she could protest, he brought his lips to hers for a long, hungry kiss, and the heat that came from him enveloped her. Not like Vandar's fire. A healing heat that sealed the two of them together.

He tightened his hold on her, and they rocked together on the bed. When he eased away and cupped his hand around her breast, she gave him a startled look.

"There are people in the house, and . . . and . . ."

"Yeah. But they can wait." He stood up and opened the window. "We're going outside. To a place where we'll be alone. Too bad we're not in my room. I have a sliding glass door, but it's only a four-foot drop from this window. Not too far."

From the top shelf of the closet, he took down what looked like a rolled-up quilt. "Sleeping bag," he explained as he threw it outside on the ground, then climbed down and held out his arms. She slung one leg over the sash before letting herself down, landing in his arms, where she had to press her mouth against his shoulder to hold back a giggle.

He grinned at her, then picked up the sleeping bag and wedged it under one arm before slinging the other arm around her shoulder as he led her away from the house, to a circle of pine trees that she'd passed on her walks. Directing her to one side of the circle, he showed her a place where they could slip through the branches.

"This is where I change."

She studied the sheltered place in appreciation. It was a private spot, the ground soft and fragrant with fallen pine needles.

After unrolling the sleeping bag, he unzipped it and laid it on the needles, making a double-wide bed. Then he reached for her, and she came into his arms again.

His mouth found hers, and he began to kiss her as he worked the buttons on the front of her shirt before pulling it off her shoulders and dropping it on the ground. After dragging his own shirt over his head and sending it to join hers, he pulled her close.

The feel of his chest hair against her breasts made her draw in a quick breath, and she pressed her cheek to his shoulder.

"This time is different," she whispered.

"Yes. Because there are no barriers between us."

It was true and so much more. The first time she hadn't known what making love would be like. The second time she'd felt frantic with the compulsion Vandar had placed on her to use their sexual connection to control Talon. But this time, it was just the two of them, knowing where they were going together.

CHAPTER
TWENTY-THREE

TALON SWAYED HER against his body, entranced by the way her hardened nipples dragged across his chest.

He had known all along that she was his life mate. At first he had fought it. Today he embraced it.

Even though he knew they still had problems to work out, he wanted this time together.

And he wanted her to know what he felt. "I couldn't make a commitment, not really. Now I want you to know how much I love you. How much I need you."

He kissed her hungrily as he worked the snap at the top of her jeans, then the zipper. When he had slid her jeans and panties down her legs, she kicked them away, then helped him off with his clothing.

Together, they came down to the surface of the sleeping bag and lay facing each other, the blue of the sky above them and the pine trees walling them off from the rest of the world as they touched and kissed.

When her hand slid down to his cock, circling and squeezing him, he let himself enjoy her touch for a few moments before lifting her hand away.

"You'll make me come."

"I want to learn what pleases you. Everything that pleases you."

"You will. We've got plenty of time."

He saw a shadow cross her face. "What?"

"We still have to . . . to deal with Vandar."

"We will," he answered, but he couldn't stand the uncertainty on her face, so he kissed his way to one of her tight nipples, biting gently, then swirling his tongue over her while he slid one hand down her body and into the warm wet folds of her sex, finding her slick and swollen for him. When he brushed his finger against the side of her clit, she sucked in a ragged breath.

"What do you call that place that you just touched?" she asked.

"Your clit. A very sweet place." As he spoke, he bent over her, parting the folds of her sex and lowering his mouth to her.

She gasped. "What are you doing?"

He lifted his head far enough to say, "What I wanted to do before. Getting a taste of you." He used his lips and his tongue on her, trying to drive every thought from her mind except the heat flaming between them.

He knew he had succeeded when she begged him, "Please. No more!"

Lifting his head, he stared at her stunned face.

He surprised her again, lying down on his back and lifting her so that she was straddling him.

From his prone position, he looked up at her and grinned.

When she tried to cover her breasts, he reached for her hands.

"It would please me to look at you when we make love," he said in a thick voice.

She swallowed. "Okay."

Her face turned serious as she raised her hips and came down on his cock, seating him firmly inside her. Once they were joined, she grinned and surprised him by contracting her inner muscles around him.

"Ah . . that's good."

She grinned again and arched her back, thrusting her breasts boldly toward him, and he could see that she had discovered she was enjoying this variation on a basic human activity.

As she looked down at him with new confidence, she began to move, and he was stunned by the intensity he saw on her face, and by what he felt.

"Oh, Talon. Oh . . ." She gasped as her movements became more frantic.

"Lean forward," he told her. "Press your clit against me."

She did, working herself against him, and he struggled to hold himself back, waiting for her to reach the peak of pleasure. When he felt her inner muscles contract in small spasms, he let himself go, joining her in a thundering climax that seemed to shake the ground around them.

When he came back to Earth, he gathered her close, holding her sweat-slick body to his.

"I love you so much," she murmured.

"I love you," he answered. "It feels wonderful to say that."

"Yes."

She snuggled against him, and he held her and stroked her, wishing they could stay where they were for a long time. But she had told him a threat still hung over them, and he wanted to wipe it out so the two of them could be truly free.

"We should go back."

She ducked her head. "Renata and the others, they'll all know what we've been doing."

"Yeah. Because it's the same thing they do when they want to show their life mate what they're feeling."

She nodded, and he held her for a while longer, then sat up.

"I think we have to face the music."

"The music?"

"It's an idiom. And I'm damned if I know where it came from. Maybe the musical theater. A performer who was nervous would have to face the orchestra pit when the curtain opened."

She laughed. "That doesn't help much. What's a musical theater? Or an orchestra pit?"

He was glad to explain the terms while they got dressed because it was a good way to distract her.

When she looked up from pulling on her clothes, there was a tentative expression on her face.

"What?"

"It's a relief to be able to ask you questions without . . . being afraid."

"Oh, sweetheart. It must have been so hard for you." He pulled her into his arms and held on tight for long moments.

When he plucked a couple of pine needles out of her hair, her expression turned shy.

"Don't worry about my family. If they're thinking anything, it's about me. They know I didn't want to bond with anyone. And now I'm well and truly snared."

"I'm not sure that helps."

As they approached the front door of the lodge, he saw a couple more cars in the driveway and knew more Marshalls had arrived.

That reality was unnerving, but he stopped worrying about his own reactions when he felt Kenna's hand tighten on his.

"We'll get through this together," he said.

"But there's a lot you don't know."

"I want to hear it."

"Maybe you won't think so when you do."

Talon squeezed her hand. "Get used to understanding that I'll be beside you. Always."

She squeezed back. "I hope I'm worthy of that."

"You are. So come save me from facing the family alone."

She made a clucking sound as he led her through the front door, then down the hall toward the living room, aware that all eyes were on them.

"You've been outside," Rinna said.

"Yeah," he answered with no further explanation, trying to act like it wasn't unnerving to find so many of his relatives and their life mates making themselves at home in his living room.

He and Kenna sat together on one of the sofas.

At least everybody was acting like they'd simply been out for a stroll, when they knew damn well it was more of a horizontal encounter.

"You haven't met Jacob and Grant," Ross said, like they hadn't burst into the bedroom a while ago to protect their mates. "Jacob and Renata are married. And Grant and Antonia."

Kenna nodded shyly.

Jacob leaned forward, addressing her. "Renata and I have been to your world. I take dogs there who have been trained to be dangerous. The healers in Sun Acres can cure them. Do you know Sun Acres?" he asked politely.

Kenna shook her head.

"It's a city to the south—in your world."

"Oh."

Talon listened, figuring they were trying to make Kenna feel comfortable. The trouble was, he couldn't really follow the conversation. He didn't know anything about her world. And he certainly hadn't been there.

Kenna glanced at him, then said, "I guess I'd better stop stalling and tell you how I got here, and why." She swallowed. "I was a free citizen of Breezewood. My father owns a shop that makes sandals and boots, and I went to the school for adepts." She glanced at Talon. "In my world, children with psychic talent go to special schools where they . . . learn to use their full potential."

Rinna smiled at her. "I went to a school like that. What is your talent?"

"I can move objects with my mind." She glanced at Talon again. "That's how I kept the tree from crushing me. And how I helped you lift it off me."

"So that's why it got suddenly lighter."

"Yes." She flushed. "And that's why the barbecue grill flew across the patio."

"Ah. I thought I'd kicked it."

Her voice grew high and strained. "And I broke into a house. Vandar ordered me to bring back things from this world, and I didn't want to steal them from you. So I took them from someone else. Only they disappeared."

"I followed you—as a wolf. Then I dug them up and took them away," Talon said. "But I was too angry to talk to you about it. So I left." He glanced up, challenging anyone to make something of that, but nobody commented.

Kenna dragged in a breath and let it out. "This time he wanted me to get you to bring me guns. And bullets. He thought you'd do it. I knew you wouldn't."

There were exclamations around the room.

"To start a war in your world?" Ross asked.

"To give to his soldiers so he can invade *this* world," Kenna said in a rush. "That's why I'm here. He wanted me to spy on you and report back to him, so he can prepare for an invasion. I . . . I'm sorry."

"Not your fault," Ross answered. "And now that you've alerted us, we can stop him."

She gave Ross a desperate look. "You don't know what you're dealing with. He's not human. He's a monster that you can't even imagine. He sends men to raid nearby cities and bring back slaves. A raiding party of his soldiers captured me about three months ago."

She gulped and went on. "When he captures you, he decides if he can use you or if you're too strong. If he thinks you're a danger to himself, he kills you right away—by drinking your blood."

Again, she heard exclamations from the people in the room.

"How many slaves does he have?"

"I . . . I think about three hundred. He gets them all together to watch him kill."

There were gasps from the women in the room.

"I'm betting they would rebel against him if they got the chance," Ross said.

"They'd be too afraid."

"What if he was . . . disabled?"

She flapped her arm in frustration. "You don't understand how much power he has."

"I felt it. When I went into that dream with you," Talon said.

Her breath hitched. "That was a dream. In real life, defying him is instant death. If you even could. I tried, after I came here. I thought maybe he was too far away to reach me, but I was wrong. Remember the migraine headaches I kept getting?"

"That's what you called them. The symptoms didn't quite fit. So I thought it was something else."

"You were right. They came from the wards he put in my mind. When I tried to tell you about him, the pain made it impossible for me to speak."

"The bastard."

"We saw him, too," Rinna said softly.

"But you don't know what he is. Not really. Nobody can," she said in a broken voice. "Unless they get close to him. And that means he's enslaved you."

When she shuddered, Talon slung his arm around her shoulder and pulled her against his side. "Don't forget, you're not alone. We'll face this together."

She looked like she could barely breathe, and he thought she'd had all she could take for now. "This is getting kind of intense," he said. "Let's go outside for a while. Just you and me."

Her grateful look made his heart turn over.

"We're going to take a few minutes," he said. Without waiting for any replies, he ushered Kenna toward the door.

Outside, the sun was just setting.

"It's so beautiful here," she murmured. "He told me this world had . . . technology and machinery. But I've never seen so many trees in my life."

"This is the kind of place a werewolf wants to live. In the woods."

"You have room to run."

"Yeah. And walk. Let's go down toward the river."

Hand in hand, they wandered down the hill.

"Do you swim there?" she asked, gesturing toward the shimmering surface.

"Mm-hmm. There's a swimming hole."

"Another term I don't know. But I can guess. That place where the water looks deep?"

"Yes. We can have some fun down there."

She gave him an apologetic look. "I can't swim."

"It's not real hard. I'll teach you. If you can't float on your own, we'll get you a noodle."

Her brow wrinkled. "Like in chicken noodle soup?"

He laughed. "No. A long, thin plastic flotation device. You can pick the color. Do you want pink or purple or yellow?"

She smiled. "Any of those."

"You rest your arms across it, and it holds you up."

She nodded, then looked up at the forest. "Will you teach me the names of the trees?"

"Sure." He pointed. "That's a red oak. And that one's a tulip poplar."

"You tell by the shape of the leaves?"

"Right. And sometimes the bark, or special things." He indicated a black locust. "That's got thorns on the trunk and branches, so don't try to climb it."

"Okay."

"There's a lot I want to show you."

"You already have."

He was enjoying the relaxed conversation when he felt a jolt of tension go through her.

"What?"

"Great Mother!"

"What's wrong?"

"Evil power," she gasped.

As she spoke, she started running back the way they'd come. He was right behind her, catching up as she ran toward the house.

CHAPTER
TWENTY-FOUR

AFRAID THAT SHE was too late already, Kenna pounded across the porch and into the living room, feeling the terrible power surging as she entered the confined space. She expected to find a bunch of people running away in all directions.

Instead, she saw something that confused her for a moment.

Everyone was gathered in a circle, holding hands, around something that glowed green and malevolent in the low light of the room.

The terrible energy Kenna felt was coming off the thing in waves.

Renata looked up as Kenna slammed into the room, followed by Talon.

"You'd better join us," she said in a strangely calm voice.

"What the hell is that?" Talon shouted.

"The talisman," Kenna gasped. "Vandar sent it here with me. You saw it in my knapsack. The green thing. Only now . . . it's grown so much bigger."

"Yes."

"It's going to explode," Renata said in the same matter-of-fact voice. "Unless we stop it."

"Run," Kenna gasped. "Get out of here."

"We can't," Renata answered. "We're containing it, and we need you and Talon."

Kenna glanced at him, wanting to order him out of the house. Maybe he saw that on her face because he stepped forward and reached for Rinna's hand, clasping it tightly and leaving a space for Kenna.

Her chest was so tight she could hardly breathe as she stepped into the circle, between Logan and Talon.

When Talon clasped her hand, it helped ground her.

"He must have planned to destroy me if I somehow got free of the compulsion to do his bidding," she whispered.

"Yes," Renata answered. "Lucky for us, Antonia felt it stirring. She told us where to find it, and we dug it out of the knapsack."

"Why did it wait so long?" Rinna murmured.

"Maybe it had to . . . build up enough energy." Kenna swallowed hard.

"I don't think we can stop it," Renata said, "but I think you can get it out of here. You're the one with the telekinetic powers."

She gasped. "Move it—with my mind?"

"Yes."

"It's too . . . heavy," she gasped, although she knew that wasn't quite the right word. It wasn't that large, but the power in its depth weighed it down.

"You don't have to do it alone. We'll help you," Renata said.

Kenna wanted to scream that she couldn't pick up the damn thing. Not with her mind. And now that she was in the room, she knew it sensed her. It was focusing on her, making her feel weak and helpless.

"That's what he wants," Renata said. "Don't let him win."

Kenna clenched her teeth. She had come so far and gained so much, and Vandar still wanted to take it all away from her.

Well, she *wouldn't* let him win the fight. More importantly, she *wouldn't* let him hurt all these other people who had come here to help her. If they died because of her, that would be the worst tragedy of all.

Renata gave her an encouraging look, and she felt strength pouring into her from everyone who surrounded the talisman, but she could feel it probing their defenses, preparing to break through.

It was like a bomb she had seen in a movie on television. Only it had a core of intelligence that Vandar had given it.

She had to get it out of here before it detonated. "Where should I put it?"

Talon supplied the answer. "The swimming hole."

He looked around the group, then inclined his head toward the west. "It's down the hill about an eighth of a mile."

Pretending a calm she didn't feel, Kenna closed her eyes, imagining that she was wrapping her hand around the green glowing talisman. Even though she wasn't really holding it, she felt a burning pain in her palm and fingers, and she knew Talon felt it, too, because he winced.

When she pulled the imaginary hand back, he shook his head. "Do it!"

She kept her eyes squeezed tight as she reached out and grasped the evil thing again. As she did, she could feel the others pouring power into her. It was a warming sensation, one she had never experienced before, not even when she had been in school. A team of friends around her all working for a common cause.

But were they strong enough?

Yes, a voice whispered in her mind, and she knew it was Renata, urging her on.

Kenna felt something inside her swell as she wrapped an invisible shield tightly around the talisman. Yet at the same time, she felt the thing churning up energy within itself, burning her flesh as it struggled to burst through the container she had created.

She knew she had to hurry and get it out of the room before it was too late, but at the same time she knew that if she acted too quickly, she wouldn't have the energy she needed from the group.

With a prayer to the Great Mother, she struggled to judge the right moment.

The talisman decided the issue for her. She felt it flare

up, and she realized that if she delayed, it would blow up in the middle of the circle.

Ignoring the burning sensation, she tightened her mental grip on the wicked object.

"Now!" she shouted as she tugged on the talisman, pulling it closer to herself, seeing it actually move across the table. The heat surged, and she almost lost her grip. But they were all dead if she let go. Like the baseball pitchers she had seen on television, she wound up the invisible arm that held the thing and hurled it away from her into the darkness outside the house. As she did, in her mind's eye, she focused on the place where the river widened and deepened.

Kenna's vision was filled with bright splotches that made it almost impossible to see the circle of faces staring at her. The buzzing in her ears blocked out sound. And she felt her body trembling violently with the effort to control the power that the others gave her.

But through it all, her mind was steady as she pictured the talisman hurtling through the air, then landing with a tremendous splash in the deepest part of the river where it sank below the surface.

Was that reality or only what she hoped to accomplish?

CHAPTER
TWENTY-FIVE

THE LODGE SHOOK as a tremendous explosion rocked the ground outside.

Dropping Logan's and Talon's hands, Kenna ran toward the door.

He grabbed for her, but she darted past him and down the hall. Outside, the night was black, but she could see a green glowing plume of water shooting into the air. It fell back to the river, and then there was silence.

"What happened?" she whispered as the others clustered around her.

"You did it," Renata said in a voice that rang above the buzzing in Kenna's ears.

She opened her mouth to speak, but she was drowned out by the voices of the others congratulating her.

"I . . . I didn't know what I was doing," she stammered as she thought back over the past few minutes.

Rinna laughed, dispelling the nervous energy. "That doesn't matter. You got that blasted thing away from us before it killed everyone."

Kenna sucked in a sharp breath, nodding. As she pictured that green jet of water again, her legs wouldn't hold her up, and she was grateful that Talon caught her arm and helped her back down the hall to a sofa.

Sitting beside her, he turned her toward him and held her tightly, stroking his hands over her back and shoulders as she struggled to control her trembling.

"You were magnificent," he murmured.

* * *

ON the other side of the portal, Vandar felt an icy knife of alarm stab into his chest.

Something had happened. Although he couldn't be sure exactly what, it left him cursing and shaking as he tried to probe for information.

He'd made Kenna think that he had an open connection with her from this side of the portal. That was only partly true. He had little direct control over her, but he had planted strong wards inside her head so that she would behave as he wished while she was in the other universe.

On her previous trip, when he'd sensed her struggling to break away, he had been able to call her back by activating one of his wards.

While she'd been here, he'd doubled the automatic triggers in her mind. And he'd been satisfied with his control.

But now . . .

He knew something was wrong.

Had she actually broken away?

He gnashed his teeth.

If she'd severed her tie with him, then his fail-safe mechanism, the talisman, had done its work, and she was dead. She wouldn't have known what was happening until it was too late. There was no way for her to save herself.

But was she really dead? Or was she simply beyond his reach?

He wanted to believe that the talisman had killed her, and she was no threat to him.

Still, he had lived too long and coped with too many emergencies to bet everything on that assumption.

After wiping away any visible trace of his uncertainty, he sent out a mental call to Swee, Wendon, and Barthime.

A few minutes later, there was a knock on his door.

"Come in."

His three key men stepped into the chamber. "Yes, master?" Swee asked, his voice obsequious.

Vandar wanted to smack the fawning expression off the man's face, but he kept his emotions under control. He had worked with Swee for years. The man was strong, but he was loyal because he'd long ago had the power to resist driven out of him.

"I want the soldiers' quarters moved near the portal."

"Sir?"

"I want the entrance to the other universe under constant guard."

"Yes, master."

"Half of the men will be on duty at all times. The rest will be sleeping nearby."

"Yes, master."

Before the adepts could leave, he stood and walked toward them, placing a hand on each of their foreheads in turn, checking their ties to him and giving them new instructions.

"YOU are very strong," Antonia said to Kenna.

"No, I . . ."

"You don't have to be modest about it. You were strong to survive your time with the monster. No one else has ever escaped from him."

Kenna didn't know how the other woman had come up with that assessment, but it sounded true.

"It's hard to imagine so many slaves doing his bidding," Renata muttered.

"Many of them are adepts—some much stronger than I am. Swee, Barthime, and Wendon are his three chief men," Kenna answered. "He'll use them and the others to fight us with their powers at the same time his soldiers are attacking us."

"But he can't be all-powerful," Ross said. "Tell us his weaknesses."

She shuddered. "I spent months with him, and I couldn't see any."

"Because he made sure his slaves never saw anything

but his strength," Talon muttered. "And if he didn't like something his slaves did, he killed them. No wonder you were scared. Anyone would be."

Hating the whole conversation, Kenna looked down at her hands. "Don't make excuses for me," she whispered.

"Don't beat yourself up!" Ross replied. "It was an impossible situation for you. Maybe if you share your experiences with us, you'll say something that we'll interpret differently."

Before she could speak, Talon jumped into the conversation. "I *have* shared her experiences," he said. "When the women helped her free herself from Vandar, I was inside her head, and I saw Vandar up close and personal in a way Kenna can't convey with narrative. He's more ruthless and more powerful than any of you can imagine."

"Yeah, then it sounds like we're stuck," Logan muttered.

Conversation swirled around her as Talon tried to explain the problem they'd face if they went up against Vandar and his adepts.

Kenna hardly listened. Something else was tugging at her, something that she'd been too busy to focus on until now.

When she shifted in her seat, Talon looked at her questioningly. "What?"

She swallowed hard. "Now that I have a little breathing space, I realize there's something I haven't told you about."

"Oh yeah?"

She hated the edge she heard in his voice and hated the way everyone was suddenly staring at her, but she said, "I think there may be . . ." She broke off, wondering how to tell them the news. It could be good or bad. She wished she knew which. "Another . . . factor."

"What?" Logan asked.

"Another being of power."

"Jesus!" Logan shot back.

"I don't know his name, but I've felt him." She dragged in a breath and let it out as she looked around the room, hoping that this group of people was open to what she had to say. And hoping again that she hadn't brought another disaster on them.

Starting again, she said, "Or, it's more like he sensed me after I came through the portal. He's the one who made the connection. I felt him, but I didn't know what he was. Now it's getting . . . more specific."

Renata gave her a sharp look. "You're not talking about someone from your world. You mean someone who's already on this side of the portal?"

"Yes."

"A man?"

She shuddered. "I'm not sure. I can't tell."

Renata stood up and walked to the window, then turned and faced them. "Jacob and I were stalked by a being of great power. A demon. He came after us time and again, down through the ages, every time we were reborn. Over and over, he destroyed us. Is this being you sense something like that?"

Kenna gave her a helpless look. "I don't know!"

Jacob leaned forward. "You're willing to trust this thing?" he pressed.

"Of course not!" She flapped her free hand in frustration. "He may be out for himself. He may be evil. He may be good, for all I can tell. The only thing I know for sure is that he found me—somehow. And he reacted to my thoughts about Vandar."

"We may be in worse trouble if we contact it," Logan muttered.

Kenna didn't want to say what she was thinking, but she knew that she had to be totally honest with these people who had broken Vandar's hold on her.

"I don't think we have any choice," she said in a barely audible voice. She swallowed. "Or maybe I should say, I don't have any choice."

"How so?" Ross asked.

"I think he's trying to find me, and I believe he will, because we're tied together in some way. Maybe through Vandar."

"How is that possible?" Talon pressed.

Her voice rose in frustration. "I don't know!"

Letting go of his hand, she stood. "I'm sorry. I know you were trying to help. And you did. But apparently I've gotten you all into more trouble than you bargained for. I'd better leave. Because if he finds me—he'll find *you*."

When she took a step toward the door, Talon also stood and grabbed her arm, holding her in place. "Sweetheart, I think it's the other way around. This is my house. They're the ones who are going to leave."

The words sounded like a challenge, and she thought from what Talon had said about his family relationships that he was protecting his territory.

Kenna looked from him to the rest of the group, seeing the sudden tension zinging back and forth among the Marshall men. Talon had told her that each werewolf was the head of his own pack. She hadn't quite understood what he meant, but in this charged moment, she was seeing the theory in action. They couldn't stop themselves from responding to the challenge.

The men all stood, their arms stiff, their hands balled into fists at their sides as they each looked at the others. She was sure they were evaluating their chances of a successful attack.

She tried to absorb what was happening. One minute they'd been part of a group. Now they were separate. And they looked like enemies.

A low growl came from one of them, and she wasn't sure which, or if it was more than one reacting to the challenge Talon had thrown out.

But she sensed that if any of them did or said the wrong thing, they would be at each other's throats.

CHAPTER
TWENTY-SIX

AS KENNA WATCHED, the rest of the women also got to their feet, each of them stepping to the side of her mate and putting a restraining hand on his shoulder. Only Ross was alone among the men, but Kenna had already seen that he had the best control.

Apparently, the women had already agreed who would speak if they found themselves in this situation.

Rinna stepped forward. "Settle down," she said in a voice that was commanding but low. "We don't have time for a turf battle. Or for werewolf grandstanding. We all know this is Talon's house, and we'll leave if that's what he really wants."

She paused and looked around at the men. "But we're facing a common enemy. Maybe more than one enemy. We know about Vandar on the other side of the portal. And there may be someone over here, too, who could hurt any of us."

All the men looked at her. Her husband, Logan, shifted uncomfortably beside her.

When he cleared his throat, Kenna tensed, because she'd decided he was the one most likely to cause trouble.

But his words surprised her.

"I tend to get hyper," he muttered, glancing at Kenna, then back to his wife. "But I know you're right. I'm glad I have you to keep me in line."

The tension in the room went down a couple of notches.

Grant also spoke. "Family is important."

"Yes," Antonia murmured, snuggling close to him.

Ross's voice turned businesslike. "So let's get back to the real problem. It's not us, it's a monster from the other universe. And maybe a monster here."

After hearing the sobering words, they all sat down, but now Kenna hoped she wasn't going to cause another flare-up.

"I created a bad situation for all of you by coming here," she murmured.

Ross turned toward her. "You didn't create anything bad. You warned us of something that's going to happen—an invasion."

She answered with a tight nod, not quite sure if she followed his logic.

He added, "The Marshall family has always been this way. Each of us wants to protect his own territory. But we're learning to adapt to the modern world."

Kenna hoped she could say the same thing.

"Can you find this man, or whatever he is?" Ross asked. "The one who's living in our world."

"He's . . . you'd call it out West. I know he lives somewhere in the big mountains."

Logan laughed. "That's a lot of territory to cover. I think you have no idea how big the United States is." He picked up his laptop computer from the floor beside his chair and typed on the keyboard, then turned the machine around. "Here's a map of the United States."

She'd seen hand-drawn maps that showed where Breezewood was in relationship to nearby cities, but she'd never seen anything like this before, and she stared at the colored patches on the screen, trying to make some sense of them.

"This is a map?"

When Talon heard her confusion, he said, "It's the whole United States. There are no details—just a color for each state."

"Um." She had learned in her prep sessions that they were in the United States. She didn't really know what that meant.

Logan tapped the screen. "We're over here in Pennsyl-

vania—this pink area along the East Coast. The Great
Plains are in the middle of the country. The mountain
states are over here—a couple of thousand miles away." As
he spoke, he swept his hand across to another area.

Talon looked from him to Kenna. "I don't think that
means too much to her."

It didn't.

"My point is, there's a lot of territory between us and
him," Logan said.

"You think we're safe because of distance?" Renata
said.

"Maybe."

"The demon always found me and Jacob. It didn't matter where we were," Renata said. "I don't think we should
just wait for this thing. We should meet him head-on."

Kenna gave her a grateful look. "If we got closer, I think
I could . . ." She lifted one shoulder. "I think if I used trial
and error, I could find him."

Logan laughed. "Sure."

"Maybe we should test the theory. We could fly to Denver," Ross suggested.

When everyone stared at him, he shrugged. "You want
to stay here, like sitting ducks?"

"We'd be on his turf if we go to him," Logan argued.

"Which will protect our homes from him," Ross said.

Kenna felt her gratitude swell. She could have been in
this alone. Ross was assuming that they would help her.

He turned to her. "Denver is a city on the plains, right at
the edge of the mountains. A good staging area." He stood.
"I'll see about chartering a plane, so we can fly there."

Her eyes widened. "Isn't that something expensive?"

"Yes, but we're in a hurry. And I don't want to waste
time." He looked around the room. "Anyone who doesn't
want to go is free to stay here, or go home."

The werewolves looked at their life mates.

"I don't want to drop out now," Rinna said. The other
women agreed. And nobody ended up backing out.

Ross walked down the hall and disappeared into one

of the bedrooms. He was back in only a few minutes to say that the trip was arranged, and they could leave from Altoona Blair County Airport.

It was all happening so fast that Kenna's mind was spinning. She'd told them about a man—or a monster—who lived in some vague area called "the West," and they were going there. She'd told them she could find him if she were closer, but had she just been grasping at a straw?

Talon took her to the bedroom, where he helped her pack some clothing and other things she would need, like her toothbrush. She wanted to grab him and hold on tight, but she knew that they didn't have a lot of time, so she simply followed his suggestions.

When they came back, she saw two of the vehicles called SUVs pulled up to the door. They divided up and climbed into the cars. Ross drove one. Grant and Antonia sat in the back. And she and Talon took the middle seat, where he helped her buckle her seat belt. As she tried to relax, she thought about how limited her experience was in this universe. She had been here for over two weeks, with an interruption when she'd gone back home, but this was the first time she had ridden in one of these machines. And the first time she had been out of the immediate area where Talon lived.

"It's about a forty-minute ride," Ross said over his shoulder as he turned from the small road that led to Talon's house onto a bigger one.

She gripped Talon's hand as the vehicle speeded up. He turned his head toward her and squeezed back. When another car roared past them, she cringed.

They reached a larger road, and the number of cars increased, all going very fast, even at night.

"Does everybody have a car?" she asked.

"Just about everyone. And most people have more than one."

She tried to relax as they picked up speed on a wider road, with many cars whizzing by.

Talon lived in the woods, but his location had given her

a false picture of this society. Outside the woods, there were huge buildings that were nothing like anything she had ever seen. It was early in the morning, and many of them were brightly lighted, telling her there was plenty of energy.

In other places, she saw acres of individual houses, and she realized that she'd had no idea how many people lived here. She was sure Vandar didn't know either. Would that make a difference when he tried to invade?

There were big green signs above the roadway, announcing what she assumed were the names of various towns and cities. When they came to a sign for the airport, Ross took that road.

"We've got a private plane," he said over his shoulder again. "That means we don't have to go through security. And we can fly directly to Denver."

They pulled up in a place where a lot of cars were parked, then got out, and walked toward a waiting airplane.

Kenna felt like she was being swept along into the unknown. The plane was a lot bigger than the SUV.

"That can fly?" she whispered to Talon.

"Yes. Don't worry."

She wanted to back away. Instead, she climbed up the short flight of stairs and dropped into one of the seats where Talon helped her with the seat belt again. Looking around, she saw that all the Marshall men and their life mates fit in easily. And there were seats left over in the back.

She sat with her heart pounding, listening to people around her talking, making plans for what happened when they encountered the being they were flying to meet.

"There's a bathroom in the back," Talon said. "But you can't get up and use it until they turn off the seat belt sign."

"Okay."

"Don't be scared. People in this world take flying for granted."

She laughed. "It's like a fairy story. About a magic carpet. Or a girl who rides off on a huge bird—or a flying horse."

He covered her hand with his. "Just relax."

The conversation faded into the background because her ears were ringing as the plane began to move, then picked up speed until it was racing down a black strip, like a highway.

When she realized it had it lifted off the ground, she grabbed the arms of her seat as she looked down at the land falling away below them. All the buildings got smaller and smaller, and it was almost impossible to see the cars.

Then she gasped.

"What?"

"The clouds. They're *under* us."

"Yeah. It's normal."

She sat gripping the seat arms, thinking that at least she could no longer see the ground so far below. Which was a mercy, because she feared they could drop out of the sky at any moment.

"We have reached our cruising altitude," a disembodied voice said. "You are free to get up and move about the cabin."

Instead of getting up, she leaned toward Talon so that her head was resting on his shoulder.

He clasped her hand, and his touch helped her relax.

"Imagine you're drifting on the clouds—and go to sleep."

She closed her eyes, sure she was too tense for that.

But maybe she did drift off, because the next thing she knew, a sharp bump made her realize they were on the ground again.

CHAPTER
TWENTY-SEVEN

RAMSAY GALLAGHER FELT the presence of the woman. He had planned to go looking for her. Now he didn't have to do it. She had come across the country to him. Not just her. Other men and women. Well, they weren't quite here yet, but they would be.

If he wanted to, he could hide himself from her, from them. But was that the best thing to do? He had a connection to the woman. He could lead her and the rest of them to him and make her think she was the one doing it.

While in fact, he was luring them to their destruction.

They were unusual. All of them. He sensed abilities that most of their race did not possess.

Well, none of that would do them any good. He would kill them—up in the mountains where nobody could see the scene of destruction. Then he would hide the evidence. When he was finished with them, the danger would be over, and he could go on with the life he had chosen for himself in his isolated mountain stronghold.

"WE have to go that way," Kenna said, pointing toward the mountains rising like a massive, jagged wall of rock in the west.

Ross, who had been conferring with Logan, stepped up to her. "You know where to find the thing?"

She shook her head. "Not exactly."

"So what are we going to do, just drive around hoping to see something?" Talon inquired, unable to keep the edge out of his voice.

She gave him an understanding look and closed her hand around his arm before turning back to Ross. "I think . . . if you let me sit beside you, I can tell you which way to drive."

When she climbed into the front seat next to Ross, Talon was stuck in the seat behind her, with Renata beside him and Jacob in the back. The rest of the contingent took the second vehicle.

He couldn't see Kenna's face, only hear the strained sound of her voice as she gave Ross directions.

They stopped at a fast food restaurant for a quick meal, then drove down Route 70 toward a place called Grand Junction. He'd never been in this part of the country before, and he felt the weight of the mountains around him. They were so much taller and steeper than the eastern ranges he was familiar with.

If they'd been in this majestic country for some other reason, he would have enjoyed the trip. He loved the natural environment, and this landscape was much different from the forests and rivers of the East where he took clients on wilderness expeditions.

It wasn't simply the scale of the mountains. The vegetation was different, too. The deciduous trees he saw were small and slender, and the pines were very tall and straight. As he looked out at the mountains, he saw what he knew was the timberline, the place where the altitude became too high for trees to grow.

Kenna interrupted his thoughts with another direction to Ross. "That way."

His cousin took a turn off the interstate onto a secondary road, toward Granby.

The late morning sky was very blue, clear of clouds. They were climbing into the mountains, and the air was thinner than he was used to.

Each time they came to a road that crossed the one they were on, Ross stopped and gave Kenna a chance to tell him which direction to take. As the day progressed, the roads became narrower and less well maintained, and finally turned to gravel.

By late afternoon, they were in what looked like virgin forest.

Ross stopped again at a road that was barely visible through what had become dense forest.

"Up there," Kenna murmured, pointing.

Talon followed her outstretched arm and saw a house built like a Swiss chalet perched on the edge of a bluff.

Ross was starting to make the turn when a flash of something above them in the sky made Talon's head jerk around. Craning his neck, he saw what looked like a great bird in the distance. It flew high in the late afternoon sky, and Talon's gaze fixed on it.

He was an expert in bird identification because his clients appreciated it when he pointed out the wildlife in an area. But he had never seen anything quite like the thing that was speeding toward them as though it had known where to find them all along and was simply waiting for them to drive into its territory.

He kept his gaze fixed on the monster. The wings were extraordinary, more like a bat. As it came closer he knew that no bat could have that wingspan.

The neck was long. The body was covered by scales that glinted silver in the afternoon sky.

As he watched, it filled the sky, then suddenly swooped down at them.

Jesus! It struck him all at once what he was seeing—a dragon from an ancient nightmare! A dragon like the monster Kenna had revealed when he'd shared her memories of the other universe.

As it descended, fire shot out of its mouth, blasting the top of the vehicle, filling the interior of the SUV with sudden heat.

Talon cursed, leaning over the seat so that he could shield Kenna as best he could.

Beside him, Renata gasped. "*Por Dios*, what was that?"

As the beast wheeled around for another assault, Ross shouted, "Out of the car. Get behind those rocks."

The doors opened, and the occupants of the SUV jumped out.

Everybody ran toward the rocks, everybody except Kenna, who rushed in the other direction. Right into the middle of the road where she was completely exposed to the creature.

Talon followed her. "Take cover."

"No! I'm through running and hiding."

His curse rang out across the mountains. When he grabbed her arm, she tried to shake him off. "Don't distract me. Go with the others."

He wanted to tell her she was crazy to try and fight this thing, but he wasn't the one who had been a slave.

She stood defiantly, her feet planted on the gravel as she raised her arms toward the great beast that was coming back toward her.

Talon had no time to contemplate his own death. All he knew was that he had to defend his mate—to the end. That was the only thought in his head as he began to tear off his clothing and say the chant that changed him from man to wolf.

What chance did a wolf have against a dragon? A beast that was five times his size.

He didn't know. But he would battle the thing with every ounce of strength and resolve he had.

He had never pushed through the change so quickly, willing his body to transform from man to wolf. The pain was blinding, but within seconds he came down on all fours and raised his head, looking for the monster.

To his horror, it had circled around to come arrowing down toward Kenna.

Talon stepped in front of his mate, baring his teeth in a snarl as the dragon plummeted toward them.

The sharp whistling sound of the monster's descent filled Talon's ears. Every self-protective instinct urged him to run for the cover of the rocks, but he stayed where he was in front of his mate as the thing dived.

CHAPTER
TWENTY-EIGHT

AS THE DRAGON shot down from the sky, Talon could see its red eyes focused on him and Kenna. Before the beast reached them, Ross, Jacob, and Grant came charging out from behind the rock, automatic pistols in their hands, firing at the dragon.

Talon saw bullets bouncing off the creature's silver scales. He howled, trying to tell his cousins to go back, but they kept firing.

In response, the monster gave a great roar, raining fire down on the three werewolves.

"No!" Renata screamed, running toward her mate.

Jacob whirled and pelted back toward her, and Ross and Grant followed, dodging and weaving through the trees to keep from getting burned.

Reversing course, the dragon came at Talon and Kenna again, sending another blast of fire down from the sky, but this time it seemed to hit an invisible barrier above their heads and bounce back at the beast.

Kenna had put up a shield!

The creature roared again, circling them, but now it didn't try to attack. It kept flying around them, flapping its great wings, and Talon thought it must be considering some other strategy.

Centuries passed as the thing circled them. Finally, it landed on the road, about twenty yards from where they waited.

It could have advanced toward them. Instead, it stood looking at them for a long moment, then backed away.

Turning, it disappeared from view around an outcropping of rock opposite where the rest of the Marshalls and their life mates had taken cover.

Long seconds passed. Then, to Talon's astonishment, a man wearing only a pair of jeans stepped out from behind the rocks. He was tall and well-built, with long dark hair, deep-set eyes, a strong chin, and well-shaped lips.

He kept his gaze fixed on Kenna. "I picked up from your mind that you come from somewhere else. Where is it?" he asked in a rough voice.

"From another universe. It runs parallel to this one."

Instead of challenging her, he nodded thoughtfully. "There is a creature like me there, and he surrounds himself with slaves?"

"Yes."

The man turned to Talon. "You showed great courage, standing with your mate. Go change. So you can join the conversation."

Talon answered with a low growl.

"I won't hurt her," the man said. "She was talking to me, in her head. I could pick up a lot of it, but not all. We need to sort this out."

Talon used his teeth to snatch up the pants he'd discarded. Dragging them across the ground, he disappeared behind a tree, where he silently said the chant that changed him from wolf to man. When he had transformed, he pulled on the pants and dashed back to the road, where he put himself between the man and Kenna.

"If you're a shifter, where did you get a pair of jeans?"

The man laughed. "That's your first question? I picked this place of confrontation. I left clothing here. My name is Ramsay Gallagher. Now. I've had a lot of names over the years."

"Yeah. Well, you were going to kill us. Why did you break off the attack?"

Gallagher gestured toward Kenna. "She stopped me. Not by force, but when I read her thoughts, I knew I had to talk to you."

"Why should we trust you not to kill us when you get what you want?" Talon demanded.

The man turned his hands palm up. "I could have killed you already. You and your friends."

"Kenna put up a shield."

His expression hardened. "Do you think that would have stopped me if I'd wanted to blast you?"

The other men had come out from behind the rocks. They were still holding their guns, pointed at Gallagher.

He flicked his gaze toward them. "You might as well put your weapons away. They won't hurt me."

"You could be bluffing," Logan challenged.

Gallagher shrugged. "Go ahead and shoot if you think it will do any good."

Logan raised his automatic.

"Put that down, you fool!" Talon shouted.

Logan glared at him. "He just challenged me."

"And you don't know if he's got some kind of shield, or if he's going to hurl a thunderbolt at you."

"Let's try to stay calm," Ross said.

Logan lowered the gun.

"We should get off the road," Gallagher said. "Why don't you all come to my house?"

"Where is it?"

Gallagher gestured toward the nearby mountain, where Talon had seen the chalet perched on the side of a cliff.

"If we go up there, we'll be trapped," he said.

"I think we're going to have to trust each other," the dragon-shifter said.

"Easy for you to say, when bullets bounce off your scales."

"What can I do to prove my good faith?"

"Let me see inside your mind," Kenna answered. "Let me find out who you are."

His gaze shot to her. "That could be dangerous."

"What can I do to you?"

"I don't know."

The tension pulled taut as they stared at each other.

Then Gallagher lifted one shoulder. "See what you can do."

"Can I touch you?"

When she took a step forward, Talon put a hand on her arm. "Stay away from him!"

"Whatever he can do, he can do it from there. I'm the one who doesn't have enough power to bridge the distance between us."

"You can get the other women to help you."

Rinna must have heard. From the corner of his eye, Talon saw her step out from behind the rock.

Logan growled deep in his throat. "I want the other women to stay where they are."

Talon nodded, knowing that his cousin was within his rights to insist on protection for his mate. If it was protection. Gallagher could probably reach them from where he was standing.

While all that was going through Talon's mind, Kenna stepped forward. It was all Talon could do to stay where he was.

There was an awkward moment when she must have been trying to decide where to touch Gallagher. Finally, she put her hands on either side of his face.

Somehow Talon stayed where he was as his mate pressed her hands to the monster's cheeks.

How she could stand to touch him was beyond Talon, but he watched in silence as she closed her eyes, breathing deeply.

Gallagher also closed his eyes, and Talon tried to imagine what was going on between them. They were two enemies trying to reach some kind of agreement. Or were they? Did their psychic abilities give them something that he and Kenna could never share?

Maybe she heard that thought in her head, because she opened her eyes and looked at him.

"This has nothing to do with us," she murmured.

He answered with a tight nod.

"Let me do my job."

He opened his mouth to say something, then closed it again. She was right; the sooner she could finish with this Vulcan mind-meld, the sooner they could settle things with Gallagher.

Talon folded his arms. He might have turned away, but he found he couldn't take his eyes off the sight of his mate touching another man so intimately.

No, not a man. A monster, he reminded himself, then struggled to put his mind into neutral so as not to interfere with what Kenna was doing.

Time seemed to stretch as she stood very still, her fingers moving on Gallagher's face, pressing a little.

Suddenly, she gasped, and her eyes snapped open. Gallagher's eyes opened, too, and they stared at each other with an intensity that made Talon's insides churn.

CHAPTER
TWENTY-NINE

"IT'S A TRICK. You're him." Kenna lowered her hands and stumbled backwards into Talon's arms. She was breathing hard, and he could feel her whole body trembling as he wrapped his arms protectively around her.

"I'm sorry. So sorry," she whispered, twisting to look at Talon, then back at Gallagher. Talon could feel her struggling to steady herself. Still her voice was high and strained when she said, "He's Vandar. Somehow he's Vandar—here. He was trying to fool me, but I figured it out."

"Christ!" Talon looked toward the rocks, wondering what their chances were of making it to shelter. And then what?

The dragon-shifter shook his head. "That's wrong. I've been here all along. In this universe. This is my home. I've never heard of this Vandar thing, until I picked him up in your mind." He gestured toward the chalet. "I live up there. I've lived there for fifty years."

Kenna had stiffened her legs. "But you could go back and forth. Vandar sent me here. And he called me back again."

Gallagher kept his voice even. "Whatever you think, I'm not him. You lived with Vandar for months. Has he disappeared for long periods of time?"

Kenna swallowed. When she spoke, doubt crept into her voice. "I . . . don't know. I suppose it's possible. I just did the job he assigned me—preserving books. I didn't see him on a regular basis. Except for the ceremonies where he killed one of us."

Talon looked from the dragon-shifter to Kenna and back again. "Why do you think he's Vandar?"

She shuddered in his arms. "Vandar told me about his early life. Gallagher's life is the same. He was the slave of a man named Halendor when he was a boy. So was Vandar. I mean, there was just one slave, not two."

Renata stepped out from behind the rock. Jacob was right behind her, gun in hand.

"Maybe both of you are right," she said in a voice that cut through the thickening atmosphere.

"How?" Gallagher demanded.

"I'm from this world," she told him. "But I'm the rein-carnation of an ancient goddess who came back to the world over and over. You don't know it, but the timeline split in 1893." Quickly, she related the story of the Chicago World's Fair and how Eric Carfoli had thrown the world into chaos by giving people psychic powers. She turned her hand palm up. "This is the confusing part. I was rein-carnated in both universes until Carfoli changed that other world. Then I was only here. So, if you're the same . . . being . . . who was alive in 1893, there would be two ver-sions of you now. One here and one there."

Kenna made a wheezing sound.

Gallagher tipped his head to the side, staring at Renata with an all-consuming focus.

"You're saying that there are two of me, one in each uni-verse?" he asked, emotions seething under the calm of his voice.

"I can't say for sure. But it would make sense. If both of you had the same early life."

His gaze turned inward. "In 1893, I met someone who . . . affected my life."

"Maybe Vandar didn't. Or maybe he did. And it came out differently."

He nodded. "We should get out of the middle of the road. Come up to the chalet and talk about it."

Talon gave him a questioning look. "You mean where you can take us prisoner?"

"Yeah, why should we trust you?" Logan asked.

Gallagher looked at the two werewolves who had challenged him. "Because I think we need to sort this out."

Renata looked at the other women. "What do you think?"

They all gathered together, holding hands, and Kenna could sense power surging among them. The sensation awed her. Since they'd first joined together, she could feel their group power building. Enough power to fight off Ramsay Gallagher? She didn't know, but she had never felt anything like that among Vandar's slaves.

One by one, they nodded.

The men stared at them.

"You have to be sure it's safe to go with him!" Logan said.

"How can we be?" Renata asked.

Ross cleared his throat. "We need to set some ground rules. Like we agree that we're all on the same side."

Talon laughed. "That will last until we have a disagreement."

Kenna jumped back into the conversation, addressing her mate and also Gallagher. "From what Renata said, I believe you're not him. And since that's true, we *are* on the same side. Vandar is planning to invade this world. If he establishes a base here, he'll come looking for you."

"And if you aren't as ruthless as he is, he'll destroy you." Logan said.

Gallagher nodded. "If what you say is true."

"It is!" Kenna insisted.

Far above them, a jet plane cut across the sky, reminding everyone that they were still part of the modern world.

"Come inside," Gallagher said. "I'll be waiting for you at the chalet." He turned and walked behind the rocks. A few moments later, the dragon leaped into the air, flying back to the chalet.

"You trust him?" Talon asked Ross.

"Yes. To a certain extent. He needs us."

"And when we've destroyed Vandar?"

"From Kenna's description of him, we can't do that by ourselves. Not if we hope to fight his adepts at the same time. I think we need Gallagher. So let's hope he's honorable."

"You think he's not a killer?" Logan demanded.

Ross turned to him. "I think he's dangerous when cornered. I'm sure he's killed to protect himself." He looked at the other werewolves, each in turn. "We'd do the same. It's part of our nature."

There was a moment of tension before the other men nodded.

"I think he doesn't kill for pleasure," Ross continued, "or to assert his power over others."

"What makes you think so?" Logan demanded.

"Instinct. And he could have already gotten us, if he'd wanted to."

"He wants information."

"And our help. Maybe he even wants to be friends. I'm guessing he's been alone for a long time."

"If you're wrong, we're in trouble," Logan muttered.

Ross turned back to him. "Any way you look at it, we're in trouble. Apparently, he discovered Kenna long before we got here. He knows about all of us now. He could come after us if he wanted, but I don't think that's how he operates. So we might as well try to set the ground rules for the relationship. While we still have some bargaining power."

There were murmurs of agreement.

"Maybe we'd better go in one car," Antonia suggested.

After Logan pulled the other vehicle to the side of the road, they all squeezed into the SUV Ross was driving.

Two of the men had to sit in the back. When they were all settled as best they could, the vehicle started up the narrow road that led to the chalet. They didn't get very far before they came to a heavy iron gate blocking the way. The mountain rose on one side, and a sheer drop fell away on the other.

"Well, I guess you don't get anyone to deliver pizza," Talon said.

"Just a moment," Gallagher's voice issued from a speaker on the gate.

The gate swung open, and they drove through. When they were on the other side, it clanked closed behind them.

"Or escape with the family jewels," Logan added.

They drove up a winding gravel road that was probably deadly in winter. Even now, the loose gravel and the lack of a guardrail made the journey treacherous.

Fifteen minutes later, they pulled into a parking area in front of the chalet. "At least there's room to turn around," Ross said.

Kenna studied the house. It was built of stone, with a high peaked roof, and she thought that it was probably bigger than it looked, with some of the structure below ground or built into the side of the mountain. She saw no other vehicles, but there was a wide garage door in front.

All of them got out, the men with their guns in their hands.

Gallagher came out the front door. He was wearing well-worn jeans and a navy T-shirt and looking totally at home in this world.

"Come in."

They followed him across the porch and into a large reception area. Kenna looked around and gasped when she saw one of the pictures hanging on the wall.

Gallagher turned toward her. "What?"

She pointed. "That picture. Vandar has the same one in his cave."

Ross walked up to the painting. "It's a Monet. Where did you get it?"

"I bought it at an auction in Paris, in the mid-1800s."

"Before the timelines split," Renata said. "So he's still got it, too."

"You're an art collector?" Ross asked, looking into the sitting room off the reception area where several more paintings hung.

Gallagher gestured. "Yes. I've got several Picassos, some Van Goghs, some Modiglianis. As well as artists who didn't turn out to be as famous." He looked back at them. "Come in and sit down. I'm sorry that I can't offer you any refreshments besides water."

"Because you drink blood," Kenna said in a gritty voice.

The room grew very silent as all of the werewolves instinctively moved closer to their mates.

Gallagher turned toward her. "Yes. In my early life, I did live on the same food as humans, and I wasn't very healthy. Then I discovered that blood was my natural sustenance."

"And you kill to get it?" Logan asked.

He gave the werewolf a hard look. "I did. But my lifestyle has evolved over the years. I don't need to kill. And I don't need to drink human blood. I maintain a herd of deer up here in the mountains. I tap them for food. Much as the Masai tribesmen in Africa tap their cattle."

Kenna stared at him. "Vandar always kills. He wants the people to be scared of him."

Gallagher turned to her. "I went through a period like that. I . . . changed. I discovered morality." Before anybody could ask another question, he said, "Let's sit down."

They walked into what Talon would have called the living room, although it was furnished much differently from his own lodge, with elegant chairs and sofas that must have come from earlier ages.

Each of the werewolves sat with his mate. And Ross and Gallagher took chairs by the window.

Gallagher turned to Kenna. "From your mind, I picked up a lot about Vandar. He thrives on power."

"And he wants more territory. Which is why he plans to come here."

"I don't really understand how he'd do that if this universe is separate from the other one," Gallagher said.

Rinna answered. "He'd come through a portal between

the worlds. The way I did. A strong group of adepts can open them."

When his brow wrinkled, she went on quickly. "Nobody here could open a portal. The other world is more primitive on an industrial level, but the psychics there are strong because they're recognized in childhood and taught to perfect their talents. Still, it takes more than one person for a task that big."

"Vandar has adepts who did that," Kenna said. "If we attacked his stronghold, they'd fight for him."

"Why?"

Talon could tell she was struggling to keep her voice steady. Gallagher might not be Vandar, but he was too close for her comfort. "Because they fear what will happen if they defy him. But it's more than that. If you're one of his slaves, he gets into your mind and forces you to do his bidding. You might want to resist, but you can't. He sent me here to spy on this world in preparation for an invasion—before Renata and the other women freed my mind from his power."

Ross said, "He wanted her to bring back guns for his soldiers to use in a conventional fight. But we don't know exactly what he has in mind. I'm assuming he'd come through and start taking over people's minds, the way he did in his own universe. We want to prevent that from happening."

"So what are you proposing exactly?" Gallagher asked.

"I wish I knew," Ross answered. "For right now, I'd like to know you're on our side."

The dragon-shifter kept his gaze steady. "Let me think about it."

"For how long?"

"You're asking me to risk my life by challenging him."

"I guess that's right," Ross answered. "Vandar has to be stopped from establishing a beachhead in this world, one way or the other."

"You should go home. I'll contact you in a few days," Gallagher said.

"Go home? So you can attack us there?" Logan asked.

"I can attack you here. I'm not going after you."

"But you may not be willing to join us," Ross clarified.

He sounded sincere when he said, "I'm sorry. I have to consider my options carefully."

RAMSAY hoped his face didn't reflect the turmoil churning inside him. The Marshalls had come here to ask for his help in exterminating a beast called Vandar, and he believed what they'd told him about the monster, especially because it wasn't all talk. He'd shared Kenna's memories, and he understood what she'd been through during her months of slavery.

He repressed a shudder. It was a little inconvenient that he was the beast in question—if you believed that timeline business. Although he had never gone as far in his hostile relations with humans as the thing that had captured Kenna, he'd come closer than he'd like to admit. But he had fought the monster inside himself and won.

Ross's voice intruded into his thoughts. "Don't wait too long."

He kept his own tone even. "Give me forty-eight hours."

"If you fly out to Pennsylvania, will it be under your own power, or do you take a jet?" the one named Logan asked, his tone mocking.

"A jet." Ramsay forced a laugh. "I don't want to end up getting shot down as an unidentified flying object."

Ross glanced at Logan, then at Ramsay. "I think we'll stay in Colorado for a few days rather than going home. That way, if you decide to join us, you can get in on the strategy session. I'll give you our hotel information when we get settled."

Logan looked like he wanted to object. But he didn't buck Ross, who was obviously the leader of the wolf pack. Ramsay wanted to ask about their relationships, but he figured there was no way to bring up the subject with the werewolves. Maybe one of the women would be willing to tell him. Or not.

It was a long time since he'd formed any close relationships with people, and he wasn't certain he could start over again.

They skipped the usual pleasantries that humans exchange on parting. Instead, the Marshalls and their mates turned and quietly left the chalet, then climbed into the SUV and started down the access road.

As he watched, he was certain they were discussing him. And the monster.

Having the Marshalls in his private refuge had been an invasion of his privacy, and he allowed relief to flood through him that they were gone. He had options. He could pull up stakes and simply disappear, and they would never find him. He'd done it before. It would be easy enough to do again.

But was that his best course of action? He thought about the extraordinary and disturbing conversation they'd just had, starting with the time line that Renata had given him. From what she said, things had started diverging in 1893. The chaos she described hadn't happened here. Thank the gods. If it had, would he have ended up like Vandar?

And what did he mean by the question?

He pictured himself walking down the hall and throwing belongings into a suitcase, like a thief escaping from the police. He could blow this place up with the charges he'd set long ago at the base of the foundation. That would obliterate any clues to his presence here—before he moved on to one of the other properties he owned.

Could the Marshalls find him?

That was an interesting question. A few years ago, the answer would have been "no." The Internet had made it more difficult to vanish into the mass of humanity.

But he wasn't going to disappear without carefully considering his options. That was why he'd asked for the forty-eight hours.

He wanted to think about the monster. And about himself. And the irony of his situation. For years he had considered that he had no enemies who could defeat him. Now there might be one—and it was himself.

Hadn't there been a cartoon character about twenty or thirty years ago who had said something like, "We have met the enemy, and it is us"?

CHAPTER
THIRTY

"WILL HE HELP us?" Renata asked as the SUV headed down the narrow gravel road with the steep drop-off on one side and the rock face on the other.

"I don't know," Ross answered as he focused on the treacherous track. "Let's see if we can get past the gate before we start speculating about anything else."

"We can shoot the hinges," Logan muttered.

"It's better if we don't have to destroy it," Ross answered.

"Yes. If he lets us go, that will be a good sign," Kenna whispered.

They stopped talking, riding in tense silence to the iron gate. Kenna felt her heart pounding. She glanced at Talon, then looked out the window, scanning the sky, half expecting to see a great winged creature circling above them.

But Van—She stopped herself from calling him by that name and started again. *He wasn't Vandar. He was Ramsay Gallagher.*

What did a change of name mean, really? Or a change in where he lived?

She felt her heart blocking her windpipe as Ross rolled down the window and reached for the button on the stanchion.

For a moment, nothing happened, and she sat stock-still in her seat. Then the gate began to swing noiselessly open on oiled hinges.

When they drove out, she felt like a fifty-pound weight had been lifted off her chest.

Nobody spoke for several minutes, then Talon asked, "How much is he like Vandar?"

She moistened her lips and answered, "I've been trying to figure that out. He looks like Vandar. I mean, when he's in his dragon form, you'd think it was him. When he's a man, he's the same in a lot of ways. The same dark hair, but Gallagher's hair is a lot longer. And the look in his eyes is different."

"You mean he doesn't look like he's deciding whether to eat you for lunch?" Talon asked.

She gave a nervous laugh. "I guess that's a good way to put it."

"The question is, can we trust him?" Logan said.

"Or, more to the point, can we work with him?" Ross amended.

"What if he turns on us?" Logan asked.

"He could have done it already."

"Agreed," Talon said. "I guess the big question for me is, can he defeat Vandar?"

"Maybe they'll end up killing each other. Then the trust problem will be out of the way," Logan answered.

Kenna shifted in her seat. "I don't like to plan on using him."

"Maybe he's thinking in terms of using us," Logan said.

She nodded, wondering how this was all going to turn out. "The problem is, we have to get rid of Vandar, whether Gallagher will help us or not."

There were murmurs of agreement around the car.

"So we'd better start making plans," Grant said.

"We can't. Until we know if Gallagher is on the team. Because he has to be an integral part of any attack," Antonia said.

This time the riders were not in complete agreement. Some of them seemed to think that they could go up against Vandar on their own.

Kenna knew they were fooling themselves. "You do it," she blurted, "and we all die. Or end up as his slaves. Then he'll get into this world, and there will be nobody to save the rest of the people."

Talon gripped her hand.

"Let's be optimistic," Ross said into the silence that followed her pronouncement.

They drove to where they'd left the other SUV, and half the team piled out and into the second vehicle.

"I'll head for Rocky Mountain National Park," Ross said. "There are some towns between here and there. We'll look for a comfortable resort in a quiet location, preferably with cabins. That way, we'll have more privacy for our planning session."

She saw Talon glance at her and felt a sudden jolt. He was thinking about privacy, but not because he wanted to make invasion plans. He was thinking about the two of them.

They rode through the unfamiliar scenery, so different from the land around Breezewood or Talon's lodge. Maybe there was no way Vandar could conquer this whole, vast land, but she didn't want to leave that to the gods—not when it could go the wrong way.

They stopped at the Mountain Escape Lodge. It had the same kind of name but it was a lot bigger than Talon's lodge. In addition to the main building, cabins were scattered in the trees around the grounds.

When Ross got out and went into the office, Talon followed. When the two werewolves came back, they both looked pleased.

"We've got a group of cabins up there," Ross said, pointing to a ridge overlooking a lake where boats were tied up at wooden boardwalks.

"It's been a long trip, so why don't we all try to relax for a few hours. I've got a larger cabin, where we can bring in dinner and have a planning session."

He dropped each of the couples off at a cabin. The moment they were inside the door and Talon had kicked it closed with his foot, he and Kenna fell into each other's arms.

She should have been thinking about how to defeat Vandar. Instead, she'd been thinking about this, because every moment alone with Talon was precious.

When he lowered his mouth to hers, she met him with an intensity that seemed to explode in a burst of heat.

They devoured each other as their hands worked at buttons, buckles, and zippers.

She hadn't even taken a look at the bedroom. All she'd seen was the rug on the wooden floor in front of the fireplace. They made it that far, falling naked together, where they held each other and rocked.

He was inside her almost as soon as they were horizontal, and she was ready for him, her hips moving as frantically as his as they pushed each other to an explosive climax. Afterwards, they lay breathing hard.

Still joined to her, he rolled them to their sides, kissing her tenderly as his hands moved over her.

She had thought the storm was over, but as he stroked and kissed her, she felt her arousal building again. He was still inside her, and she could feel him hardening again as her inner muscles made involuntary little clenching movements around him.

He grinned down at her. "That's nice."

"I didn't know it could be like this," she whispered.

"Neither did I."

She stared at him in wonder. "But you must have . . ." She let the sentence trail off.

"It's *never* been like this. Because we belong to each other—a werewolf and his life mate."

She couldn't stop herself from saying, "What if it all ends in a few days?"

"It won't!"

"But what if it does?"

"Then we will have had this together." He gave her a fierce look. "I thought I was going to lose you on the road when that thing came swooping down."

"I thought I would lose you when you jumped in front of me. You couldn't fight him!"

"But I had to try."

She felt her desperation surging as she found his mouth again and began to kiss him with an urgency that shocked her. He was her mate, and she was going to lead him into danger. Perhaps fatal danger.

"No," he answered, and she knew that the intimacy had given him access to her mind. "We'll win."

She let herself absorb his certainty, because maybe that would be enough for the two of them.

He bent to suck one of her taut nipples into his mouth using his lips, his tongue, and his teeth while he pulled and twisted the other with his thumb and forefinger, building the heat rushing through her veins.

As he did, he moved his hips, just a little, just enough to inflame her.

When she surged against him, he slipped one hand down her back, clasping her hips. "Stay still."

It was difficult to obey when she wanted to push for completion. But she did as he asked, letting him build their need slowly, until it was impossible to simply stay passive.

She reached around him, stroking and kneading his ass, hearing his growl of approval.

They made the decision at the same time, both of them suddenly moving with frantic urgency. Climax rolled over them, pressing them together as it lifted them into a place high above the mountains where the air was almost too thin to breathe.

They clung to each other, finally drifting off to sleep in each other's arms. Some time later, a ringing noise woke her, and she blinked, trying to remember where she was.

"The phone," Talon said, getting up and answering.

He talked for a few moments, then hung up. "Ross is getting the meeting started in half an hour."

"Then let's hurry. I don't want to walk in late and have everybody staring at me again, knowing I've been making love. They'll think that's all we do."

He laughed.

"I see that doesn't bother you at all. You're a man."

"Yeah. But I'll hurry up, because that's what you want to do."

She grabbed her clothes and made a quick trip to the

bathroom, then combed her hair, wishing she had a little of the makeup women used in this world.

Talon appeared in the mirror in back of her. "You're beautiful."

When she looked uncertain, he turned her toward him. "Never doubt yourself."

She met his eyes. "I had the confidence beaten out of me by Vandar. Well, not literally. He didn't actually hit me. But you know what I mean."

"Yeah. And we'll make sure he doesn't do it to anyone else—ever again."

They walked to Ross's cabin, where they were the first to arrive. And that made her uncomfortable, too.

"Can I help you set up the meal?" she asked Talon's cousin, amazed that a man was doing domestic work.

He answered easily, "Sure. I'm not that great at this kind of thing. But I knew what to buy at the grocery store down the road—from get-togethers my mate and I have had. Plastic plates and cutlery. Meat for the guys. Salads for the women."

He began setting up. After watching for a moment, Kenna made herself busy helping put out the plates and utensils. As the other women came in, they joined her, and she felt good about the way they worked together.

When the others had all arrived and helped themselves to food and drinks, they pulled chairs and sofas into a circle where they could discuss the problem.

"Are we talking about opening a new portal?" Rinna asked.

"Is that too difficult a way to start off?" Ross asked.

"I'd prefer to use my energy to fight the adepts," she answered.

Ross looked at Kenna. "How many does he have?"

She considered the slave population. "Maybe fifty or sixty. But only a few have great power."

"And how many soldiers?"

"Also fifty or sixty. Swee, Barthime, and Wendor are the chief adepts. They opened the portal." She stopped and thought. "With help, I guess, because they told me it took ten men. They also prepared me for the trip here."

Ross nodded. "They're not the only ones who opened a portal. There's one near Jacob's home in Maryland."

Her eyes widened. "I didn't think about there being another one."

"That's where Rinna first came through." Ross paused for a moment. "But in this case, I don't think we should use it, given the difficulty of traveling through the badlands. That would also drain too much of our energy."

"Okay. Let's assume we'll use the portal that Vandar's adepts opened."

Ross turned to Kenna. "Do you think he'll have adepts at the portal, or just soldiers?"

"I think he's not expecting adepts from our world. So I'm guessing he'll just have soldiers. But I can't be sure," she added quickly.

"Then let's assume we can overpower a conventional force with wolves and our superior weapons," Ross said.

"Then what?" Logan asked.

"Then we subdue the rest of the soldiers and the adepts."

"How?"

"We're going to need Sara and Olivia," Ross answered. "Those are the wives of my brothers, Adam and Sam. Sam changed his last name to Morgan when he moved to California."

"Will they want to risk getting into this?" Kenna asked.

"I think so, when they hear an evil monster from the other universe wants to take over *this* world."

Antonia cleared her throat, and everyone turned toward her.

"There's something we haven't discussed," she said. "Is this too big to handle by ourselves? I mean, have you considered telling someone in the U.S. government?"

The group was silent for several moments. Ross finally answered. "I've thought of it. I'd like to get help, but there are too many problems. We'd have to reveal that there *is* another universe parallel to this one. Who would believe that? If they did, what kind of panic would it create?" He stopped and made a rough sound. "And would the government try to exploit it?"

There were murmurs of agreement around the room.

"And then there's the danger of revealing who we are," Antonia's mate, Grant, said.

The other men nodded.

"So I think we're stuck with handling it on our own," Ross said.

"I was just posing the question," Antonia murmured.

"I know. And it was something we had to consider," Ross answered. "But at the end of the day, we can't."

"Which means we need more concrete plans," Logan said. "And better intelligence. We've worked together as a team before, but never fighting such a large force." He glanced at Talon. "Well, the rest of us have worked together."

"I'm with you," Talon snapped.

"He's the one who initially called me," Ross reminded them.

"What about Vandar's soldiers?" Talon asked. "Won't they be right at the entrance to the portal?"

Kenna thought about that. "When I came through a few days ago, some of them came to guard me, but only the adepts entered the cave with me. The soldiers were outside, so they couldn't see what I was doing."

"Okay," Talon answered. "So let's get back to Vandar himself. Will he make us come into his lair to get him?"

"He's not going to hide from you. He'll put on a show of force," a voice answered from the doorway.

Everybody turned to see that Ramsay Gallagher had stepped into the cabin.

"How did you get here?" Ross asked. "I didn't tell you where we were."

"I noticed that little oversight."

Kenna knit her fingers together so hard that they ached, and her knuckles turned white. "You didn't have to tell him," she said in a strained voice. "He knows. Because of me." She gulped. "Now that we've done that mind thing, I guess I can't hide from him."

CHAPTER
THIRTY-ONE

MITCH SUTTON WAS about to step out of the woods when he heard the sound of a vehicle coming up the long drive that led to Talon Marshall's house.

He'd stayed away since the big dog had chased him. Now he was back—prepared to finish what he'd started.

Before he could approach the house, a couple of SUVs pulled up in the driveway, and a whole crowd got out. Men and women.

Were they customers? People who were coming here at the start of a wilderness trip?

He peered at the men. Most of them were similar types. Tall, rangy, and dark-haired. Maybe Marshall was having a family get-together, which was bad timing for a fire. Or a robbery.

Time to get the hell out of here for a while.

AFTER unlocking the door, Talon stood on the porch, sniffing the air. Once again, he thought that it didn't smell quite right, like there was someone lurking in the woods who shouldn't be there.

"Smell that?" he asked his cousins.

"I'm not sure," Ross answered. "You know this area better than we do."

"I'm wondering if that guy who tried to burn the place down is back."

"Mitch Sutton," Ross said.

Talon's head jerked toward him. "You know his name?"

"I got a police detective friend to run the plate you gave me. With everything that was going on, I forgot to tell you about it."

"No problem."

Talon and Grant morphed to wolf form and went out to have a look around. Twenty minutes later, when they'd changed back, Talon said, "I think he's been here. But he's probably left. I guess we spooked him."

"We'll keep up the patrols," Ross said. "I'll take the next one."

"Yeah. Thanks."

"Do you think we could focus on the Vandar problem?" Ramsay Gallagher asked in a tight voice.

Talon studied the tension around the other man's eyes. *Man?* Well, he'd better not fall into the trap of seeing this guy as human. Of course, there were people who would say the same thing about the Marshalls.

"You're anxious to tangle with your other self?"

"No. But I think we have to get it over with, before things get worse."

Talon nodded. They'd cooked up a plan as they'd flown back from Denver. It had sounded good in theory. But how well was it going to play out?

Another car came up the driveway, and he turned to see two more of his relatives get out. From what Ross had said, it must be Adam Marshall and Sam Morgan—and their life mates Sara and Olivia.

Both wives had strong powers, and they were going to join the other life mates. He didn't like the idea of sending the women into danger, but he couldn't come up with another plan, not when Vandar had a bunch of adepts on the other side of the portal waiting to do battle with anyone who challenged him.

In the living room, they brought the newcomers up to speed on the plans they'd made. Logan and Rinna were missing from the group. They'd gone back to Maryland to use the other portal. Not for a direct attack on Vandar. They were going to nearby Sun Acres, where Rinna had been born and raised. Their mission was to talk with Griffin, the head of the city council. If Sun Acres could send a contingent of adepts north to the edge of Vandar's territory, they could join up with the Marshall women and help disable the dragon-shifter's adepts.

Rinna and Logan had elected to cross the badlands—the wild and lawless area between the cities—on dirt bikes. Although the machines were an anomaly in the other universe, Logan had insisted that riding would be safer than traveling on foot. Actually, from what Talon had seen, it looked like his cousin had been itching for an excuse to ride the bikes there.

Jacob was also missing from the group. He'd gone off to collect some of the supplies they'd need for the assault on Vandar's stronghold.

Talon cut Ramsay Gallagher a glance. On the one hand, everybody understood that they needed him to pull off this operation. On the other hand, nobody was comfortable with his level of power. Kenna had described Vandar in vivid terms, and Gallagher was just as dangerous. There was still no guarantee that he wouldn't turn on them, once he'd taken care of the other dragon-shifter. *If* he could take care of the other dragon-shifter. That was another question. Apparently, Vandar had developed the cutthroat side of his personality, while Gallagher seemed to have made himself more human. They hoped.

Talon bit back a sigh. There was nothing they could do about Gallagher until the time came. They'd just have to hope he was as tough as Vandar.

Ross looked at his watch. "I assume that Logan and Rinna have gone through the portal. As we agreed, we'll give them six hours to collect some allies and get into position at the edge of Vandar's territory. And we should get some rest."

Talon watched Kenna stand, thinking that they could have a few more hours of private time together. But just as she started down the hall, Jacob came in, and he realized that he needed to stay for the men's planning session. "You go on," he said to his mate. "To my bedroom. I'll be along after I see what Jacob managed to get."

She gave him a long look, then turned, and walked slowly down the hall. As he watched, it was all he could do to keep from following her. But he knew that he couldn't leave the pack now. Not when they were still making plans.

The pack!

When he had time, he should examine how much his perspective had changed over the past few weeks. If he lived long enough.

He cut off that thought and focused on what the other men had to say. As Logan had pointed out, they'd all worked together before, and he needed to learn some of their protocols.

Since they couldn't speak to each other as wolves, Ross had devised a system of signals, including bird whistles. He'd also outfitted each of them with a small, flat backpack where they could carry clothing to put on after they changed back to human form.

After the other werewolves had filled him in, the meeting broke up. Wondering what Kenna was going to say, he tiptoed down the hall to the master bedroom. His mate was lying in his bed on her back, sleeping soundly. He stood for a long moment, looking down at her, longing to climb into bed with her and take her in his arms. But they'd already had a couple of difficult days, and it wasn't going to get any easier tomorrow. Better to let her get some sleep.

So he continued down the hall to one of the empty rooms. After kicking off his shoes, he lay down with shirt and jeans. In case someone needed him, he left the door ajar.

RAMSAY Gallagher closed the door to one of the bedrooms. Crossing to the bed, he lay down, relieved to be alone. He'd let them think he'd help them kill Vandar.

Now he was wondering, was that really what he wanted to do?

What if it didn't work out that way?

Vandar was *him*. Or they'd been the same being until the timelines had diverged. Could he really kill his other self? What if the "monster" wasn't as bad as Kenna thought? Or what if he had good reasons for his current behavior?

And what about the strange reality Ramsay was facing? He was going to meet another version of himself. Suppose they liked each other? Understood each other? What if it turned out they joined against the humans?

He honestly didn't know how this would go once the two of them met.

He had better stay open. To betraying himself? Or betraying the humans?

MAYBE Talon was the one beyond exhaustion. The next thing he knew, the sun was streaming in the window, and Kenna was standing over him, an accusing look on her face.

"You didn't wake me."

"You needed to sleep. We both did."

When she ducked her head and started to turn away, his hand whipped out and grabbed her by the wrist. With a tug, he pulled her down so that she was lying on top of him. His arms went around her, and he held on tight.

"Never doubt how much I want you. How much I want to build a life with you." As he spoke, his hands moved over her, caressing her, molding her body to his.

In response, she moved against him, bringing his blood to a boiling point. He was about to pull off her shirt when a throat-clearing noise made his head jerk toward the door. Antonia was standing in the doorway.

"Sorry to interrupt," she murmured.

He knew she couldn't see them, but he still saw Kenna's face redden.

"We'll be there in a few minutes," he called out.

When they were alone again, Kenna started to get up. But he held on to her. "Stay here for a little while."

"It all comes down to today," she whispered.

"Yeah. And we're going to stop the bastard once and for all."

"We hope."

"We will! So let's get the show on the road." He laughed. "Another strange expression."

When they stepped into the living room, Ross was filling in Lance and Savannah, who had just arrived. Lance was another cousin; Savannah was his mate. To Talon's way of thinking, she should be the most nervous. Unlike the rest of the women, she hadn't been born with special powers. But the other life mates had been working with her over the past couple of years, and it seemed that she could fit into the nexus of power that they generated together.

"We should eat before we go through," Rinna said.

"I don't know if I can swallow anything," Kenna murmured.

"You have to eat a little—to keep your strength up."

They all went into the dining room, where a buffet was waiting. The men, except for Gallagher, ate their usual meat. The women ate more lightly. Nobody had much to say, since they'd already discussed what was going to happen when they got to the other side of the portal.

OFFICERS Ken Eckert and Frank Milner pulled up in front of the Winslow house. Ordinarily, the lieutenant wouldn't have sent them out to investigate a minor robbery. But this incident might be connected with the box of money that had turned up in the woods in the nearby state park. And then there was the added piece of strange information. When Winslow had called, he'd mentioned a green fountain of light down by the river.

When Eckert knocked, a lanky man wearing a running suit answered the door. Behind him stood a redheaded woman and two redheaded little girls.

"Mr. Winslow?" Eckert asked.

"Yes."

"Can we come in?"

"Sure." He stepped aside. Eckert and his partner followed him into a living room decorated in relentless country kitsch.

"Come sit down. Thanks for showing up so promptly. We came up to the cabin on Tuesday. It took a while to realize several things were missing."

Mrs. Winslow glanced at the little girls. "Why don't you go to your room and play? This will only take a few minutes."

"Mom, we want to watch," the older one whined.

"This is adult stuff. You go to your room now," Winslow said.

The kids left, dragging their feet. When they were gone, Eckert read off a list of stolen items.

"Yes. I know that's not much, but the door was locked. I'm worried that someone has the key."

Yeah, Eckert thought. *And you're getting VIP service from us.*

"You don't have one under a rock outside?" he asked.

"No."

"How long since you've been here?"

"A month."

"Any evidence that someone was living in the house?"

"Not unless they cleaned up really well," the woman answered.

Milner took out a kit and dusted the kitchen and the bathroom for fingerprints, of which there were many, but probably mostly from the family.

"And what about the green light you reported?" Eckert asked.

"I was out on the back deck when I saw it," the husband said. "It was like fireworks. It went up in an arc, from that direction." He pointed toward Talon Marshall's house. "Then it plunged into the river. The ground shook, and a big spout of green water shot up."

"And you've never seen or felt anything like it before?"

Winslow shook his head. "No. It was weird."

"Anything else you want to tell us?"

"Nothing I can think of now. But I appreciate your coming out here."

"Not a problem."

Eckert and Milner both stood, and Winslow walked them to the door.

When they were back in the cruiser, Milner said, "Maybe they're exaggerating about the ground shaking."

"You think the bank robber was in there—camping out?"

Milner shrugged. "It's a strange kind of robbery."

"Yeah." He started the engine. "We should go over to the Marshall lodge and see if he knows anything about that light."

"Or maybe we should poke around in the woods where he said he found that box. Then pay him a visit. He's hiding something."

"What?"

Milner shrugged again. "I'd like to find out."

AFTER breakfast, Talon and Lance changed to wolf form. Then Kenna led the way toward the rock formation that hid the doorway between the worlds, the men carrying the supplies they'd bought and the wolves wearing the packs Ross had provided.

Turning his head, Lance licked Kenna's arm and gave her a wolf's grin.

"The cave on the other side will give you cover," she murmured.

He nodded against her hand, then turned to Logan. The two of them were going in first as werewolves, to assess the troop numbers, because they were less likely to be attacked. Lance was going to stay with the women.

If it seemed that the force in the parallel universe was too great, Talon and Lance would retreat to the portal, where Grant would be waiting for them to open the doorway again. If they didn't come back in fifteen minutes, the others would come through and attack.

Talon made a low growling sound, telling Kenna it was time. She walked toward the rock formation and reached to press her palm against the place that would open the portal.

He kept very still, watching the rock thin. This was new to him, and it was astonishing to see what looked like a solid wall disappear.

He and Logan were poised to enter when they both spotted a guy who looked like a Roman soldier lying on a blanket near the portal.

Apparently, he'd snuck in here to take a nap.

Looking up, the soldier gasped when he saw two wolves stepping through what had been solid rock. But he recovered quickly. Leaping to his feet, he raised the spear in his hand and threw it directly at Talon.

CHAPTER

THIRTY-TWO

TALON DODGED TO the side, hearing Kenna scream behind him. The spear clattered against the ground as he growled deep in his throat and leaped through the opening, taking the man down and going for his neck. He knew this soldier had nothing against him personally, but he also knew from Kenna that Vandar's forces were trained to kill any invaders. So his powerful teeth crunched through flesh and bone as hot blood spurted into his mouth.

Behind him, a snarling Lance took down another warrior who had been sleeping at his post.

They'd worked out an invasion plan, but the soldier at the portal had screwed it all up.

As Talon and Logan burst from the cave onto blackened land that looked like it had been destroyed by a volcanic eruption, Ross and Grant stepped in front of the wolves.

Talon saw Ramsay Gallagher come through, too. Then he disappeared from sight.

The main body of the soldiers dashed toward the invaders, probably confident that they could take them down. But they didn't know what was in store for them.

Ross and Lance, who had already put on gas masks, waited until the warriors were thirty feet away, then lobbed tear gas grenades at the advancing troops.

At the same time, Kenna and Savanna, also protected by masks, rushed to the waiting werewolves. The life mates each put a mask on a wolf.

Talon watched the unfolding scene with awe. He had studied the effects of tear gas. He knew it caused burning skin, lungs, and eyes, but he'd never actually seen it in action.

As the white cloud hit the soldiers, they began to cough and sneeze, their noses running as they clawed at their faces.

Many cried out as they dropped their spears and knives and tried to run.

But the wolves were ready to prevent their escape from the field of battle. They leaped on the backs of the warriors, knocking them to the ground.

Grant, Lance, and Ross ran forward, shooting their automatic weapons.

The battle was over almost before it had started.

Talon knew the effects of the gas would wear off quickly. With his paw, he pushed the edge of the mask aside. When he felt no ill effects, he clawed it off his face.

Kenna, who had also removed her mask, came up beside him. Kneeling down, she threw her arms around his neck.

He heard her make a low sound. "I'm sorry. I didn't know soldiers would be in the cave."

He pawed the ground, wanting to tell her that it wasn't her fault.

"Now we've lost the element of surprise," she murmured.

Talon gave a wolf's shrug, turning his attention to the men scattered on the battlefield. Had they taken out all of them? Or had Vandar left some of his troops to guard the cave where the slaves lived?

As he started forward, a great winged shape appeared in the air above them.

Vandar!

The monster roared as it circled above the massacred troops.

AS the defending dragon appeared on the scene, Ramsay Gallagher felt a thrill of anticipation.

Renata believed that he and the other dragon had been

born into the same body. Now he would find out if it was
true.

He wanted to step into the open and wave his arm to
attract Vandar's attention.

But not yet. Not until he found out how his other self
would deal with the invaders.

WHEN Vandar spotted Kenna and Talon, he roared and
changed course, aiming for them. Swooping low, he sent
out a stream of fire that singed the already blackened
ground in front of them, the hate-filled expression on his
face making Talon's blood run cold.

With a growl, he put himself between his mate and the
monster, urging her back toward the safety of the portal
cave. But the fire wasn't the only weapon at Vandar's dis-
posal. As Talon led Kenna toward shelter, a bolt of pain
slashed through his head. It felt like someone had cut
through his skull with an ax, hacking away at his mind,
each stroke almost bringing him to his knees.

He stumbled, then fell.

"Get up," Kenna cried out, her voice high and strained.
"You have to get up."

In a daze, he turned his head toward her, amazed that
she was still on her feet when the pain inside his skull
almost wiped out rational thought.

But she must be able to shield herself, at least partially.
Catching him under the front legs, she tugged him back
toward the portal. Before they reached its shelter, another
bolt of fire shot from the beast's snout, this time singeing
Talon's fur.

Kenna cried out as the monster wheeled around, preparing to come at them again with another blast of brimstone.
This time it was going to fry them both.

Before the beast could muster more firepower, a mighty
roar made it turn in the air as another dragon came wing-
ing out from behind the mountain, its silver scales glinting
in the morning sun.

Vandar screeched in shock as he saw a mirror image of himself bearing down on him.

His full attention was now on the new enemy, and to Talon's profound relief, the pain in his head suddenly cut off.

Vandar recovered quickly, this time directing his fire toward the dragon that had invaded his territory.

Did he have any idea who it was?

Transfixed, Talon watched the two beasts circle each other, both of their tails whipping, both of them sending out a stream of fire, and both of them missing the other as they maneuvered for position.

Talon wanted to stay focused on the battle, but he knew that Gallagher was giving them the chance they needed.

In back of him, the rest of the invading force came out of the portal cave, and they went into the formation they'd agreed upon. The women clustered in the middle, and the wolves and men formed a circle around them, guarding their front, back, and flanks.

As they advanced across the blackened land, Talon glanced behind them to make sure all of the soldiers were neutralized.

When one of them staggered to his feet, Talon turned and raced back, knocked him down, and gouged out his throat. Then he pawed among the other warriors. A few were still alive, and as soon as he made sure that they were no threat, he raced back to the main group.

As they approached the cave where the slaves lived, about forty men and women, all clad in white, stepped from the shadows. Three men stood defiantly at the front of the group. They must be the ones Kenna had mentioned: Swee, Barthime, and Wendon.

One of the leaders shouted, "Go back."

"Vandar is finished," Ross answered. "Surrender before it's too late."

The man looked toward the sky, seeing the two dragons circling each other. For a moment, Talon thought the adept might cut his losses. The notion evaporated as his face turned grim with determination.

Seconds later, a blast of psychic energy hit Talon. It was something like what Vandar had thrown at them, but different. This was more diffuse, aimed at his whole body, not just his head. It wasn't as intense, but the blow was enough to stop him in his tracks.

The others also stopped, then staggered as another bolt hit them.

"Quickly," Rinna called. "They have great power. Close ranks."

The whole group moved into a tighter formation so that they were all touching.

Talon could feel the others in the invasion party pressing in around him, and he could also feel the women sending a wave of psychic energy toward the adepts at the cave entrance.

In defense, they also pulled into a tighter formation.

"Swee," Kenna called out. "I've escaped from Vandar. If I can do it, so can all of you. I've brought people to help you."

"Only Vandar can help us," the man shouted back.

IN the sky above the blackened land, Ramsay Gallagher circled the other dragon.

At first they had simply struck out at each other with fire and mental jabs. But as they wheeled in the sky, he heard a silent question come from the other beast.

Who are you? Where did you come from?

I am you. From the other universe.

Impossible.

Who else could I be? As he spoke, he opened his mind to his other self, sharing his thoughts with an intimacy that he had never experienced before, not even with Kenna.

He caught the silent gasp as Vandar took in his early history.

The same.

Yes.

How?

This world changed.

He focused his thoughts on the last part of the nineteenth century.

When Vandar understood where their lives diverged, he roared, wheeling in the air, his tail lashing. *I suffered at the hands of the new psychics. They hunted me down like an animal. They caged me. I barely escaped with my life.*

We have both suffered over the years. Don't make this all about you.

You. Me. We are the same. Thank the gods you found me. Now we can rule this world together. And the other world.

I have no desire to rule. Especially not with you. I know what you have done here.

I survived.

By making slaves of people you stole from their homes.

I paid them back for what they did to me.

Not the people down there. They didn't have a chance against you.

Vandar roared again. *You are either with me or against me.*

I will not join you.

Then die! Vandar lunged in the air, tail lashing as he shot a stream of fire at the invader. Ramsay had been prepared for the attack. As he dodged aside, Vandar shot past him.

Turning, Ramsay took off, leading the other dragon away from the people. He didn't know if he could win the fight. He had been ruthless in his time, but he had changed, and he recognized that he lacked the killer instinct of his other self.

AS the two dragons flew toward the mountain, Renata raised her hand toward the sky. At this distance, it was impossible to tell which was which. But her voice held the conviction of the righteous. "Your master cannot survive."

"He always survives," the adept spokesman answered.

They all watched as one of the dragons caught up with the other, spewing out fire.

Was Vandar fleeing? Or had Gallagher found out he was no match for the other beast?

When the two dragons had disappeared from view, Talon turned his attention back to the adepts at the mouth of the cave.

The Marshall women were strong, but there were more of Vandar's people, and they must have practiced for an attack. Or they were more desperate because they feared that if they failed, their master would kill them in his horrible way.

Talon had thought he was prepared for this conflict, but he hadn't really been able to imagine the reality of a battle that was fought with bolts of energy rather than tooth and claw—or guns.

His whole body felt as though it had turned to boiling lead. At the same time, a terrible hopelessness gripped him. Even as it wrapped him in its embrace, he knew that the adepts were sending it toward him.

Fighting the sensation, he bent his head, maneuvered the whistle into his mouth, and blew a long blast. Then he broke away from the group, staggering toward the slaves, thinking that he could take some of them down and weaken the attack.

Lance caught up with him, and they both struggled toward the cave where the defenders looked at him with alarm.

"Go after the wolves," the spokesman shouted.

The adepts changed the focus of their attack, aiming for him and Lance. Somehow the two of them kept staggering toward Vandar's people, who were now advancing on them, sending out a steady wave of energy. The pain was almost too much to bear, yet Talon knew that at least he and Logan were taking the focus off the women, who might be able to do something if they weren't under the worst of the attack.

Before he reached the adepts, he went down on his front paws.

Behind him, someone shouted, "No," and he was sure

that Kenna had tried to break away from the group and get
to him, but he knew that she had to stay with the others.
Together, the women had a chance. If they lost contact with
Kenna, their strength would diminish.

The defenders gave Talon and Logan one more blast,
and he rolled to his side, unable to move.

Then they must have turned their attention back to the
women and their mates, because he heard groans and cries
from the Marshalls.

They'd thought they could conquer Vandar's adepts, but
they'd been wrong.

Talon struggled to turn his head. When he did, he saw
the other invaders going down. Across the blackened land,
his eyes met Kenna's. Her lips moved, but he couldn't catch
what she was saying. He thought it might be "good-bye."

He wanted to howl in sorrow, but even that was beyond
him now.

ON the other side of the portal, Mitch Sutton crept closer
to the place where the group of people and a couple of the
dangerous big dogs had disappeared. It looked like they'd
used a magic trick. Making a piece of rock wall vanish. Or
maybe it hadn't actually been rock.

He'd stayed way back until they disappeared. But he'd
been watching everything with high-powered binoculars.

The men and women had been in a hell of a hurry. Like
somebody was after them.

Was one of the guys Talon Marshall? It was hard to
tell, because there was a whole bunch of men, and all of
them could have been his brother or his cousin. But he saw
someone he recognized for sure. The woman who should
have burned up in the lodge. She'd screwed him up, and she
was on his shit list, just like Marshall.

Jeez! Maybe Marshall hadn't turned the money over to
the cops after all. Maybe he'd hidden it, and now he was
going to get it.

But how had they gone through the wall? As far as he

could see, it had something to do with the woman pressing her palm against a spot on the rock.

He hefted the Glock in his hand. They had to come back, hopefully with the money. And when they did, he could cut them down before they knew what had hit them. He was about to head for a screen of brambles when he heard something rustling to his right. Peeking out from behind the tree where he was standing, he saw gray-clad figures coming up the hill at a good clip.

Jesus! The fuzz.

So that's why Marshall's friends had been in a hurry. They were dodging the cops, and Mitch had come back at the damn wrong time. Again.

Christ! Was he never going to get a break?

He looked wildly around. Could he get the hell out of here before the guy spotted him? Or was it already too late?

The officer stopped and looked down the hill, and Mitch thought he had a chance for a getaway. Then he saw another cop coming from the other direction, cutting him off.

Shit.

He waited with his heart pounding. When they drew abreast of each other, he ran toward the rock, hoping against hope he was doing the right thing.

Shifting his gun to his left hand, he pressed his right hand to the same place where the woman had pressed, flattening his palm against the stone the way she had. When nothing happened, he clenched his teeth and moved his hand a little to the right, feeling a tingling sensation. Seconds later, the rock in front of him began to change.

It was going away! Just like before. Just like magic!

He stared in wonder at the solid wall that suddenly wasn't so solid. There was a dark cave beyond. As far as he could tell, it was empty. And farther on, the tunnel seemed to bend. But he could see some light filtering in.

This is spooky. Should he go in? Or what?

Behind him, someone shouted, "Police. Stop."

Not likely. With no choice now, he stepped through the

opening. It closed behind him, and he smiled. He'd been looking through the binoculars and seen the woman press the rock. The cops weren't close enough to have seen him do it, and they were at the wrong angle to figure out where he'd gone.

Could he be sure of that? Maybe he'd better get out of the cave in case they came through.

When he started down the dark tunnel, he almost tripped over a limp body lying on the ground.

Shit! Something had happened here. Something bad.

Moving more cautiously, he took a few more steps and kicked another body.

Cursing again, he stopped, staring toward the light ahead of him. He wanted to go back, but the cops were probably right outside now. Maybe they'd even figure out how to get in here.

The only way to go was forward. Slowly, Mitch crept to the mouth of the cave where he stared out at a scene that robbed him of breath.

What the hell?

He'd been in the Pennsylvania woods. Now he was staring at a blackened plain, with a bunch of dead guys lying on the ground. They looked like they were actors in a costume drama, only he had the sinking feeling that what he was looking at was horribly real.

Making a desperate decision, he turned and ran back the way he'd come. But the wall had closed behind him, and when he pressed his hand against the vertical surface, nothing happened.

CHAPTER
THIRTY-THREE

ECKERT AND MILNER ran forward.

When they reached the granite wall, they searched for some crevice where the guy could be hiding.

"Where the hell did he go?"

"The sun was in my eyes, but there was something funny about the way he just vanished."

When they failed to find a hiding place in the rock, they looked for a tunnel but found nothing.

"Could he have gotten around the other side?"

"If he did, he's probably long gone."

"I'm pretty sure it wasn't Marshall," Eckert said. "Too short and thick."

"Yeah."

They split up, one moving to the right, the other to the left, searching the woods.

TALON could see Vandar's adepts advancing on them, confidence on their faces now, even when the outcome of the battle in the sky was unknown.

With every fiber of his being, he tried to reach out to Kenna's mind. Then, in that charged moment, he heard her voice inside his head.

Talon, I love you.

I love you.

Making a superhuman effort, he struggled to face her. They had shared paradise on Earth together, and he wanted her to be the last thing he saw. But as he fought to turn, he realized that the ground below him was vibrating.

What?

To the south, he saw a cloud of dust rising. The vibrations grew, and he wondered what was happening. An earthquake?

As he stared at the dust cloud, he made out a group of horses and riders galloping toward them. He didn't know who it was. Had Vandar stationed reinforcements out of sight?

The slaves turned toward the riders, and the expressions on their faces told Talon that it wasn't anyone they were expecting.

When he saw who it was, hope leaped inside him. In the lead were Rinna and Logan along with a dark-haired man and a woman with long golden hair. They must be Rinna's friends, Griffin and Zarah.

As the reinforcements approached, the people around him straightened. The women stretched out their hands toward the cave, and Talon was shocked to see streams of energy flowing from them toward Vandar's slaves.

The dragon-shifter's adepts crowded closer together, sending back a wave of power, but it wasn't as strong as what they'd previously mustered.

As the horsemen drew up, Talon saw that some of them were soldiers, dressed much like Vandar's troops.

The civilians stepped quickly into the circle, clasping hands with the Marshalls. There were moments of confusion when Talon felt the energy shifting around him as the newcomers got acclimated to the group. He could feel power jumping and coiling in the air.

Vandar's adepts took advantage of the disconnection, hurling a new blast that sent agony screeching along his nerve endings.

Even as he fought the pain, the energy from the Marshall group stabilized. He felt it expand and shoot outward toward Vandar's adepts.

The effect was almost instantaneous. They went down on their knees, gasping, some of them trying to crawl away to escape the punishment that their rivals had inflicted.

But the Marshall women and their new allies kept up the pressure until Vandar's minions were immobilized. Most of them lay on their backs, gasping for breath. Some had gone absolutely still, and Talon wondered if they had survived the attack.

While the others hurried toward the slaves, he trotted to a spot behind a low outcropping of rock, where he slipped out of his backpack and quickly said the chant that changed him from wolf to man. After pulling on his shirt, pants, and shoes, he stepped back into the open and hurried toward his mate.

Kenna rushed forward, and he hugged her to him with a surge of gladness. She held him just as tightly as she asked, "Are you all right?"

"Yes. Are you?"

"Yes."

They embraced for a long moment, and his hands ran over her as he assured himself that she was unharmed, but he knew they shouldn't stand out here in the open. Looking up, he shaded his eyes with his hand as he scanned the sky, but he couldn't spot the dragons. Had they killed each other, or were they simply out of sight?

"What now?" he asked.

The others had already closed in on Vandar's adepts, but Kenna had waited for him. She gestured toward the slaves.

"They're still dangerous. They will be, until we know Vandar is dead."

"What are you going to do?"

"I don't—" She stopped suddenly and whirled toward the portal. Talon followed her gaze and went still. A man wearing a dark T-shirt and jeans stood at the entrance to the parallel universe with a gun in his hand.

"It's him," Kenna gasped. "The man with the gas can."

The newcomer's gaze snapped to her. "You! There's something weird about you. Where are we?" he asked in a gravelly voice. "And why the fuck can't I get out the way I came in?"

Talon and Kenna exchanged a glance. The portal was blocked? Probably by Vandar's adepts—to keep anyone from getting out until he was ready.

Talon kept his focus on the gun. From the brief conversation, he knew this was the man who had been stalking him for weeks. Ross had said his name was Mitch Sutton. Talon wasn't going to let him know he'd pegged him.

Instead, he simply asked, "What are you doing here?"

Sutton pointed the weapon at Talon's chest. "I'll ask the questions." He gestured with his free hand. "Answer me, you bastard. What the fuck kind of place is this?"

"We're in another universe."

"Do you expect me to believe that?"

Talon turned his hands palms up. "Does this look like Pennsylvania?"

"Get me out of here. With the swag you stole from me."

Talon processed that. The guy thought the box with the cash was here? *Okay. Good.*

From the corner of his eye, he saw the fixed expression on Kenna's face. It was the look she got when she was doing something—mental.

"It was your money?" he asked, stalling for time.

"Fuckin' right."

"I'll get you the cash, and I'll open the doorway, if you let us go."

"Deal. Where's the dough?"

"In the cave."

"Then get it!"

"Sure."

Talon and Kenna passed the robber, heading for the cave. Just as they reached the entrance, Sutton cried out in surprise, scrabbling to keep his balance. Talon turned to see him lifting off the ground. Grabbing Kenna, Talon pushed her down, out of the line of fire.

But instead of shooting at them, the man flew backwards, his arms wheeling, then folding inward.

"No," he screamed. "Stop."

The gun discharged as he hit the ground, and he made a wheezing sound.

Talon rushed forward, crouching over Sutton.

Blood spread from a hole in the center of his shirt.

Kenna came up beside him.

"It looks like he's been shot in the heart. Did you do that?" Talon asked.

She dragged in a breath and let it out. "I directed it, but I felt Rinna and Renata in the background, sending enough energy to me."

The other two women approached them.

"Thank you," Talon said.

"We saw you were in danger," Rinna answered. "Is he one of Vandar's slaves? Where did he get the gun?" she asked, pointing to the man lying dead on the ground.

"He's from the other universe. He robbed a bank and buried the money," Talon answered. "When I was out for a run in the woods, I found the stash and turned it in to the cops. Unfortunately, he's been making trouble for me ever since."

Talon gave a harsh laugh. "His mistake, stepping into Vandar's territory." He looked at Kenna. "You understand that's why the soldiers were in there? Vandar had the adepts close the portal on this side, so no one could escape."

She stared at him. "I didn't think of that."

"We'll open it later," Rinna said.

After a final look at Sutton, they turned away and walked back to the rest of the group.

Kenna lagged back. When they were alone again, she turned to Talon. "I . . . never killed before."

"But you had the strength to do it."

"It's wrong."

"Not when somebody is trying to kill you. Like the adepts."

She nodded.

"Thanks to you, we're rid of him. But there's still work to do here."

She nodded again, and they returned to the group.

Vandar's adepts were lying on the ground. A few were dead. Most looked frightened.

The three leaders gave Kenna a murderous look. "You can't win," one of them growled.

"You're wrong, Swee," she answered, but Talon heard the edge of doubt in her voice.

"We're holding them immobile," Renata said. "Until we find out about the dragons."

Talon looked up, shading his eyes. But he couldn't see either of the beasts. "I'd like to know about them myself." He turned to Kenna. "You've been in contact with Gallagher. Is he still alive?"

She went still, her vision turning inward. "I . . . don't know."

"But you were . . . connected to him. He said he could find you."

She shook her head. "I lost track of him when we came here. I was focused on them," she said, gesturing toward the slaves.

"Can you reach him?"

"I . . . don't know."

She closed her eyes, her hands clenching at her sides as she did something with her mind that he couldn't even imagine.

Finally, she opened her eyes and looked at him. "I'm sorry. I don't know what happened. Maybe he's dead. Or maybe he's too focused on the fight."

Talon nodded, wishing she could give him some information.

Ross joined the conversation. "Until we find out what happened with the dragons, somebody is going to have to keep the adepts under control."

"Yeah," Talon answered, feeling the tension among his cousins and their life mates. They all understood that if Gallagher lost the fight, their situation was precarious.

Kenna shuddered, and he knew she was thinking about the monster who had been her master for months.

But when she spoke, it wasn't of Vandar. "There will be people hiding in the cave. They'll be worried about what's going on. Are they going to be punished? Killed?"

Talon sighed. "I guess we'll have to go in after them."

"It's not one big open space," Kenna said. "There are corridors and rooms."

"Will the people in there have weapons?" Ross asked.

Kenna shook her head. "Vandar kept weapons away from everyone except the soldiers. But if the people are frightened, they could have gotten into the armory. Or they could have taken knives from the kitchen."

Lance cleared his throat. Like Talon, he'd changed from wolf to human form. "It would be nice if we could tell them their master is dead."

"Yes," Kenna murmured.

They had just turned toward the cave when a flash of movement in the sky made them all look up. A dragon was flying toward them. A dragon with silver scales and a bleeding wound on his underside.

"Vandar," Swee cried out, a look of triumph in his eyes. "I told you he would come back."

Ross raised the machine gun he was carrying, sighting on the approaching beast.

CHAPTER
THIRTY-FOUR

"NO! WAIT," KENNA cried out.

After tense seconds, Ross lowered his arm. But he kept the gun at the ready. *For all the good it would do him*, Kenna thought, remembering the last time the werewolves had tried to shoot the dragon.

The great beast continued toward them, but she saw it was faltering in its flight.

If it was Vandar, he would rain down fire on them and free his adepts.

If it was Gallagher, it looked like he was in serious trouble. Could he even land without injuring himself?

As the dragon drew closer, there was no blast of fire. Somehow the beast made a soft landing, then lay panting on the dark ground.

When Kenna darted forward, Talon tried to grab her, but she slipped from his grasp and ran to the monster, putting her hand on his huge head.

"Ramsay," she cried. "It's you, isn't it?"

The creature's whole body shook. It opened its mouth, but nothing came out besides a long moan.

Kenna knelt beside him. "Don't try to talk."

The dragon clacked its huge teeth together, its chest heaving.

Talon moved to her side. "I can't talk when I'm in wolf form. I'm sure he can't talk as a dragon."

She nodded. "He's in pain."

"Yes."

The great beast shuddered as it scraped at the cinders

under its claws. Then, before their eyes, he began to shift
his form. The scales, claws, and fangs disappeared. His
body began to shrink into the form of a man. Moments
later, Ramsay Gallagher lay panting on the ground. His
skin was pale as paste, a huge gash swept across his middle,
and one shoulder was burned.

"It looks like you were in a hell of a fight," Talon
muttered.

Ramsay's eyes were out of focus, but when Talon
gripped his arm, he met his eye.

"Is Vandar dead?"

"Yes," Ramsay gasped out. "He's to . . . the right . . .
around the mountain." His body was shaking now.

"Thank the Great Mother," Kenna said. Turning to
the adepts, she shouted in triumph, "This is the other
dragon-shifter, Ramsay Gallagher. Vandar is dead."

Without waiting for a reply, she knelt by the wounded
shifter.

While Renata and Rinna stayed with the adepts to
secure them with psychic restraint, the rest of the women
joined the group around Ramsay.

After introducing herself and explaining that she had
some healing powers, Zarah knelt and put her hands on the
shifter's head and shoulder, then drew in a quick breath.
"He's in bad shape. But I hope we can save him."

Zarah unfolded several blankets she'd brought. After
laying one beside him, they gently rolled him onto it, then
covered him with another.

As she knelt beside him, Zarah lit a small lamp. Kenna
had seen that before and knew it was a focus for the woman's powers.

"Form a circle around him," she murmured, "and we'll
see what we can do."

Zarah's lips moved as she stroked one hand on the
dragon-shifter's forehead.

Kenna felt a low hum of energy flowing around them
that made her skin tingle.

"Great Mother, let him live," she whispered. She had

been terrified that Ramsay was like Vandar. Now she knew how different he was, and how much he had sacrificed for her and everyone else here. He had killed Vandar. Killed himself in a way. And she couldn't imagine how horrible that would be.

Slowly, Ramsay's skin color grew pinker, and his breathing became less labored.

He had looked near death. Now it seemed as if Zarah had worked a miracle. She pulled down the blanket enough to see his shoulder and the gash across his chest and belly. Both of them had begun to heal.

Gallagher looked down at his chest, then turned his head toward Zarah. "Thank you."

She found his hand and clasped her fingers with his. "You fought him and won. That was . . . extraordinary."

He answered with a small nod.

"And Vandar's slaves are free," Zarah added.

"You'd better take care of them." He closed his eyes and drew into himself, and Kenna could see he didn't want to talk about the fight with his other self. From the looks of him, it had been a battle that both dragons had known they must win to live.

Rinna stayed with Ramsay, and the others walked back to Vandar's adepts, who were still lying on the ground, under the control of the men.

Kenna gave the leaders a hard look. "Swee, Wendon, Barthime. Your master is dead."

The men glared at her.

"Why should I believe you?" Swee growled.

"Why should I lie?"

"You want him to be dead."

"Don't you?" She stared at him. "You were never harsh with me. I thought you were suffering under his control, the way I was."

"I thought you were doing the master's bidding."

"You helped me memorize all those facts. Let me help you now."

"You should have stayed in the other universe."

"This may be more difficult than you imagine," the dark-haired man who had led the horsemen said. "I'm Griffin," he added. "Head of the Sun Acres council."

"I'm . . . honored that you came to help us," Kenna stammered, awed that the leader of a city had risked so much for them.

"You did me a favor. I knew there were problems in this area. I had heard people were being stolen from their cities. The beast could have attacked us."

He raised his voice and spoke to the adepts. "I can help you get back to your cities. And if you were slaves before you were brought here, I can offer you a place as free men and women in Sun Acres."

Most of them looked grateful.

Swee, Barthime, and Wendon still looked defiant, and she wondered if they could ever live in normal society.

When she heard a noise behind her, she turned and saw Ramsay staggering toward them, a blanket draped over his shoulder like a toga. It was clear he could barely stay on his feet, but he wasn't letting Rinna help him walk. Instead, she trailed behind, ready to steady him if he stumbled.

He stopped a few feet from the adepts. "I am called Ramsay Gallagher. I am Vandar's twin brother. We were separated for many years."

Swee glared at him defiantly. "Then where were you? Why are you coming here *now*?"

"I was living in the alternate universe. The universe where you sent Kenna."

The adept glanced at her, then back at the dragon-shifter.

"I sensed her presence," Ramsay continued. "Because of her connection with Vandar, I think. When I came back here and met your master, I knew the two of us could never exist in the same time line."

"If you're his brother, you could have killed him anytime. Why now?" Wendon challenged.

"At the beginning, we were very much alike. Over the years, we grew apart."

Kenna listened to the explanation. It wasn't strictly the truth, but it would do. Probably, the adept wouldn't believe the real truth, anyway.

"Accept that he is dead," Ramsay said, his voice wavering slightly.

"Bring me his body!"

Kenna glanced at Griffin. "Can we do that?"

"I don't know. It depends on where he's lying. Maybe we can bring his head."

Knowing that Ramsay had done what he could, Kenna took his arm. "You were badly wounded when you fought him. You need to lie down. You should go into the cave where you can be comfortable."

"I have no interest in his cave," he shot back. "I want to get as far from his damn lair as I can."

"Then maybe you could go back to the smaller cave where the portal is located."

He thought for a moment, then nodded. "All right. And perhaps one of you can bring me some clothes."

Ross handed him the pack he'd been carrying.

Gallagher took it and started back. Kenna would have gone with him, until she saw Talon give her a long look. She'd formed a very intimate relationship with the dragon-shifter when they'd melded their minds back in the mountain country. They had never been physically intimate, but they had been tied together in a way that nobody else could share.

Stopping, she turned to her mate. "He's my friend. That's all."

Talon answered with a tight nod, then walked over to Ross and Griffin.

Kenna came back and joined the group. "Ramsay's weak. And he doesn't like having anyone see him at less than his best."

"Too bad," Talon muttered.

Kenna touched Talon's arm. "Can we talk for a minute?"

He looked like he wanted to protest. Instead, he followed her a few yards away. "Don't be jealous of him," she said in a low voice.

"I'm not!"

"I would be, if I had watched you meld your mind with another woman." She kept her gaze fixed on him. "The most important thing that ever happened to me was finding you and bonding with you. Ramsay will never come between us. I'm thinking that Zarah and the other women can help me break the link with him, but I can't take the time to do it now. There are still too many of Vandar's slaves that need to be found. They've got to be hiding in the cave." She gave him an open look. "I don't want to go in there by myself. Will you come with me?"

"Of course."

When she went to tell the others where they were going, Swee gave her a murderous look, and she turned swiftly away.

Without glancing back, she and Talon walked into the rock-bound antechamber. The cool air made her shudder.

"This place gives me a spooky feeling," Talon whispered.

"A lot of bad things happened here. To me and the other slaves."

He closed his hand around her arm. "You don't have to do it. Let's get someone else to search the cave."

She wanted to agree, but she knew she still had work to do. Cupping her hands around her mouth, she called out, "This is Kenna. I used to be one of Vandar's slaves. You may know me. I worked in the library. Vandar is dead. You can come out. It's all right."

"And his adepts are neutralized. They can't hurt you, either," Talon added, then lowered his voice and said, "Tell them what happened to you."

She looked at him, then called out again. "This is Kenna again. Vandar sent me on a mission. You might not know where I went. But it was to another universe. I met some people there who could help us. They killed Vandar." She paused for several seconds, then said, "Please come out."

After a few more seconds, Talon heard a shuffling noise to his right. A woman in a white dress appeared.

"Lina," Kenna said. "Thank you for trusting me."

"Is it really true?" the woman asked.

"Yes. Go on outside." Kenna stepped forward and hugged the other woman. "My friends are there. And they have the adepts under control."

"Nobody can control them," Lina whispered.

"My friends are stronger. Some of them are from this universe. From a city called Sun Acres. But some of them are from the other side of the portal," she said, like that would give them powers. Of course, the opposite was usually true, but Lina didn't know it.

The woman gave a tiny nod.

"Do you know where the others are hiding?" Talon asked her.

"Some are down there," she said, pointing to a room farther along the corridor. Then she walked cautiously toward the cave entrance.

When she was gone, Kenna took a few more steps into the cave, then stopped short.

"What?" Talon asked.

"I feel danger . . . but I don't know where it's coming from."

"Then let's go back."

She looked up and down the tunnel, expecting one of the slaves to come charging out at them with a knife in his hand.

"Is it my imagination, or is the floor vibrating under our feet?" Talon asked.

"I feel it, too." Panic gripped her. "We have to go back. Before it's too late."

As she spoke, a huge crack appeared in the ceiling right above her head, and small chunks of rock began to fall around her.

CHAPTER
THIRTY-FIVE

KENNA'S GAZE MET Talon's, and she knew in that terrible moment that she was going to die. After all this.

But she hadn't counted on her mate's werewolf reflexes.

He grabbed her, pulling her out of the way and throwing his body over hers to shield her as the cave shook around them and rock rained down.

When the ground stopped trembling, they were lying just beyond a pile of rubble.

"You saved me," she whispered.

He clutched her tighter. "Thank God."

They clung together, her arms moving over his back and shoulders as she reassured herself that her mate was unharmed, and he did the same.

"What the hell happened?" Talon finally asked.

Until that moment, she hadn't put it all together, but as the picture fell into place, she caught her breath.

"It was Swee, Wendon, and Barthime. They used their psychic powers to bring the ceiling down—on top of me."

"But they were being . . . guarded."

"Yes."

The sound of feet in the cave made them both turn. Zarah and Renata ran toward them.

"Are you all right?" Renata gasped out, looking over their shoulders at the chunks of rock lying on the floor.

"Yes," Kenna answered.

"Thank the Great Mother."

"Let's get the hell out of the cave," Talon suggested, his voice gritty. "Before something else goes wrong."

Kenna nodded, and they all started back to the exit.

Renata looked embarrassed. "I'm sorry. The power came from the three chief adepts."

"I know," Kenna answered. "But how could they do it?"

"We could feel that they were up to something, but we didn't know what it was. We tried to stop them, but we couldn't do it." She gulped. "They were prepared to die to accomplish their goal."

Kenna started running to the mouth of the cave. As soon as she saw the men who had tried to kill her, she gasped. They were all lying on the ground, their faces contorted in pain, their bodies unmoving.

She dragged in a breath and let it out. "I guess that was Vandar's final plan to get me, if all else failed."

"Yeah, like the talisman," Talon answered. He reached for her again and clasped her to him, and she swayed in his arms as the extent of Vandar's hatred sank in.

Finally, she said, "We still have to get the rest of the slaves out of the cave."

"But you don't have to do it personally," Griffin answered. "I'll have my men go in there."

Talon looked glad to hear the suggestion.

But Kenna felt her chest tighten. "The slaves will think they're Vandar's soldiers."

"Not for long," Talon muttered. Unable to leave it at that, he bent toward her and added, "Do you think you could stay out of danger for a little while? For me?"

Catching the deep emotion in his voice, she took a moment to steady herself. "Yes. For you."

"Then let's go home."

"Home?" She gave him a long look. "You mean, to your world?"

His gaze stayed fixed on her. "I hope you want to go there with me."

"Gods, yes." She swallowed. "But I'd like my parents to know I'm okay."

"We can send a messenger to Breezewood," Griffin said. "Then, when the situation here has settled down, you can visit them in person."

"I'd be very grateful. Thank you so much," Kenna said. "My father is Becker. He has a boot and sandal shop very close to the city gate. You don't mind sending someone?"

"Of course not. And when you come back, I suggest going through at the portal near Logan and Rinna's house. If you travel to Sun Acres together, that will be safer. Then we can send you with a party to Breezewood."

"Thank you," Kenna replied, overwhelmed at the way these people were willing to help her.

As she looked around, she saw that everybody was finally starting to relax. And Talon looked eager to leave.

"Ready?" he asked.

"Very ready," she answered. Finally, it was sinking in that she was free to do what she wanted.

The Marshalls spent a few more minutes discussing the cleanup operation with Griffin, who was obviously an excellent administrator.

Talon glanced toward the small cave that hid the portal. "Can we get back through?"

"Rinna, Olivia, and Antonia already took the seal off," Griffin answered.

Kenna kicked up the blackened ground with one foot. "He could have sealed it from the other side, too," she murmured. "Why did he let me back in?"

Talon's jaw tightened. "Arrogance, I assume. He was sure he could deal with a mere mortal like you. He was wrong."

"He could have dealt with me." Kenna looked around at the people who had come through with her and the ones from her world who had joined them. "All of you made the difference. Thank you so much."

"He was a threat to all of us," Ross answered, then added, "Ramsay Gallagher went back to our world while you were in the cave."

"This place disturbs him," Kenna said. "He doesn't

like to think that he could have become like Vandar." She looked at Talon, but he only gave her a small nod.

"Renata explained that he's the same being," Griffin said. "That he was also in your universe where he'd lived for centuries."

"Yes. It's a weird concept," Kenna answered.

They made plans to get together in the next month. After the men shook hands and the women embraced, the Marshalls and their mates started back to the portal.

Once again, Kenna opened it, this time feeling a sense of wonder that she was leaving this place as a free woman.

AFTER stepping through, Talon took a deep breath and let it out. "I'm always glad to get back from a trip." He laughed. "Never more than today."

"Yeah," Ross agreed.

They all started down the hill to the lodge, but they had only covered a small part of the distance when Talon heard sounds coming from the forest.

"Christ, now what?" he muttered.

They all tensed when two police officers stepped into view.

"Stop right there," one of them called out.

"What's going on?" Ross asked in a low voice.

"It's the two cops who interviewed me about the money Mitch Sutton stole," Talon said, also speaking so his voice wouldn't carry. Kenna moved closer to him, and he knew a confrontation with the authorities was the last thing she wanted.

"Let me handle this," he said.

"Okay," Ross answered.

Both officers stepped up to them, giving them a hard look.

"Where have you been?" the one named Eckert asked.

Talon didn't miss a beat. "I've been teaching some of my family wilderness camping techniques."

The cop gave them all a long look, probably taking

in their disheveled appearance. "Oh yeah, where's your campsite?"

"We don't have one. We've been foraging and sleeping where we could."

"Did you see a guy around here acting suspicious?" Eckert asked. "He's about five-eight. Dark hair. We didn't get close enough to see his eye color. Dressed in a dark T-shirt and jeans."

"No."

"He was poking around the rocks up there in back of you. Then he disappeared. You're sure you didn't see him?"

"Absolutely. We just got here."

"And what about a green streak of light in the sky a few nights ago. Do you know anything about that?"

"No. Maybe it was kids setting off firecrackers?" Talon gestured toward the people with him. "I worked this gang pretty hard, and we'd like to get home and shower."

The cops looked at each other, then back at him. "You'll be here if we need you?"

"Unless I'm out on a trip."

Without waiting for permission, Talon stepped around them. The rest of the group followed.

Beside him, Kenna breathed out a deep sigh. "Don't we have to . . . respect them?" she whispered when they were fifty yards away.

"In this world, they have to respect us."

The group walked into the lodge, where they repaired to different bedroom suites to clean up.

A half hour later, when they were back in the living room, Ross said, "I have a contact who created an ID for Rinna. I can do the same for Kenna, if you want."

"I'd appreciate it." Talon had been wondering how they were going to handle that.

"I have a camera in my car. Let me take her picture."

They took some shots. When Ross showed them to Kenna, she marveled at the likeness.

But it was clear everyone was anxious to leave. And Talon was anxious to have them out of the way. He had forged a relationship with his family, but it wasn't something he could deal with on a daily basis.

After another round of handshaking and hugging, the others finally left.

Talon and Kenna stood on the porch, watching the last car pull away.

"Alone at last," he said, pulling his mate into a close embrace.

She raised her face toward his. "I couldn't have escaped from Vandar without you and your family."

"And the world would be in danger if you hadn't told us his plans." He cleared his throat. "What happened to Gallagher?"

"I don't know. I can't sense him. And not because the life mates did anything to prevent it. I have the feeling he was injured worse than we realized, and he didn't want us to know it."

"Will he live?"

"I hope so. But I think he may be . . . damaged."

"What do you mean?"

"That he may have lost some of his powers." She looked up at Talon. "I know you didn't like my bond with him, but it was only temporary. And it wasn't . . . intimate in the way . . . we are."

"I saw you with him, and I wanted you all to myself."

"You have me." She swallowed hard. "I know you thought I would never trust you."

"I didn't understand what was wrong. Now I realize what you were going through."

"And you."

He lowered his head to hers for a long, passionate kiss.

When he moved his lips back a few inches, they both dragged in several breaths.

Smiling, he trailed his hands down to her ass so that he could press his erection to her middle.

In answer, she swayed against him, and he gave her a wolfish grin. "You're going to love playing down at the swimming hole in your birthday suit."

"My . . ." She stopped and grinned. "Okay, I get that."

"But not in broad daylight, of course."

"Nobody can see us inside your circle of pines," she murmured.

"That used to be my private space."

She looked uncertain. "Do you mind . . ."

"Actually, I love sharing it with you. That and everything else I have."

"The most important thing is sharing yourself," she whispered.

"I've learned that. From you."

Linking his hand with hers, he led her down the steps and toward the private circle, loving this woman. And knowing that the life they would build together would be richer than he could ever have imagined.

Keep reading for an excerpt from

SKIN GAME
BY AVA GRAY

Available November 2009
from Berkley Sensation!

KYRA HELD THE guy's balls in the palm of her hand. Literally.

Just for a second as she brushed by him, but it was enough. His eyes widened, and she knew he took the touch as a sign he'd get lucky after he won her last hundred bucks. The crumpled bill lay underneath his, weighted by a cube of pool chalk.

Poor, stupid mark.

She slid him a slow smile as she racked for their fourth and final contest. His friends stood with beers in their hands, half-smiling in anticipation of a sure thing. In a seedy place like this, they had only an old table with worn felt near the right corner, making it necessary to compensate. That wouldn't slow her up this game, though.

Her opponent had years of practice on this particular table. A scruffy, hard-drinking son of a bitch like him had no better skill, nothing else going for him. No, calling himself reigning champ at Suds Beer Factory defined him. She counted on that.

Spinning her cue stick between her palms, she paused before taking the first shot. "You want to make this interesting?"

Her voice had often been called throaty. Kyra sounded like she smoked unfiltered Camels and drank too many whiskey sours. In fact, she did neither. That was just one of nature's cons, more flash for the package to distract people from what lay underneath.

"Darlin'," drawled one of the barflies, "it already is."

Now somebody would comment on the sweet curve of her ass or the way she filled out her jeans. Kyra managed not to roll her eyes, but it was a near thing. If she ever sunk so low that she needed a boost by picking up a man in a place like this, she hoped somebody would shoot her and put her out of her misery.

The man she'd been reeling in for the past hour couldn't resist asking, as she'd known he couldn't. People were so damn predictable. "What'd you have in mind?"

"Double or nothing."

"You don't have the cash," he scoffed.

Her smile didn't falter. "No, but I have a fully restored 1971 Mercury Marquis parked outside. It's nice, fresh powder blue paint. You'd get a good chunk for it."

"That's yours? Big ride for a little thing like you," her opponent said. Chet, she thought his name was.

For that comment alone she wanted to smash his nose through his forehead, but he'd feel the hit worse in his wallet. It wasn't like he used his brain much, after all. Kyra made herself smile as she put her keys on top of the two bills.

A stocky guy near the bar shook his head, a crop of coarse brown curls bristling from beneath his baseball cap. "Don't take the lady's ride. She probably has a gambling problem . . . Don't know when to quit even when she can't win."

"I never walk away from a bet." She hadn't affirmed what he'd said, but these yokels would never notice the difference. "What about you? Scared?" she mocked gently.

Oh, that would never stand. As a chorus of *oooh*s arose from his friends, Chet shook his head. "It's your funeral, lady. You're on."

Finally. She never knew how long a boost would last, so she needed to get this game in the bag, or she really *would* lose her ride. Since the car was the only thing she owned, that would be catastrophic.

Kyra broke then, a perfect scatter. The red three slipped into a pocket, deciding whether she'd shoot solids or stripes.

Four more shots lined up for her, and she called them in a neutral tone.

A con could go south pretty fast if she didn't play it right. Chet might suspect he'd been hustled when she was done, but men seldom started a fight with "a little thing like her." If they did, they found themselves unpleasantly surprised—after she tapped the toughest among them.

Bank, carom, and suddenly she'd sunk half the balls on the table. Suds got really quiet and someone muttered, "I call lemonade."

"Yep," another guy said. "She's torching him."

If she hadn't been worried about the clock running out, she might have stalled a shot and put a ball in jail just to let Chet use his cue, but she needed to wrap things up. She rounded the table, using his own skill against him. Kyra sank the next shot easily, as she knew everything about this game and this particular table. She didn't bother with showy play; the point was to win, not to impress.

The bar was dead quiet when she pointed to the far left pocket, called it, and banked the eight ball toward it. She narrowed her eyes as its roll slowed. She hadn't noticed the faint wear near that pocket as well, but it didn't matter. Chet had learned to compensate over long years of practice; thus, so had she.

The black ball sank with a quiet plunk.

"I believe that's a dime in all," she said with a smile. "Cash only."

A dime was a thousand bucks. Kyra knew pool hall slang because she'd worked this particular con a lot. Now it just remained to be seen whether he'd pay up politely.

"You played me," Chet growled.

She pretended to misunderstand, opening her eyes wide. "So I did. I won, too."

This was the moment of truth. Most guys wouldn't take a swing at her, no matter how mad they were. She'd run across some real sons of bitches in her travels, though. So Kyra braced herself.

"Pay the lady," came a low, rough voice from the back of the bar. "Unless you want people to call you a welsher."

With a muttered curse, Chet handed back all the money he'd won, plus a few hundred more. Kyra smiled, then claimed her keys and the last two bills beneath the chalk cube. She thumbed the white rabbit's foot on her key chain, as she did after every successful con. Superstition had its place.

"Table's all yours, boys. Thanks for the fun!"

Before the mood could turn from puzzled to hostile, she grabbed her denim bag and headed out. It was best to hop into the Marquis and hustle down the road. Nobody prevented her from pushing past the front door and into the humid kiss of Louisiana twilight. Wild jasmine growing on a broken-down fence scented the air.

Kyra cast a look back at the timber road house. Places like this made up her bread and butter. *So many suckers, so little time.* She loved the euphoria of getting away clean.

Then she heard the crunch of footsteps on the gravel behind her.

Shit, she thought. *I knew it was too good to be true.*

She picked up the pace to no avail. A hand on her arm spun her around, and she found herself craning her head back to see who had ahold of her. At five foot four, she was neither petite nor average, and he topped her by a foot. More interesting, he hadn't been involved in the game.

"What did you do in there?" She recognized his voice—a cross between black velvet and a buzz saw—he'd demanded Chet pay up. The guy had been drinking alone near the back, but she hadn't gotten a good look at him.

She'd remember a face like this, hard angles, softened by a spill of midnight hair and eyes so dark they seemed to drink the light, black pools with azure lightning in their depths. He had skin like old mahogany, weathered but lovely. But his fine, unusual looks didn't give him an excuse to touch her.

Thanks to this ass, she'd be lucky if she didn't wind up in the fetal position, groaning through a migraine. With a prowess she must've snagged from him, Kyra neatly broke his grip on her forearm. Surprise flickered in his gaze, as if he recognized the maneuver but didn't understand how she'd done it. Well, hell, she didn't know how either, and sometimes it got damn confusing, but it was a living.

"I won a pool game. And now I'm leaving." Her tone dared him to try something, especially when she sensed the deadly readiness in her muscles. She knew without a doubt she could snap somebody's neck. *Comforting.* It'd be better if she wasn't nearby when the skill she'd stolen reverted to him.

"You think so?" He fell into step, alarmingly casual as they came up to her car.

"Who's going to stop me?"

"This is a nice ride," he observed. Suddenly he had a knife in his hand, but instead of threatening her with it, which she could've handled, he traced it down the front whitewall. "And I guess *I* could stop you." Understatement.

"Yeah." She wouldn't even breathe without his permission. Those Diamond Back tires had set her back a pretty penny in South Carolina, but nothing was too good for the Marquis. It was all she had left of her daddy, after all. "Just what do you want from me?"

TEN minutes with you up against a wall.

For a second, Reyes thought he'd spoken out loud, but she wouldn't be regarding him with the same mix of wariness and puzzlement in her tawny eyes if he had. Up close, he saw freckles smattered her nose and cheeks, making her look young and vulnerable. He'd bet she played that for all she was worth.

Not tall, but she gave the impression of being leggy, lean along with it. She wore her strawberry blond hair in a wavy nimbus to her shoulders. Her jeans were old, torn at the knees, but her boots looked expensive.

And he absolutely couldn't explain his vicious urge to grab her with both hands, mark her with his teeth, and ride her until she begged for mercy. Maybe it was because he couldn't picture her crying uncle; spirit in a woman made his heart kick like a half-broke horse, and she'd shown such a roguish blend of guile and confidence inside the bar.

The first three games, she hadn't been able to play worth shit. He'd watched his share of hustlers over the years, and he always knew when a player stalled. They had a tell in the way they handled the cues, something. But this woman, he'd have sworn she barely knew how to hold the stick. Until that last game. Until she turned into a tournament player before his eyes, like magic.

Reyes didn't believe in magic.

She'd done something when he touched her. He felt different. Energy coursed through him with no outlet, as if a customary corollary had suddenly been blocked. He felt slower, too, as if his muscles had forgotten how to move.

Just as well he hadn't intended to do anything here at Suds. He never acted without all the facts, and he needed to know more about this woman. It worked on him like a compulsion. He wanted to know her better than his own name.

Like most impulses, he'd resist it, taking satisfaction instead in leashing his appetites. Reyes almost enjoyed letting the longing build to fever pitch, only to turn his back on it. He never let hunger overwhelm him anymore. But for the first time in years, temptation tugged. She smelled like coconut oil and sunny days. He wondered what she'd do if he leaned down to breathe the scent of her. Would she fight? Scream?

"We'll take a ride," he said easily. "You probably *should* get away from here. Once those rednecks figure things out, they'll come running."

"You're not getting in my car."

Smart woman. But that wouldn't do her any good, not when he already knew her weakness. Attachments, whether to people, places, or things, only led to trouble.

He applied a little pressure on the tire. "Both of us go. Or neither. They're going to think I was your silent partner since I made them pay up, and I'm not taking a beating for you. But if you want to get away, I'd hurry. Sounds like they're getting riled inside."

No lie. Reyes heard shouting. Soon the men she'd swindled would come pouring out, looking to take the money back and maybe a pound of flesh. Chet had probably worked himself up to thinking she owed him sex to make up for the heaping helping of emasculation she'd served with a smile. This couldn't have fallen out better if he'd planned it.

She swore. What a mouth she had, but everything sounded better when spoken in a husky undertone. "Come on. I'm only taking you as far as Lake Charles, and if you spill a drop of anything on Myrna's upholstery, I'll kill you with my bare hands."

"Myrna?"

The woman shot him a look that said it wasn't the time to talk about the name of her car. By the time she got the keys in the ignition, he'd settled into the passenger seat. She handled the big car with careless expertise, backing out in a spit of gravel.

Just in time, too.

The bar door flew open, and six men swarmed out. One chucked a beer bottle at them, and it smashed against the fender. To his amusement, the hellcat spat another curse and reversed hard into the lot, like she'd happily run *all* the rednecks down. They apparently thought so, too, because they scattered, fell on their asses. She shifted gears and then stuck her hand out the window, flashing the finger as they fishtailed out onto Rural Route 9.

"Myrna Loy," she said, as if they'd never been interrupted. "I'm nuts about her."

It took him a minute to place the name, and then connect it to her car. He tended to connect the dots, not make tangential leaps. Logic, not Rorschach blots.

"You like her movies then?" This wasn't going at all as he'd planned. She still hadn't even answered his original question. He prided himself on being adaptable, however;

it made him the best at what he did. So he'd circle back to it soon enough.

Before answering, she adjusted the radio and tuned it to KBON, filling the car with zydeco music and rushing wind. "Love them. Have you ever seen *The Thin Man*?"

"I'm afraid not. Good?"

Her smile flashed, a dimple in her right cheek. "Fantastic. She and William Powell were *the* couple back then. So suave and charming. When I was a kid, I wanted to be Nora Charles."

Nick and Nora Charles—the two names popped into his head as a matched set. Where had he heard them before? It would come; he had a nearly eidetic memory.

"Dashiell Hammett." He finally remembered. "I read the book a long time ago. I prefer Mickey Spillane."

She glared at him out of the corner of her eye, green eyes practically throwing sparks. "Heresy. I should throw you out of the car."

Reyes tried to picture that. Nobody ever made him do anything he didn't want to. Odd, she didn't seem in the least intimidated. Nothing in her manner indicated she was worried about acquiring a passenger his size, armed with a knife. She ought to be tense, sweating, and when things didn't add up, it troubled him. It was like she knew something he didn't. And he hated that feeling.

He slid the blade back into his boot. Threatening her ran counterproductive to his aims at this point, so he improvised. "So, what did you do back at the bar? Or maybe I should ask *how* did you do it?"

That would give her a reason to be wary of him, thinking he'd noticed something askew. Which he had, of course, but it wasn't the big picture. Honesty often provided the best smoke screen for his other endeavors.

She lifted a shoulder. "Maybe you should."

"So how did you do it?"

"Do what?"

He had the feeling she could continue this line of circular conversation all night. Well, it didn't matter. In time, he'd wear her down. She didn't realize it, but she'd gained his company for a while.

That was something of a specialty of his—breaking down barriers, building trust. Reyes bet she'd yield what he needed to know before too much longer. A softness about her mouth said she liked what she saw when she looked at him. He was used to that, but this woman made him *want* to use sex, a tactic he seldom employed these days. Too many complications, too many variables.

"What's your name, anyway?" He played the rootless hitchhiker with a familiarity born of experience. That impression would be reinforced by his appearance and his lack of personal belongings. "And thanks for the lift."

"You didn't exactly give me a choice." Her husky voice sent a pleasurable spike along his nervous system straight down to his groin. Reyes shifted, unwilling to let the erection gain full-flag status.

"No, I didn't. You love your whitewalls too much to gamble with them."

"I love this car," she corrected, stroking a hand along the blue dashboard.

Reyes watched her fingers with a clawing hunger that astounded him. He wanted them on his chest, his abdomen . . . lower. He wanted two weeks with her in a hotel room, nothing but bare skin and cool, white sheets. Despite iron discipline, his penis swelled all the way up, straining his zipper.

"I can see that." His voice rumbled low, even for him.

"Isn't she a beaut?"

"Sure is."

So are you. But he didn't say that out loud. It was too soon. Like a wild thing, she would be skittish, slow to gentle. She *still* hadn't told him her name. Such a way she had about her—appearing to give away everything, when in fact, it granted nothing—could've come only through years of practice.

All in all, Kyra Marie Beckwith was a lot more intriguing than her dossier let on. Too bad he had to kill her.

Also from
Usa Today Bestselling Author

REBECCA YORK

THE MOON SERIES

KILLING MOON

EDGE OF THE MOON

WITCHING MOON

CRIMSON MOON

SHADOW OF THE MOON

NEW MOON

GHOST MOON

ETERNAL MOON

"Action-packed...
and filled with sexual tension."
—*The Best Reviews*

penguin.com